THE BRAZEN BLUESTOCKING

#1 The Duchess Society Series

BY

TRACY SUMNER

WOLF PUBLISHING

The Brazen Bluestocking by Tracy Sumner

Published by WOLF Publishing UG

Copyright © 2021 Tracy Sumner
Text by Tracy Sumner
Edited by Christy Carlyle
Cover Art by Victoria Cooper
Paperback ISBN: 978-3-98536-018-5
Hard Cover ISBN: 978-3-98536-019-2
Ebook ISBN: 978-3-98536-017-8

WOLF Publishing - This is us:

Two sisters, two personalities.. But only one big love!

Diving into a world of dreams..
    ...Romance, heartfelt emotions, lovable and witty characters, some humor, and some mystery! Because we want it all! Historical Romance at its best!

Visit our website to learn all about us, our authors and books!

Sign up to our mailing list to receive first hand information on new releases, freebies and promotions as well as exclusive giveaways and sneak-peeks!

WWW.WOLF-PUBLISHING.COM

Also by Tracy Sumner

The Duchess Society Series

The DUCHESS SOCIETY is a steamy new Regency-era series. Come along for a scandalous ride with the incorrigible ladies of the Duchess Society as they tame the wicked rogues of London! Second chance, marriage of convenience, enemies to lovers, forbidden love, passion, scandal, ROMANCE.

If you enjoy depraved dukes, erstwhile earls and sexy scoundrels, untamed bluestockings and rebellious society misses, the DUCHESS SOCIETY is the series for you!

#1 The Brazen Bluestocking

#2 The Scandalous Vixen

#3 The Wicked Wallflower

#4 One Wedding and an Earl

#5 Two Scandals and a Scot

Prequel to the series: The Ice Duchess

Christmas novella: The Governess Gamble

THE BRAZEN BLUESTOCKING

My heart is, and always will be, yours.
-Jane Austen

Chapter One

Limehouse Basin, London, 1822

S he'd taken this assignment on a dare.

A dare to herself.

Unbridled curiosity had driven her, the kind that killed cats. When it was just another promise-of-rain winter day. Another dismal society marriage the Duchess Society was overseeing.

Another uninspiring man to investigate.

Hildegard Templeton told herself everything was normal. The warehouse had looked perfectly ordinary from the grimy cobblestones her post-chaise deposited her on. A sign swinging fearlessly in the briny gust ripping off the Thames—*Streeter, Macauley & Company*—confirming she'd arrived at the correct location. A standard, salt-wrecked dwelling set amongst tea shops and taverns, silk merchants and ropemakers. Surrounded by shouting children, overladen carts, horses, dogs, vendors selling sweetmeats and pies, and the slap of sails against ships' masts. A chaotic but essential locality, with cargo headed all over England but landing in this grubby spit of dockyard first.

When she'd stepped inside, she halted in place, realizing her blunder in assuming anything about Tobias Streeter was *normal*.

Hildy knew nothing about architecture but knew this was not the norm for a refurbished warehouse bordering the Limehouse Basin Lock. A suspect neighborhood her post-boy hadn't been pleased to drive into—or be asked to wait *in* while she conducted her business. Honestly, the building was a marvel of iron joists, girders, and cast-iron columns with ornamental heads. With a splash of elegant color—crimson and black. What she imagined a gentleman's club might look like, a refined yet dodgy sensibility she found utterly... *charming*. And entirely unnecessary for a building housing a naval merchant's headquarters.

Her exhalation left her in a vaporous cloud, and she gazed around with a feeling she didn't like as the piquant scent of a spice she identified as Asian in origin enveloped her.

A feeling she wasn't accustomed to.

Miscalculation.

As she would admit only to her business partner, Georgiana, the newly minted Duchess of Markham: *I fear I've botched the entire project*. She'd taken society's slander as truth—shipping magnate, Romani blood, profligate bounder, and the most noteworthy moniker the *ton* had ever come up with—and made up her mind about the man, concocting a wobbly plan unsupported by proper research. A proposal built on assumptions instead of *fact*. Sloppy dealings were very unlike her. Ambition to secure the agreement to advise the Earl of Hastings's five daughters as they traveled along their matrimonial journey—the eldest currently set on marrying the profligate bounder—had risen above common sense.

Hildy took a breath scented with exotic spice and tidal mud and stepped deeper into the warehouse, locking her apprehension out of sight. She wasn't going to back down now, not when she had *five* delightful but wholly unsupervised women who would make terrific disasters of their marriages without the Duchess Society to guide them.

Marriages much like her parents' were an aberration staining her memories until she wanted none of the institution. They needed her, these girls, and she needed *them*. To prove her life wasn't a tale as ordinary as the building she'd expected to find herself in this morning—

society outcast, bluestocking. Spinster. Not that it mattered what they thought of her; she'd rejected the expectations the *ton* had placed on her from the first moment.

"Looking for Streeter, are ya?"

Hildy turned in a swirl of flounces and worsted wool she wished she'd rejected for this visit when a simple day dress would have sufficed. Perhaps one borrowed from her maid.

The man who'd stumbled upon her lingering in the entrance to the warehouse was tall enough to have her arching her neck to view him from beneath her bonnet's lime silk brim. And built like one of those ships moored at the wharf outside. "Tobias Streeter, yes."

The brute gave the tawny hair lying across his brow a swipe, removed the cheroot from his lips, and extinguished it beneath the toe of his muddy boot in a gesture she didn't think the architect of this impressive building would appreciate. "He expecting ya?"

They make them rude in the East End, Hildy decided with a sigh. "Possibly." If he'd been alerted by his future father-in-law, *yes*.

"Who's calling?" he asked gruffly, digging in his pocket and coming up with another cheroot, even as the bitter aroma from the first still enveloped them. "Apologies for asking, but we don't get many of your kind round here. Some kinds"—he chuckled at his joke and swiped the tapered end of the cheroot across his bottom lip—"just not *your* kind."

Hildy shifted the folio she clutched from one gloved hand to the other. Her palms had started to perspire beneath kid leather. This man was playing with her, and she didn't like participating in games she wasn't sure she could win. "Lady Hildegard Templeton," she supplied, using the honorific when she rarely did. "Of the Duchess Society."

The impolite brute arrested his effort to remove a tinderbox from his tattered coat pocket. "The Mad Matchmaker," he whispered, his cheroot hitting the glossy planks beneath their feet. Horrified, he backed up a step as if she had a contagious disease.

A rush of blood flooded her. *Temper*, she warned herself. *Not here.* The blush lit her cheeks, and she cursed the man standing stunned before her for causing it. "That ridiculous sobriquet is not something I respond—"

"Sobriquet," a voice full of laughter and arrogance intoned from behind her. "Go back to unloading the shipment from Spain, Alton. I have this."

When she turned to face the man she assumed was Tobias Streeter, she wanted to be in control because that was how this day was going to go. Confident. Poised. Looking like a businesswoman, not a lady. Not a *matchmaker*—which she *wasn't*. She longed to tell him what she thought of the rude entry to his establishment when he hadn't known she was coming.

Instead, she felt flushed and damp, unprepared based on a split-second judgment of the glorious building she stood in. Adding to that, the niggling sense that she'd made a colossal error in calculating her opponent.

And then Hildy merely felt *thunderstruck*.

Because, as he stepped out of the shadows and into the glow cast from the garnet sconce at his side, she realized with a heavy heart that Tobias Streeter, the Rogue King of Limehouse Basin, was the most attractive man she'd ever seen.

Which wasn't an asset. She was considered attractive as well—she surmised with a complete and utter lack of vanity—and she'd only found it to be a *trap*.

"I wondered if you'd actually venture into the abyss, luv," he said idly, tugging a kerchief from his back pocket and across his sweaty brow.

He had a streak of graphite on his left cheek, and his hands were a further mess. Additionally, he'd made no effort to contain the twisted collar of his shirt. The top two bone buttons were undone, and the flash of olive skin drew her gaze when she wished it wouldn't. No coat, no waistcoat. He was unprepared for visitors. However, if she were being fair, she'd given him no notice he was to have one.

"Those feral phaeton rides through Hyde Park I read about in the *Gazette* must be true. They say you're a daredevil at heart, Templeton, a feminine trait the *ton* despises, am I right? Gossip that I'd lay odds you don't welcome any more than that charming nickname your poisonous brethren saddled you with." He tucked the length of stained cloth in his waistband to crudely dangle, drawing her eye to his trim waist.

"They can't understand anyone of means who doesn't simply sit back and enjoy it."

"I'm, well..." Hildy fumbled, then wished she'd waited another moment to gather her thoughts. "I'm here on business. As you know. Or guessed."

His gaze dropped to the folio in her hand, his lips quirking sourly. "My sordid past is bundled up in that tidy file, I'm guessing."

No, actually, she wanted to admit but thankfully didn't. *I've gone into this all wrong.*

She ran through the facts detailed on the sheet in her wafer-thin folio that were not facts at all. Royal Navy hero of some sort, a conflict in India he didn't discuss publicly. Powerful friends in the East India Company, hence his move into trade upon his return to England. Ruthless, having built his empire one brick at a time. Father rumored to be titled, mother of Romani stock, at least a smidgen, which was all it took to be completely ostracized.

Insanely handsome had never factored into her research.

And she'd assumed this would be an uncomplicated assignment.

"Tobias Streeter," he murmured, halting before her. Almost as tall as his brutish gatekeeper, Hildy kept her head tilted to capture his gaze. Which she was going to capture. And *hold*. Hazy light from a careless sun washed over him from windows set at all angles, allowing her to peruse at her leisure.

She didn't fool herself; it was an opportunity he *allowed*.

Skin the color of lightly brewed tea. Eyes the shade of a juicy green apple you shined against your sleeve and then couldn't help but take a quick bite of—the glow from the sconce turning them a deep emerald while she stared. Highlighted by a set of thick lashes any woman would be jealous of. Jaw hard, lips full, breath scented with mint and tea. Not brandy or scotch, another misstep had she presumed it.

When, of course, she'd presumed it.

As he patiently accepted her appraisal, his hand rose, and his index finger, just the calloused tip, trailed her cheek to tuck a stray strand behind her ear.

The hands of a man who worked with them.

Played with them.

She shivered, a shallow exhalation she couldn't contain rushing forth in a steamy puff. Parts of the ground story were open from quay to yard for transit handling, and glacial gusts were whistling through like a train on tracks.

"Alton," he instructed without glancing away from her, though he dropped his hand to his side. "Close the doors at the back, will you? And bring tea to my office."

"Tea," Alton echoed. "*Tea?*"

Streeter's breath fanned her face, warming her to her toes. "Isn't that what ladies drink over business dealings? If ladies even *do* business. Perhaps it's what they drink over spirited discussions about watercolors or their latest gown."

She gripped the folio until her knuckles ached, feeling like a ball of yarn being tossed between two cats. "Make no special accommodations. I'll have whatever it is you guzzle during business dealings, Mr. Streeter."

He laughed, then caught himself with the slightest downward tilt of his lips. She'd surprised them both somehow. It was the first chess move she'd won in this match. "We guzzle malt whiskey then," he murmured and turned, seeming to expect her to follow.

She recorded details as she shadowed him across the vast space crowded with shipping crates and assorted stacks of rope and tools, to a small room at the back overlooking the pier. His shirt was untucked on one side, the kerchief he'd wiped his face with slapping his thigh. His clothing was finely made but not skillfully enough to hide a muscular build most men used built-in padding to establish. Dark hair, *no*, more than dark. Black as tar, curling over his rumpled shirt collar and around his ears. So pitch dark, she imagined she could see cobalt streaks in it, like a flame gone mad.

Hair that called a woman's fingers to tangle in it, no matter the woman.

The gods had allotted this conceited beast an inequitable share of beauty, that was certain. And for the first time in her *life*, Hildy was caught up in an attraction.

His office was another unsurprising surprise.

A roaring fire in the hearth chasing away the chill. A Carlton House desk flanked by two armchairs roomy enough to fit Streeter or his man of business, Alton. A Hepplewhite desk, or a passable imitation. A colorful Aubusson covering the floor, nothing threadbare and old because it had lost its value. Her heart skipped as she stepped inside the space, confirmation that she'd indeed misjudged. Shelf upon shelf of leather-bound books bracketed the walls. Walking to a row, she checked the spines with a searching review. Cracked but good, each and every one of them. Architecture, commerce, mathematics, chemistry. Nothing entertaining, nothing playful. The library of a man with a mind.

While Streeter moved to a sideboard that had likely come from the king's castoffs, and poured them a drink from a bottle whose label she didn't recognize, she circled the room, inspecting.

Holding both glasses in one hand, he situated himself not at his desk but on the edge of an overturned crate beside it, his long legs stretched before him. Sipping from his while holding hers, his steely gaze tracked her. Fortunately, she realized from the travel-weary Wellington he tapped lightly on the carpet, her examination of his private space was making him uneasy. With an aggrieved grunt, he yanked the kerchief from his waistband and tossed it needlessly to the floor.

Finally, she sighed in relief, a *weakness*. If he didn't like to be studied, he must have *something* to hide. She'd been hired, in part, to find out what.

"This isn't one of your frivolous races through the park." He leaned to place her glass on the corner of his desk. Hers to take, or not, when she passed. The only charitable thing he'd done was pour it for her. "Right now, I have two men guarding your traveling chariot parked outside, lest someone rob you blind. The thing is as yellow as a ripe banana, which catches the eye. They'll slice the velvet from the squabs and resell it two blocks over for fast profit. Your post-boy looked ready to expire when we got to him. Guessing he's never had to sit on his duff while waiting for his mistress to complete business in the East End. A slightly larger *man* might better fit the bill next time."

Post-boys were all she could afford.

Hildy released the satin chin strap and slid her bonnet from her head. Her coiffure, unsteady on a good day as her maid's vision was dreadful, collapsed with the removal, and a wave of hair just a shade darker than the sun fell past her shoulders. Streeter blinked, his fingers tightening around his glass. She noticed the insignificant gesture while wondering if the fevered awareness filling the air was only in *her* mind.

Halting by his desk, she reached for her drink with a nod in his direction. The scent of soap and spice drifted to her, his unique mix. "This warehouse, it's quite unusual. Magnificent, actually. I've never seen the like."

"I'll be sure to tell the architect the daughter of an earl approves." His gaze cool, giving away absolutely nothing, he dug a bamboo toothpick from his trouser pocket and jammed it between his teeth, working it from side to side between a pair of very firm lips. At her raised brow, he shrugged. "Stopped smoking. It's enough to breathe London's coal-laden air without asking for more trouble."

Hildy dropped the folio, which held little of value aside from her employment contract with the Earl of Hastings, in the armchair and lifted the glass to her lips. The whiskey was smooth, smoky—*good*. "This is excellent," she mused, licking her lips and watching Streeter's hand again tense around his tumbler.

"Thank you. It's my own formula," he said after a charged silence, a dent appearing next to his mouth. Not so much a dimple. Two of which she had herself, a feature people had commented on her entire life.

His was more of an elevated smirk.

"Yours?" Continuing her journey around the room, Hildy paused by a framed blueprint of this warehouse. Beside it was another detailed sketch, a building she didn't recognize. Architectural schematics drawn by someone very talented. She couldn't miss the initials, *TS*, in the lower right corner.

Frowning, she tilted her glass, staring into it as if the amber liquor would provide answers to an increasingly enigmatic puzzle. Aside from disappointing her family and society, she'd never done anything remarkable. *Been* anything remarkable.

When faced with remarkability, she wasn't sure she trusted it.

Streeter stacked his boots one atop the other, the crate creaking beneath him. "A business venture, a distillery going south financially that I found myself uncommonly intrigued by, once I handed over an astounding amount of blunt to keep it afloat *and* demanded I be invited into the process. Usually, I invest, then step away if the enterprise is well-managed, which it often isn't, but this..." Bringing the glass to his lips, he drank around the toothpick. Quite a feat. She couldn't look away from the show of masculine bravado if she'd been ordered to at the end of a pistol. "It's straightforward chemistry, the brewing of malt. But, lud, what a challenge, seeking perfection."

Finessing his glass into an empty spot next to him on the crate, he wiggled the toothpick from his lips and pointed it at her. A crude signal that he was ready to begin negotiations. "Isn't seeking perfection your business too, luv? The *ideal* bloke, without shortcomings. I've yet to see such a man, but the Mad Matchmaker is fabled to work miracles, so maybe there's a chance for me."

Seating herself in the chair absent her paperwork, Hildy set her glass on the desk and worked her gloves free, one deliberate finger at a time. If he believed he could chase her away with his bullying attitude, he hadn't done suitable research into his opponent's background. Last year, the Duchess Society had completed an assignment, confidential in nature but rumored nonetheless, for the royal family. Madness, power, fantastic wealth, love gained, love lost. This handsome scoundrel and his trifling reach for society's acceptance, she could handle.

Although she realized she was silently reminding herself of the fact, not stating it outright.

"Nothing to do with perfection and rarely anything to do with love, Mr. Streeter. The betrothals I support are, like the marriage you're proposing with Lady Matilda Delacour-Baynham, a business agreement. Unless I'm mistaken from the discussions I've had with her and her father, the Earl of Hastings."

He twirled the toothpick between his fingers like a magician. "You have it dead on. Holy hell, I'm not looking for love. Don't fill the chit's head with that rubbish. The words mean nothing to me. They never have. Society only sells the idea to make the necessity of unions such as these more acceptable."

Well, *that* sounded personal. "Lady Matilda—"

"Mattie wants freedom. If you know her, she's told you what she's interested in. The only thing. Medicine." He laughed and sent the toothpick spinning. "An earl's daughter, can you conjure it? When no female can be a physician and certainly not a legitimate lady. To use one of your brethren's expressions, it's beyond the pale."

He winked at her, *winked*, and she was reasonably certain he didn't mean it playfully.

"I have funds, more than she can spend in a lifetime. More than I can. She wants to use a trifling bit to rescue her father, a man currently drowning, and I do mean drowning, in debt? Fine. Finance her hobby of practicing medicine? Also fine. Or her *dream*, if you're the visionary sort. Let her safely prowl these corridors and others on the rookery trail, delivering babes, bandaging wounds, swabbing fevered brows. They have no one else, the desperate souls I live amongst. She'll be an angel in their midst. And me, the one controlling the deliverance. Deliverance for *her* from your upmarket bunch. Who, other than finding ways to creatively lose capital, do nothing but sit around on their arses making up nicknames for those who *prosper*."

"What's in it for you?" Hildy whispered, not sure she knew. Was Tobias Streeter, rookery bandit, shipping titan, this eager to marry into a crowd that indeed sat on their toffs all day dreaming up pointless monikers? When she'd been trying to escape them her entire *life*?

He jabbed the toothpick in her direction, his smile positively savage. "Don't worry about what I need. I don't make deals where I don't profit, luv."

A caged tiger set loose on society. That's what he was. Half of London was secretly fawning over him while refusing him admittance to their sacred drawing rooms.

Not so fussy about admittance to their beds, she'd bet.

He slipped the toothpick home between his stubbornly compressed lips. "Templeton, you of all people should understand her predicament, being somewhat peculiar yourself. Boxed in by society's expectations, unless I'm missing my guess, which I usually don't. I understand, do you see? It's why the girl trusts me. Why, maybe, I trust *her*.

"I know what it's like to be found lacking for elements beyond your control. Where you were born, the color of your skin. Being delivered on the wrong side of some addled viscount's blanket. Think nothing of intelligence or courage, wit or ingenuity, *talent*, only the blue blood, or lack of it, running beneath that no one sees unless you slice them open."

Hildy smoothed her hand down her bodice and laid her gloves in a neat tangle on her knee, Streeter chasing every move with his intense, sea-green gaze. That blasted blue blood he spoke of kept her tangled in a web, day in and day out. He didn't need to enlighten her. Resignedly, she nodded to the folio lying like a spent weapon between them.

"Let's discuss specifics, shall we? Hastings wants you to court his daughter properly. Even if Lady... um, Mattie doesn't require it, *he* does. Flowers, gifts, trinkets. Courtship rituals. The servants gossip, and everyone in London then knows what's what, so this is an essential, seemingly trivial part of the process. I'll assist with the selection. He'd also like certain businesses you're involved with downplayed, so to speak. The unsavory enterprises. At least until the first babe is born. Rogue King of Limehouse Basin isn't exactly what he desired for his darling girl. But you, obviously, got to her first."

"At least I'm not an ivory-turner," he whispered beneath his breath.

She tilted her head in confusion.

"Her father cheats at dice, my naïve hoyden. I do many cursed things, but cheating is not one. Every gaming hell in town is after him." Streeter growled and, snatching up his glass, polished off the contents. Lord, she wished he'd button his collar. The view was becoming a distraction. "There's more to this agreement. I can see from the brutal twist of those comely lips of yours. More edges to be smoothed away like sandpaper to rough timber. Go on, spit it out. I can take a ruthless assessment."

Hildy controlled, through diligence born of her own beatdowns, the urge to raise her hand to cover her lips. *Comely* ones that had begun to sting pleasantly at his backhanded compliment. "Aside from your agreement that my solicitors—in addition to yours and the earl's—will review all contracts to ensure fairness for both parties, there is the matter of Miss Henson."

He whispered a curse against crystal and was unapologetic when his narrowed gaze met hers. He lowered his glass until it rested on his flat belly. "So, I'm to play the holy man until the ceremony?" Then he muttered something she didn't catch. Or didn't want to. *For a wife who prefers women.*

Hildy made a mental note to investigate that disastrous possibility, although it made no difference. Lady Matilda—Mattie—had to get married to someone. A *male* someone. Why not this beautiful devil who seemed to actually *like* her? Heavens, Hildy thought in despair. The Duchess Society couldn't weather the storm should a scandal of that magnitude come to light. It was illegal, which was absurd, of course, but that was the case. There were whisperings of such goings-on, relationships on the sly.

Rumors with the power to destroy one's *life.*

It was decided at that moment, with dust motes swirling through fading wintry sunlight, in a startlingly elegant office in the middle of a slum. This marriage, between a lady who wanted to be a doctor but couldn't and a tenacious blackguard who wanted high society tucked neatly in his pocket, had to happen. Or Hildy and her enterprise to save the women of London from gross matrimonial injustice was *finished.*

Too, she would go belly up without funds coming in to pay the bills —and coming in *soon.*

Streeter rocked forward, his Wellingtons dusting the floor, upsetting the shipping crate until she feared it would collapse beneath him. "I return the question because it's a valuable one. Besides a hefty fee that Hastings can't afford and will eventually derive from other sources, namely the source sharing this stale malt air with you, what's in it for you? Dealing with me isn't going to be easy. Ask my partners, should you be able to locate them. Mattie isn't much better from what I know of her. Her spirit is part of the reason I believed she'd be the right woman for the job."

Hildy chewed on her bottom lip, an abominable habit, then glanced up to find Streeter's gaze had gone vacant around the edges. The way a man's does when he's *thinking* about things. She wasn't, saints above, imagining the thread of attraction strung between them like ship's netting. He felt it, too. "I'll be candid."

"Please do," he whispered, bringing himself back from his musing, his cheeks slightly tinged. His breathing maybe, *maybe*, churning faster.

"When I arrived, I would've said I was doing it to secure future business with the Earl of Hastings. He has five daughters, as you know, and no wife to guide them. A line of inept governesses, another quitting every week it seems. My proposal?

"I guide him to appropriate men for the remaining four since Mattie has you on the hook. *Decent* men my people have investigated thoroughly. Then assist with the negotiations, so his daughters are protected, pay my coal bill, and we're both happy." Hildy ran her finger over a nap in the chair's velvet, her gaze dropping to record her progress. "Frankly, I need the money as I wasn't left a large inheritance, more a burden. An ever-maturing residence and staff and no funds allocated for preservation.

"And I'm not planning to marry myself, so survival falls directly to me. Likewise, I do this to benefit the young women I work with, if you must know, not simply as a business venture. You have no idea how lacking they are simply from being isolated from any discussions outside the appropriate tea to serve. They're forced to sign contracts they can't even begin to understand—*lifelong*, binding contracts—with no assistance."

The toothpick bounced in Streeter's mouth as he bit down on it. "What's changed?"

Digging her fingertips into the chair's cushion, she decided to tell him. "I'm *bored* with earls and viscounts in fretful need of an heir to carry on a line that should cease production. In need of capital to salvage a crumbling empire. A rumored Romani bastard who's hiding what he really wants, and I'm the person hired to find out what?" She snapped her fingers, a weight lifting as she spoke the truth. "Now, there's a challenge."

For a breathless second, Streeter's face erased of expression. Like a fist swept across a mirror's vapor. She'd stunned him—and her pulse soared. Foolishly, categorically. Then a broad smile, a *sincere* smile, sent the dent in his cheek pinging. His teeth flashed in wonderfully startling contrast to his olive skin. "Well, damn, I can be surprised." He saluted her with the glass he'd picked up only to find it empty. "A worthy opponent steps out of the mist."

"I'm not an opponent," she murmured, knowing she was.

With a sigh of regret, perhaps because she'd gone back to fibbing, he braced his hand on his thigh and rose to his feet. She watched him cross the room because she couldn't help herself. Tall, broad yet lean, an awe-inspiring physique even in mussed clothing. He moved with an innate grace even a duke wouldn't necessarily have possessed. Natural and unassuming. The stuff one was born with—or without. Elegance that simply was.

He stopped before another of the schematic drawings, an imposing brick structure laid out with mathematical precision she suspected existed only in the sketch. "What if I say no to working with you? Refuse your kind service. Toss it back to Hastings like a flaming ember, pitting his desperation against my ambition."

Hildy understood after a moment's panic that this was part of the negotiation. That the correct response, or non-response, was vital. Retrieving her glass, she took a generous pull, smooth liquor chasing away the chill. "Is it any different than working with your"—she gestured over her shoulder to the warehouse—"bountiful trading partners? We'll be in business together. End of story."

He paused, studying her in a way few men had dared to even while telling her how beautiful she was. Men she'd never wanted to undress her with their eyes, as the saying went. A phrase that until this second had held no meaning.

A peculiar tension, the awareness from earlier, roared between them as if Alton had reopened the doors and let the Thames rush in. As if Tobias Streeter had laid his hands on her. An experience she had no familiarity with which to visualize.

"End of story," he murmured joylessly and turned back to his sketch.

She deposited her folio on his desk, the thump ringing through the room. Outside, a dockworker's shout and the rub and bump of a ship sliding into harbor pierced the hush. He was equally damaged, she could see. And very good at hiding it. They were alike in this regard, a mysterious element only another wounded animal would recognize.

Making the call on instinct alone, Hildy nonetheless made it.

Tobias Streeter wasn't a fiend. He wasn't an abuser like her father. He was just a man.

A man she was willing to polish until he shone like the crown jewels. "There will be events. Part of your engagement and introduction to the *ton*, as it were. You'll likely need some instruction."

He tapped the sketch three times before shifting to lean his shoulder against the wall in a negligent slump she no longer counted as factual. "I clean up well. Never fear," he said, his voice laced with scorn. Who it was directed at, she wasn't sure. "I'll review the contract in that tasteful folio of yours this evening, then we'll discuss the details tomorrow afternoon. I'll send a carriage with a coachman ready to protect you should the need arise, not those lads just out of the schoolroom you have manning your conveyance."

Glancing to a clock on the mantel that had been cautiously ticking off time, his smile thinned, frigid enough to freeze water. "I'm sorry to rush you out, but I have a meeting in ten minutes that will, if successful, net me close to a thousand pounds. My men will escort you home. Your chariot can follow along for fun." His jaw tensed when she started to argue, and he pushed off the wall with a growl. "Not on my watch, Templeton. Not in my township. Don't even *begin*."

However, stubborn chit that she was, she did begin, opening her mouth to tell him who was managing this campaign to show London how bloody wonderful a husband he would be.

"Tea and some of them lemony biscuits from the baker on the corner, coming right up," Alton proclaimed, stumbling into the room, a silver teapot she wondered where in heaven's name he'd located clutched in a meaty fist and two mismatched china cups balanced in the other. Halting, he took one look at his employer's thunderous expression, slapped the cups on the first available surface, and hustled Hildy from the office.

The teapot was still in his hand as Streeter's coach rolled down the congested lane with her an unwilling captive inside. She suppressed a clumsy laugh to see a coat of arms, painted over but visible, on the carriage's door.

Another aristocrat who'd lost his fortune to the Rogue King.

Hildy collapsed against the plush squabs of the finest transport she'd ever ridden in, realizing she hadn't asked Tobias Streeter how he planned to profit from a marriage he didn't want.

Chapter Two

I f Tobias didn't know himself better, he'd say he was looking for
trouble.

He stared out over Dunbar Wharf from his preferred position on the roof of his warehouse, a structure he'd poured his heart,
creativity, and funds into until the dwelling was more alive to him than
the souls he encountered on the tangled streets below. For a chilling
moment, Hildegard Templeton, perhaps the comeliest woman he'd
ever met, had understood.

He'd seen the expression on her face when he sneaked up on her on
the floor below. Wonder. Admiration. Because the dwelling *was* a
marvel, even if most didn't give it a second look. Everything a hood-
lum-cum-architect fantasized about. Not the kind of emotion, frankly,
he'd ever put on a woman's face outside the bedchamber.

Wonder aplenty there.

He chuckled and took a sip of whiskey, a smooth sting lighting his
throat. It was just his luck that his warden was beautiful.

The sun was dipping low on the horizon, throwing a wash of
violent color across the Limehouse sky. The docks were quietening for
the night, workers having left for home or the countless public houses

situated temptingly along their route. Leaving only the marshmen toiling into the darkness, maintaining the river walls. It was low tide; the fertile scent of tidal mud and waste drifted past him on a steady gust that tore at his hair and clothing. The limekilns that had given the area its name were long gone, but he often imagined he could smell scorched lime in the air, a lingering reminder of what had been. Not what *was*.

So much had changed since he'd roamed these alleyways and dank lanes as a boy. With the opening of the masterpiece of waterway engineering, Regent's Canal, two years earlier, the riverside districts along the bustling channel were thriving. Silk merchants, coffeehouses, spice vendors, sailmakers, shipbuilders, ropemakers. Name a business either related to the ships that brought merchandise into port or the actual merchandise, and there you had it. The essence that was his snug hamlet. He could buy blood oranges on one corner and faille taffeta on another, then pop into a teahouse for the sweetest leaves Asia had to offer in between.

It was his superb luck, if the Mad Matchmaker's beauty was a rotten bit, that the Royal Navy had given him the chance to make contacts in India he'd come home and used appropriately. They hadn't cared about his Romani blood. Britain had been perfectly willing for him to die for their cause, tainted lineage or no. Yet, he wasn't a man to waste an opportunity or hold a longer than estimable grudge.

So, he'd taken his battle scars and his knowledge of the shipping industry and created a kingdom.

There weren't many items sold on Bond Street, in fact, that his company hadn't touched. In fact, the *ton* drank his whiskey, ate his fruit, slept on his sheets while treating him as less than the man he was.

In a year, maybe two, they'd welcome him in the only way he gave a damn they do.

Live, shop, and work in the buildings he'd designed. As one of them, because he planned to give them no choice in the matter. He was going to march right into their party.

And he was going to do it *soon*.

Their respect, no, their *approval*, he cared less than nothing about.

"How'd I know I'd find you up here, mate? Surveying your territory, yeah. You and your love for this hole. It's enchanting, it is. When I grew up here too and now find myself slogging along beside ya, and it's yet to grow on me."

Tobias glanced over his shoulder in time to see his partner, Xander Macauley, cross the roof, the ever-present cheroot pilfered from the Welsh shipment that had arrived this morning tucked neatly between his lips. His mouth was tilted in that half-smile, which meant he was pleased about something.

Tobias looked away with a sigh, suspecting his partner's pleasure was going to arrive at his expense.

"Lovely night, innit?" Macauley released a whistling, smoky breath. "Look at that rubbish floating around down there, not a care in the world. Like you for a moment when I walked out here. Almost carried away by the ripping river wind, I was. Didn't hear me, just staring out with a lost expression. One of the vicious nobs out for our blood could've shoved you over the side and left me to my lonesome with a business you're quickly losing favor with."

Tobias sipped from finely cut crystal without comment. One of his partner's statements was false, one true. No one would get through the mercenaries guarding the entrances to the warehouse at rotating intervals. However, he *hadn't* heard Macauley approach. But he'd known Hildegard Templeton had entered his space before his men let him know he had a visitor. A ripple of awareness he'd only experienced once before—on a battlefield in Kanpur. "I'm not losing favor. I'm wearied," he finally said because he had to say something.

Wearied with five floors of merchandise, valuable items he could toss in a hearth and not feel the loss. Emotionally or financially. Then he remembered the crate of Bristol blue vases, similar to the one his father had given his mother, ah, thirty years ago, that he'd unloaded this morning. A treasure his mother had been unable to part with, even if it would've put food in their mouths for a week. Hopeless devotion his father hadn't deserved.

It seemed daft, but unpacking crates like the gangly, famished thirteen-year-old lad he'd been calmed him, a calming task Lady Hildegard had interrupted. A task he had a hundred men to do now. She'd seen his clothing, the sweat on his face, the grime on his fingers, and cast her verdict. While examining the space he'd designed, the architectural sketches on his office walls, none of it matched up in her mind.

Her confusion had been cheerily palpable.

And her eyes were not far off from the haunting blue of that damned glass.

Macauley grunted and sucked hard on his cheroot. Then plucked it free of his lips and gestured to the blazing sunset sweetening their lowly part of the world. "When you use important words like wearied, I know there's a viscount's offspring in there somewhere." He touched the bridge of his nose offhandedly. "You know the spectacles make me cagey. I can't see your eyes behind the lenses. Almost look like another bloke in them, too. A bloke who don't belong on the docks."

Tobias resisted the urge to remove his spectacles and tuck them away in his coat pocket. A battle injury had brought frequent headaches and necessitated the need.

And nightmares.

He mustn't forget that his time in the navy had brought not only headaches but nightmares. In the midnight hours, India didn't let him go.

Macauley kicked at a tar bubble, shifting from boot to boot, ready to reveal his reason for coming to the roof when he had a moderate fear of heights. "Alton said the matchmaker was a stunner."

Tobias swore and spun around, heading for the iron staircase that led into the bowels of the warehouse.

"Don't get high on the ropes, Street," Macauley panted, jamming his cheroot out on the waist-high wall as he passed it. "According to Gerrie, the bloke who escorted her home, she has eyes like sapphires. Sounds like nonsense to me, but a man has to ask."

It wasn't her eyes that'd hooked him, Tobias contended and took the stairs at a dangerous skip. Though they'd been relatively remarkable. She had *dimples*. Two very serious ones sitting on either side of her mouth. Frown or smile, they remained. No man could look at those for long and not yearn to place his lips over them. No man on *earth*.

Ripping his coat off, he tossed it to the floor, grabbed the crowbar propped against the brick wall, and set to work on one of the crates that had arrived this afternoon.

Macauley scowled when he reached his partner, leaning in to muscle the lid free as Tobias worked the crowbar between a narrow gap in the slats and gave it a violent twist. Once they'd opened the crate, he dug through the straw, coming up with a pink teacup. "We could be doing more amusing things with our time this evening if you get my meaning. Dice, drink, women, in that order."

Tobias wedged the crowbar beneath his armpit and dug around in his pocket for a toothpick, wondering if he'd be able to keep himself from begging Macauley for a cheroot. "I have to let Juliet go."

Macauley paused, the lid sliding from his hands to hit the floor. "Bloody hell, that cracked matchmaker is already changing things. She thinks one woman is *enough*?"

Tobias laid the crowbar aside, picked up the violently ugly teacup, and rotated it in his hands. "What was I thinking, buying this?" Chucking it back in the crate, he released an aggrieved breath through his teeth. "Maybe I'll try the pearl tiara again. Worked well with Rebecca. She was only furious with me for a month. Rather a unique farewell gift versus the standard necklace."

Macauley exhaled despairingly and backed up a step, sprawling on an unopened crate. "I hear the Duke of Winchester gave his bit of muslin a castle as a sendoff."

Tobias went back to unpacking a crate he'd no interest in revealing the contents of. But the task kept his face averted from his indelicate but intuitive partner and best friend. "Part of the engagement process. No mistress. For now."

"This nosy chit's so attractive my eyes are gonna bleed, I know it. Alton's sluggish sure, but he's not stupid. You'd never surrender this easily if there wasn't something else, even if you don't want to admit it, wrapped up in the deal."

Tobias uncovered a packet of silk thread, colors dyeing the sunset currently sheltering his kingdom. "Matilda Delacour-Baynham's my future. The Mad Matchmaker is simply a business associate, to define the relationship since you seem to need a definition."

"It's a disaster mixing with these upper-crust toffs above what we're already doing. Buying up the legacies they're losing faster than we can secure them. This scheme..." He dropped his head to his hands and massaged his temples. "You're thinking to oblige yourself to the gentry for *life*."

I'm obliging myself with my designs, not my marriage. Matrimony was merely a dimension on his life's blueprint. Working the toothpick between his lips, he ran his thumb along the silken threads. He couldn't get a single thought out of his mind—a spot of trouble should he be unable to erase it.

Hildegard Templeton had been attracted to him, too.

Her cobalt gaze hadn't strayed from him once, except to review his sketches. "An earl's daughter is a fast step above gentry, Mac." The irony didn't escape him.

"Christ," Macauley whispered into his hands.

Tobias picked at a sliver on the crate, breaking it off and tossing it to the floor. "Talking with her was like shooting that flintlock pistol in the alley behind the mercantile when we were lads. Our bare feet sliding over the cobbles as we sought to steady our aim. A rush. This feeling of being swept up in something larger than me and my ridiculous problems. On my toes, Mac. On. My. *Toes*."

Macauley swore and vaulted to a stand, pointing accusingly. "You *like* her."

Tobias gave his spectacles a nudge, the word *like* rolling around his brain. Hildegard Templeton had strolled about his office pretty as you please, her flaxen hair a tragedy, her plump lips coated with *his* whiskey. Her outdated gown a delicate flutter trailing along behind her. The scent of lavender, enough to tease but not overwhelm, filling his most personal of spaces. Her gaze was absolutely *overflowing* with intelligence. For a second there, he'd had a primal urge to back her into the wall when she passed him and kiss that confident smirk from her face. "Respect is the word I'd choose."

"Ah, blimey," Macauley muttered. "That's worse."

Tobias leaned to pick up the lid from the floor and wrestled it back into place. An industrious and unique female, creating an emboldened organization for those on the cusp of marriage. Best not to tell his partner that she'd left her bonnet in his office, and in a moment of weakness, he'd lifted it to his nose and drawn the deepest breath he had all day. "Quit worrying. We don't see eye to eye. For God's sake, she's a do-gooder."

"So are you, Street, so are you."

His head came up, his gaze fixing on his partner's. "No, I'm *not*," he gritted between clenched teeth, sounding all of twelve.

Macauley held his hand out and ticked off the points on his fingers. "Repeated requests for review of sanitation in the district. Arranging for men to escort ladies home from the textile factory when their shifts are over. Supporting the Salmon Lane Mission's orphanage. How many of those boys do we have working for us anyhow? Deliveries of food to those in need, twice a week at last count. The list of families getting supplies growing every time until we're feeding everyone from South West India Dock to Dunbar Wharf."

Tobias took a rushed step forward, curling his hands into fists at his side. "If you ever breathe a word—"

"I'll put you into the dirt, Street. Don't make me show you. How many times have I bruised that pretty face of yours, eh? You're the brains, agreed by all. But I'm"—he jacked his thumb to his chest—"the muscle. Besides, this is another of your pointless arguments, as everyone knows. It's why we move through these streets like emperors. Don't call you King for nothing. Problem is, you still feel like the hungry boy who's broken into a house, set to rob someone blind for his own survival, only to realize, it's *my* house now."

"Then you understand why I want this. Entrance into their ranks is the way to get it. The committee is making a decision in a month, picking a collection of architects to work on the housing development project, so time is ticking for me to get a foothold. They have my initial sketches, and they're good. But I'm untrained, formally anyway. No Cambridge, no Oxford, but I've read every book on the subject coming out of there and then some. I'm not one of them." He pushed when he could see he needed to, a skill that had carried him far. "It would mean working with John Nash, Mac."

Macauley rocked back on the heels of his boots, his expression grim. "I didn't think Park Crescent was all that splendid, truthfully. Maybe this Nash nob is overrated."

Tobias laughed, and the band around his chest released. He wasn't alone in this. Since Xander Macauley had saved him from a brutal beating when they were boys of no more than eight or nine, just two streets over from the business that had made them staggeringly wealthy, they'd been a team. "It's bloody brilliant, Mac. And so is he. This is my chance to do what I've always longed to do, aside from the import business. And the distillery, which has been surprisingly fascinating. I never expected to like chemistry so much."

Macauley slipped his timepiece from his fob pocket and snapped the etched silver lid open, his shoulders slumping like they did when his friend was off on another caper. "So, you're fine and dandy to work with this infernal matchmaker? Have her sticking her pointy nose in your business and *mine*. Molding us like bloody clay into some shape as hideous as that teacup you unpacked earlier? She's got her own troubles. Rumors about her father, if you haven't heard them. A nasty sod. Bandied about because the *ton* loves nothing more than reducing one of their own. Society outcast in her own way. But preferred, not awarded, if you get my meaning, so they still receive her."

There was more to Lady Hildegard than presented. That's why he was intrigued. Tobias never confronted a riddle he didn't yearn to solve. Only fair, because she was trying her admitted hardest to solve *him*. "Place a man on her. Gerrie, come to think of it. Clever, and he looks the toff part. Tell him he has to *blend*. Check his clothing before he walks out the door. You may have to help him."

Macauley flipped his timepiece from hand to hand, the chain attached to it slapping his belly. "Protection?"

"She came to Limehouse with two post-boys who looked like they were a year out of leading strings." Removing his spectacles, he polished the lenses on the sleeve of his shirt. He liked them, even if Macauley didn't. They were a reliable weight on his nose and gave the feeling that he was a step closer to the future, one step away from the past, when he was wearing them. "Plus, then we'll know where she goes. Advance notice when she's snooping."

"If she finds out?"

Tobias slipped the toothpick free and pointed it menacingly at his partner. "She better not."

"You sound frightened, Street. Of a *woman*."

Tobias shrugged the taunt off and strode from the room, unwilling to tell Xander Macauley, a man who knew almost everything about him, that he was indeed scared of a woman.

Chapter Three

T he waterfront was a beehive of activity, the foggy morning layered with a multitude of exotic scents and the foul language of stevedores hoisting crates atop their broad shoulders. Hildy turned in a slow circle, surrounded by a remarkable assortment of goods arriving from around the globe. Tea from the East Indies, wine from the Mediterranean, timber from Russia, spices from Asia, tobacco from America. Their mixture was a fragrance unlike any she'd encountered. She swiveled at a man's hoarse shout as a crate slipped from its hoist and crashed to the ground, a rainbow of soaps, cigars, and lengths of lace spilling out over the mud-spattered cobblestones.

A crate with *Streeter, Macauley & Company* seared in black lettering on the side.

When Hildy glanced back, it was to find Lady Matilda Delacour-Baynham's feather-and-ribbon-hatted head disappearing into a crowd of dockworkers, the cedar apothecary box she held banging her hip. Cursing softly beneath her breath, Hildy lifted the hem of her woolen gown from the muck and dashed after Tobias Streeter's willful fiancée, her parasol tapping the ground with each step as a roar of conversation, arguments, and laughter trailed after her.

They'd been scheduled to meet at the Duchess Society office to discuss the next steps in the engagement proceedings until her charge summoned Hildy to another location.

Two mornings in a row spent on the Limehouse docks. That was a first.

"Do you see stall number fourteen?" Matilda asked when Hildy reached her.

They'd entered a low-level timber structure where trade was being conducted on a lesser scale. A mysterious, in-a-dark-corner scale. One booth they passed showcased candles stacked on a rough wooden counter, the next bags of sugar and salt. Still others sold chocolate, tea, and strips of leather. Cases of wine, rum, brandy. Money changing hands, conversation rapid. "What *is* this place?"

Matilda—or *Mattie*, as Hildy was coming to think of her, mostly against her will—popped to her toes to gaze over the horde traversing the single, narrow aisle of the improvised market. She was a tall woman and could likely see over a great many heads using this method, where it would have gotten Hildy and her meager stature nowhere. "It's a market for items damaged in transit. Only known to those in the shipping trade. It changes location if merchants are trying to evade paying taxes." Her voice dropped to a whisper. "I imagine some of the items are not actually damaged but sold here anyway."

"Smuggling," Hildy breathed and took a closer look at the mountain of goods scattered around her.

"*Civilized* smuggling."

"Mr. Streeter knows about this?" She pointed her parasol at a makeshift counter piled high with merchandise. "Products off his ships ending up here instead of where they were supposed to arrive?"

Matilda glanced at her, a startled laugh rolling from her lips. "He's the one who told me about it. I'm here to purchase medicinal herbs, as I'm also trained as a homeopathic chemist. Unofficially, that is. He said he smashed the crate, then marked it damaged himself. Isn't that charming?"

Charming? Hildy gathered her cloak at her neck, her exasperated breath fogging the air. The man was a complete and utter scoundrel.

Highlighting the challenge she faced trying to fashion him for society. "Stall fourteen holds the herbs, I'm assuming."

"Exactly," Matilda replied and marched away as if she knew where she was going.

They circled the marketplace twice before Matilda decided to send one of her footmen to inquire about the location of this cryptic stall. A gap-toothed sailor, with a curious expression that indicated he didn't often see women in this area, directed them to a murky back corner. When Hildy glanced over her shoulder as they walked away, he was still watching them, a penetrating gleam in his eyes.

"Don't worry, Lady Hildegard," Matilda said as they stopped before the unmarked, unmanned stall the sailor had indicated.

She placed her apothecary box atop the timber board serving as a counter and flipped the brass lock. Inside were a multitude of glass bottles and sharp instruments Hildy was afraid to ask the use of. "We're protected should that seaman decide to cause trouble, which it looks like he might. He has shifty eyes. Because I travel into areas much worse than these to offer medical attention, Mr. Streeter supplied me with footmen he claims can kill a man in between taking bites of an iced bun. Without injuring the bun.

"Rather bloodthirsty, I admit, although I appreciate the sentiment. Just between us, I've had one or two perilous encounters in the rookeries of late. I'm often called as a midwife when I'm more of an untrained physician, but as a female who wishes to be something in a world wishing women would be *nothing*, one does what one can." She leaned over the stall's slanted baseboard, searching for the vendor who would supply her with herbs. "And with that face of yours, we can't travel with too much protection. I agree with my intended on that score."

"What is this? You and Mr. Streeter talked about me?"

Matilda raised a brow, her lips pursed in an inflexible line Hildy suspected she was going to spend the next month softening. "Didn't the two of you talk about *me*?"

Hildy sighed and flicked her gloved fingers in an ageless sign of capitulation. *Fine.*

A man popped up from behind the booth, where he'd been organizing his products below sight. His grin was missing more teeth than the sailor's. "Well, well. Ladies, as in two. Daughter of an earl I'm to be selling my product to. Streeter tol' me to expect the one, so this is a passing surprise." He gave his mustache a twirl, then bowed, his presentation worthy of the stage. "Johnny Plint, locator of unique merchandise, is happy to serve, happy to serve. A king needs a joyful queen. Indeed, he does."

Matilda preened like a cat who'd licked a bowl clean of cream. "Queen," she whispered. "I like the sound of that almost as much as doctor."

The locator of unique merchandise hesitated, his expression pensive. Then he pointed rudely to Hildy, his mouth hitching in a crooked smile that further exposed his dental complexities. "Huh. I woulda picked her fer the queen."

Hildy's cheeks caught fire. And for some horrifying reason, Tobias Streeter's apple-green eyes floated like a mocking whisper through her mind. When she'd done nothing but *secretly*—down deep where no one would ever know—find him attractive.

Intriguing. Intelligent.

Leagues different than what she'd anticipated.

But not hers. She would never, ever, *ever* be anyone's queen. Anyone's *wife*.

"Goodness, no," Matilda said after a tense pause, in the frank way young people have of sounding confident and absurd in the same breath, "she's too old to be a queen. She's simply helping the king become a gentleman. The Mad Matchmaker. I'm sure you've read about her in the gossip sheets. *The Times* columnist particularly loves to discuss her."

She shrugged without concern, pulling a bottle in her case free, glancing at it with a sigh, then returning it to its spot. "Because my father insists upon a gentleman when I rather appreciate the nomadic bent my future husband displays. Although I don't truly wish to marry, but women are given no choice in this world, are they? And it's not as if I've met many noteworthy men in Mayfair ballrooms. Milquetoast bunch. Completely uninterested in my professional aspirations while Mr. Streeter *admires* them. So, he is the best I can perhaps hope for."

Johnny's brow cocked, his gaze crawling Hildy's way. As if to say, *anything to add? Because this troublesome chit barely knows the bloke she's wedding.*

Consequently, as Matilda bargained gleefully for rare medicinal herbs like lovage, then valerian and goldenseal, Hildy silently but staunchly defended herself, tapping the toe of her slipper on the grimy straw scattered across the ground. She could've married; she'd been asked. *Twice*. Kissed poorly, *once*, but it had been a kiss—Viscount Lindell—contact she recalled as all teeth and too much spittle. In her youth, she'd had a season and the frivolity that went with it. Balls, opera, theatre, flowers, ear-bending musicales. Awkward conversation and reprobates who'd never lifted their gaze above her bosom.

Those few short months had taught her a lot about herself. And men. They didn't want a woman with an independent nature and keen business sense whose dowry was flimsy at best.

Even if the woman was moderately attractive.

Hildy was practical about her looks. The result as much chance as a propitious roll of the dice. She often felt guilty about her attractiveness as it was the only thing in her life that she'd used to her advantage but not worked for. However, women had few weapons at their disposal; who was she to deny such a powerful one? There were social benefits should she have wished to claim them. Her beauty had secured the proposals she'd received, for instance. Neither man who'd asked for her hand in marriage had particularly liked or *known* her. But those close calls, imagining sharing a man's life and bed, had forced her to acknowledge something about herself. Her beauty had brought wisdom in its own odd way.

After escaping her father's brutal household, she'd determined she didn't *want* to be beholden to a man ever again. Unless it was for a love story unlike any written in the stars; a romantic, implausible ideal she expected to occur about as much as she expected Tobias Streeter to turn himself around enough to be presented at George's court.

There were possibilities in life—and then there were *miracles*.

Hildy fumed and blew an ostrich feather from her frayed bonnet out of her face. Helping the Rogue King become a gentleman was an *addendum* to her agreement with Matilda's father. To Hildy's mind, anyway. The main thrust being negotiating this ungrateful girl's marital contract so her future was as secure as her cunning fiancé would allow. For instance, Matilda would have visitation rights with her children should a divorce, rare but possible, occur. Unlike many, *most*, of her naïve contemporaries.

This was not a typical situation. For the first time in the history of the Duchess Society, Hildy had agreed to mold a man into more manageable societal clay. Usually, she only worked with the men already cast and hardened. She frowned. That sounded rather debauched.

Of course, the four Delacour-Baynham daughters tripping along behind Matilda had weighed into Hildy's decision. If nothing else, she was an apt businesswoman.

Matilda tugged on her sleeve, pulling Hildy from her musings. She shook a bag of what looked like ragweed before Hildy's face, clearly delighted. "This diuretic is a marvel for disorders of the stomach and feverish attacks, especially for cases of colic. I have a family with a flat-ulent baby in Shoreditch, the mother having gotten no sleep for weeks. I haven't been able to locate lovage for over a year." Her smile was breathtaking and genuine, the first Hildy had seen from her. Trans-forming a rather plain girl to a near beauty. "This herb will improve her life almost immediately."

"Why are you doing this? Agreeing to marry someone you don't love?" A vulnerable sensation flooded Hildy. She'd asked as a woman. Not a guide. Not a tutor. Not a paid assistant. The query from one earl's daughter to another. Her curiosity scared her because she helped women marry for convenience every day of the week except Sunday and never thought twice about it as long as they were safeguarded.

Matilda's bright gingerbread gaze slid high before returning to Hildy. She placed her herbs in her apothecary cabinet and snapped it shut, flipping the brass lock. "He told you." She held out her hand when Hildy would have argued, *lied*, saying Tobias Streeter hadn't divulged anything private about his intended. "I can't be who I am. Society doesn't accept it, or truthfully, they're repulsed by the notion. Although the *ton* doesn't accept my interest in medicine either, it's not punishable by law. Or even something so shocking my family will discard me over. They simply find my *hobby* eccentric and mildly objectionable. The other would ruin every one of my sisters, ruin my family name forever. Ruin everything. So, as many others have before me, I'll live a partially false life."

Hildy stepped aside to avoid being struck by a seaman careening down the aisle with a crate of smuggled brandy in his arms. "But Tobias Streeter," she whispered, hoping Johnny Plint didn't run straight to him and tell him the Mad Matchmaker was talking his fiancée out of marriage. "He's..."

Impossible. Unpredictable.

Provoking. Clever. Magnificent.

Only a woman who wanted a fight on her hands was going to take on the Rogue King.

"Not you, too." Matilda grabbed her apothecary case, her gaze fiery when it landed on Hildy. She moved them away three paces, her voice falling to a tight whisper. "He knows about me and doesn't care. Didn't blink when I told him I don't favor men. I've never admitted that to anyone. You're the second. Congratulations. A Romani by-blow made me feel normal when the rest of society, a ruthless club he's intent on joining so he can fulfill his dream, would have—" She swallowed and did what Hildy was hoping to show Tobias Streeter how to do.

Right before Hildy's eyes, Lady Matilda Delacour-Baynham hardened like pottery in a kiln as the real person slipped away, a talent taught to every child born to the aristocracy. "We have a deal, Lady Hildegard. I give him legitimacy, and he gives me *freedom*. Funds to practice medicine in whatever way I can in an age that doesn't look fondly upon women who desire anything outside the norm. Desire anything at all! I almost love him, I think, for agreeing to this. And frankly, being so kind during the discussions. So much he's giving up only to gain an earl's bewildered daughter. When truly I don't want to marry anyone. I'm a bad bet. *You*, of all people, should understand."

Her pulse tripping, Hildy tapped her parasol against her soiled slipper, humbled by Matilda's—*Mattie's*—emotional confession. She did, of course, understand. Although, aside from the Duchess Society, she wasn't sure she'd ever loved anything enough to fight for it. "I asked him to relieve himself of his mistress, at least until a babe is born.

After that, it's your battle should you choose to wage it. I felt you should know."

Matilda snorted softly, her amber gaze sparking. "It bothers you, does it? That he has a woman he runs to? While I'm relieved."

Stunned by the question, Hildy stared at Matilda, the fierce chill in the air penetrating her woolen cloak and making her shiver. Did it bother her? She didn't know him, or herself, well enough to say. For example, what were these dreams his fiancée spoke of?

Tobias Streeter didn't look like a dreamer, not for one lazy *minute*.

Matilda settled her case by her hip, tipping her head in consideration. "He's attractive enough, certainly. If you find him appealing, no one could blame you. Women throw themselves at his feet every day. I've seen it."

Hildy stepped into the web, her mouth opening to assert *he's beautiful* before she realized what she was about. "I'm going to help you," she said instead, folding her fingers around her parasol handle in a grip so tight it hurt. "I can help you. I *want* to help you." She'd started this business to improve women's lives. That had not changed because Lady Matilda was a tough customer.

"And four sisters after me. For business. For your Duchess Society."

Hildy nodded and wrote the word *yes* with her pointed parasol tip in the straw at her feet. "Only business," she echoed faintly as Tobias Streeter's handsome face swam before her eyes.

She wondered if the blatant falsehood showed.

Chapter Four

T he next morning, Hildy stood in the arched entrance of the
converted storeroom-to-office she'd been shown to, hoping a
minute spent drawing the leaden, malt-tinged distillery air
into her lungs would shake her out of her reverie. The three-story
brick structure was set off the Thames on a winding lane hosting a
variety of nondescript but well-maintained warehouses. All owned,
she'd wager, by Streeter, Macauley & Company.

The future looked hopeful on this neat block as it did nowhere else
in Limehouse. Tobias Streeter's influence was fearsome in this locality,
should one know to look for it.

Feeling like a voyeur, she studied the man in question with a flutter
in her belly she neither welcomed nor recognized. Tobias was standing
behind a drafting table, drawing on a sheet of foolscap, a metal-edged
ruler guiding his path across the page. The muscles in his arms were
flexing with the movement, his upper body covered in nothing but a
wrinkled cotton shirt of excellent quality. The collar again open at the
neck, exposing a slice of golden skin to her hungry gaze. A gust from
the cracked casement danced through the room, tugging at the ends of
a loose cravat dangling around his neck. Placing the graphite pencil

between his teeth, he leaned in and over his work, and a lank strand of jet hair fell into his face.

It hit her while she stood there, amassing details. There was more to this man than anyone knew. His space, each one she'd entered, was full of his vibrant personality. She felt like an explorer who'd uncovered a rare, wondrous treasure.

She lost herself watching him sketch, one line extending to another across the page, his mumbled observations inaudible as he positioned a compass and completed a tight circle, then ironed his hand over the sheet with a smile. He had beautiful hands, the fingers long and slim like a pianist's. Or a sculptor's. Chiseled forearms disappeared into carelessly rolled sleeves. Broad chest, lean waist. She couldn't see his legs because of the table, but she'd looked her fill in his warehouse two short days ago.

He was built like a man who used his body.

Although, his penetrating study was reminiscent of a man who used his *mind*.

She squinted, her breath fading. An inked illustration of a quill surrounded by a moon and four stars lay like a birthmark on the inside of his right wrist. Small, the symbol no bigger than a half crown, but something she'd never seen before. On any man. She made a helpless noise, a throaty gasp that sounded all too feminine and caused him to glance up.

Oh.

Her heart dropped, the tattoo forgotten when she caught sight of his spectacles.

The lit taper on the drafting table winked off the lenses, flooding his emerald eyes with bursts of gold and amber. Before he killed the emotion by dropping the pencil from his teeth to his hand and looking down, he'd revealed a gaze brimming with captivation and pleasure, a man spellbound by his task.

In love with his work, if not the woman he planned to marry.

He should've appeared a ruffian playing a part, fashioning a ruse of some sort when instead he looked utterly appealing—like no man she'd ever known. She simply had no comparison. Tobias Streeter rejected every box she shoved him in.

Gentleman, delinquent, scholar, charlatan.

"You're early," he said gruffly, seemingly stung by her catching him unaware. Before he'd had time to arrange a glib façade to present to her. "And once again, unsafely alone. The most unchaperoned woman in London, you are, luv."

"My age has slain the need for a maid to follow along for no good reason other than propriety. For which my disheartening reputation and I are grateful." She tilted her chin to indicate the way she'd come. "Footmen, nevertheless, as in two, are as we speak stalking your tasting room. As you recommended, I decided to employ menacing ones. Though I can hardly afford the luxury. Hulking brutes soft on conversation but ready to brawl if I so much as flick my pinkie. You may want to send your factotum to check on them. When I left, they were in desperate search of an open bottle of your malt."

He frowned, an endearing wrinkle forming between his brows. "You followed my advice?"

"How could I argue? You were right. I've left the gangly post-boys behind since my travels have suddenly become, well, more adventurous. I'm guessing the next stop will be a meeting on the deck of one of your ships. I'll need *five* hulking brutes to protect me there."

He dropped the graphite pencil to the desk with a snap. "You're admitting I'm right?"

"There *is* a first for everything, Mr. Streeter."

Tobias dragged his stubbled jaw across his shoulder, then seemed to remember his state of dress and twisted to snatch his coat off the hook behind him. His overlong hair glimmered cobalt in the taper's glow.

"Haircut," she murmured when the comment had been meant as a whisper in her mind.

He paused, his arm entangled in his coat sleeve, his apple-green gaze, now free of suspicion over females' motives, seizing hers and holding. "Excuse me?"

Chewing on her lip to avoid liberating a smile—something he wouldn't appreciate—she gestured to the folio, *her* folio, balanced on the corner of his table. The very *tiptop* corner, as if he'd given it and her plans for him minor accommodation in his world. "I would like to make an addendum to the list of items to complete before the marriage. Before you sign our agreement, and I have no professional leg to stand upon." She pointed to his head, then drew a circle in the air with her finger. "Haircut. Yours."

His jaw flexed as he continued muscling into his coat without comment.

Hildy plucked the folio off the table and gestured to the imposing leather armchair situated in the middle of the room. "May I?"

"Certainly, Templeton," he said flatly while straightening his lapels. "Whatever lights your wick."

She frowned at the vulgar reference but refused to engage in battle —*not yet*—and settled into a butter-soft armchair as grand as any in Windsor Castle. Aside from the sour aroma of malt fermentation, the room also smelled faintly of beeswax, ink, and an exotic spice no doubt just unloaded from one of his ships. She noted this as she wiggled a list free from her folio and smoothed it on the console table at her side, trying diligently *not* to ponder if the spice would cling to his lustrous hair and golden skin or be noticeable if she pressed her nose to either.

If she were to do that. Which she wasn't ever going to. The fact that his office space smelled like a dream, meaning he likely did too, mattered little.

Trying to get back on track, Hildy glanced around, searching for a quill.

"Top left drawer, luv. Quill and inkwell. So, you're readily able to add to my list of improvements."

She could see her image reflected in the glossy mahogany surface as she freed the writing implements from their tasteful confinement. Quality, every piece of furniture in every room he graced. Smuggling was evidently a thriving profession.

"The haircut is merely a suggestion. We're striving to blend you into the environs, not make you stand out. You've worn the renegade routine thin as gossamer." She dipped the quill in the well and tapped the excess ink free. "I thought, for ease of acceptance, we would tread the gentleman's route. Or as close as humanly possible. For the benefit of the Earl of Hastings, if nothing else. This melodrama, parading you around like a prize stallion for the *ton's* inspection, is at his request."

"For the benefit of your dashed society, you mean. Securing the four chits Hastings has following behind my darling doctor. A notion that will strike fear in the hearts of men. The Mad Matchmaker on the loose." He grunted curtly on his way to the sideboard tucked in the corner of the room. Another gorgeous piece worthy of royalty—satinwood, if she didn't miss her guess.

Glass clinked against crystal, then a tumbler containing liquor close to the color of his skin appeared beside her. Although Tobias continued his journey, circling the room twice while she made notes in her folio. Finally, he halted before her, bracing his arm on the drafting table in a languid slump she wondered if he'd practiced before a mirror. He looked styled for visitors and, at the same time, windblown and vivacious as if he'd just arrived from a fantastic voyage on one of his ships.

She sighed and tucked a strand of hair that had gotten loose from her chignon behind her ear. "Your valet can do the trim. Light on the sides, marginal reduction in the back. You act as if it's an amputation."

"I object to anyone telling me what to do." He took a deliberate sip, his boot—Hoby, without question—tapping the floor in a graceful rhythm at the edge of her vision. "And I have no valet."

Without glancing up, she made another notation. *Acquire valet.*

"What else do you have planned? Aside from ordering me to sack my mistress of long-standing, distance myself from profitable yet dubious businesses, and oh, yes, cut my hair. Add to that a seasoned valet arriving in my household tomorrow morning, I suspect. Another person to demean my activities, but the joy is that it'll be from within my own *home*."

Hildy drew a quill surrounded by a moon and star in the column, then flushing, took a taut breath and looked up. One phrase had stung like a needle piercing her skin. "Long-standing?"

"Fair enough. A month." He hid a smile behind his glass, then shrugged, and let it free. He actually grinned, the gesture shaving years off his face until she could see a glimmer of a boy in his rounded cheeks and that appealing dent beside his mouth. A revelation she didn't require to fan the flames of her attraction.

She huffed and glanced back at her list, irrational jealousy cutting a wide path through her. "Other items to work on. Gifts for your intended. Review of titles and proper address. Evaluation of your staff, as you'll need more in residence with a wife arriving shortly. Attendance at a ball—"

His glass smacked the drafting table with a bang. "*No* bloody balls. And it's not the clothing keeping me away because I have them."

Hildy counted to five, then eyed him with a cool smile. "This event is being held by my dearest friend and partner, the Duchess of Markham. In ten days, giving us time to make certain arrangements. It's an ideal opportunity to introduce you in a manner befitting a man marrying an earl's daughter. Due to the ball being held in the winter, a reduced crowd of vultures will be in attendance." When she could see he wasn't swayed, she pushed. Patient persistence was a skill. "They're actually quite lovely people, the duke and duchess. Markham is almost as unconventional as you. He loves geology and his duchess, and that's about it. Furthermore, it's a masquerade. Consider it a gentle launch."

Tobias slipped a toothpick from his pocket and wedged it between his lips. It bobbed as he thought. His mouth was *very* pleasing, she decided. Sensual yet stubborn. She bet he could kiss the varnish off a silver teapot if he tried. "So, they won't know who I am? Then what's the point?"

Hildy stalled, her gaze helplessly taking him in from head to toe. She gestured to his height, feebly, and touched her nose where spectacles would have hit, indicating his eyes. The last touch was to her wrist, the tattoo. None of which made any sense to anyone but her. "They'll know."

He'd recorded her deliberation, her bold appraisal, with patent stillness. After a moment of rousing silence—the bite of attraction in the air warmer than the heat rising off the banked fire in the hearth—he leaned out without losing contact with the table, almost bending over her, his finger going to the drawing of the quill, star, and moon she'd drawn on the sheet. He tapped it once and sat back, removing the toothpick and laying it aside.

"I spent summers as a boy with my cousins on the Romani caravans. I sketched into the night until we lost light. My grandmother, *púridaia*, made me go to sleep with a promise that everything would be there when I woke. Every day, the same comforting routine. Surrounded by family and that roaring campfire, a sea of stars, the moon guiding us." He tilted his head, staring abstractedly at the ceiling as if an image of the convoy was painted there.

"They're a whimsical people, the Rom, unafraid to dream, happy to lose hours to it. I'd never encountered such freedom and have never again found it. Sometimes I want to run back, sleep under the stars, and let the world revolve around me. But after all this time, I don't belong there, and I certainly don't belong here. The scant amount of blue blood in my veins is tainted, almost worse than having none. I have a toehold in two extraordinarily disparate worlds, welcome in neither."

"So, the rumors are true," Hildy whispered, struck by his raw honesty when men rarely disclosed their thoughts, feelings, beliefs. Especially to a woman. She'd never known a man to be sincere and had no idea how to respond.

Tobias hummed a nonanswer, then smiled in a self-deprecating way, his gaze lowering as if he'd shared too much. Perhaps he had. "Not to be indiscreet, but the mystery surrounding me, which I find amusing *and* puzzling, has helped me acquire lots of things. Personal and professional. I built an empire with fast hands and a convenient naval profession granting me contacts around the world. Ones I've used to procure a boundless assortment of merchandise. Some legal, some... not. But it wasn't the empire I longed for. Which is where you step in. Why I'm allowing this charade, as it were." He exhaled and adjusted his spectacles when they needed no adjustment. "It's the reason Mattie and I are players in this absurd game."

Hildy frowned, unsure she understood, adding a question mark after the word *masquerade* on her list.

Sitting back, he rolled his shoulders, giving her a candid assessment. Lifting his glass, he peered inside before placing it by his side. Reading her and judging himself. *How much to tell?* Finally, he held out his hand, and she blinked, staring at the slim fingers she'd dreamed of the night before. It was *his* hand she'd imagined when she touched herself in her darkened bedchamber, losing herself to the fantasy. A startling reality that should've had her summoning her partner, begging

Georgiana to take over this assignment before she woke and rang for tea.

"Frightened yet?" Tobias whispered, his smile diabolical. "Or are you willing to take the dare?"

Her gaze skipped to his starkly beautiful face. *Yes, terrified.* Then she grasped his hand and let him tug her to her feet.

He escorted her to the other side of the drafting table and positioned her rather indelicately between his spread legs, his front warming her back until it was as if she stood in a burning ember. Goosebumps rose on her arms and chest, sensation mounting inside her. To speak sensibly would have been a challenge, so she remained silent, waiting for sensibility to surpass feeling.

Flicking aside a metal triangle and a wooden ruler with Belcher Bros. stamped on the inset, Tobias dashed his hand across the blueprint laid out before her. "I'm completing a proposal set to secure my involvement with a series of projects for John Nash, now that he's completed Park Crescent and Marylebone Park."

Hildy reached to trace a section of the design, an immense veranda supported by columns. "Doric," she said and pulled her hand back before she actually touched the vellum. *John Nash.* Heavens, Tobias Streeter's ambition—and his talent, she surmised from the beautifully detailed architectural plan—knew no bounds.

He caught her hand when he still held her other one and pressed her fingers to the paper. "Roman Doric." Following the lines he'd drawn, his breath streaked past her cheek. "Greek are fluted, Roman plain."

Her toes curled inside her slippers, and a scent she hadn't detected before, something foreign and enticing that must have drifted from his skin, lit a blaze inside her. "The warehouse. The architect you said you'd tell when I mentioned I liked the design. It's you."

He hummed again, mercifully stepping back enough to give her room to breathe. Casually dropping one hand while keeping hold of the other. "My little secret. *Our* little secret, luv."

"How does Nash's committee tie into your marriage?"

"The assembled team will be announced in five weeks, one week after the wedding. I was advised that having the Earl of Hastings on my side in a familial capacity would be enormously beneficial. My architectural proposal was outstanding, etcetera, etcetera. However, I'm known as a smuggler in certain circles and the bastard of a viscount in others, which presented a negative bias. Truthfully, the Romani blood isn't proving terribly helpful either."

He let loose a mocking sound that could've been a laugh or a sigh and rocked from one foot to the other in those elegant boots. "You see, since my beloved father has never seen fit to acknowledge me, and I would *perish* before asking him to, I must make this happen for myself. On my own. As it's been with everything else. Straight from my family's caravan to a Limehouse distillery and beyond."

So, that's why he's doing it.

Matilda hoped to gain the freedom to pursue her dream. Tobias hoped to gain the credibility to pursue his.

Hildy stared at the plans, her mind awash with a thunderous mix of awe and dread, elation and hopelessness. Grand—and not just the buildings he wanted to erect.

Tobias Streeter was shooting very, very high.

She glanced over her shoulder, wondering if he realized he still held her hand. She'd left her gloves in her carriage, and the callouses on his fingertips drove a shaft of greedy desire through her that she was ill-advised to feel. "Any more secrets I should know about as we enter into this business arrangement? I like to be prepared."

Proving he knew he still touched her, he drew a sluggish circle on her wrist as his shrewd gaze devoured her, searching for facets she didn't want to share. After a lingering heartbeat of inspection, he shook his head. "I've shared my secrets, my lady. What of yours?"

The ungainly shrug rolled off her shoulder before she could call it back. "I'm what you see, nothing more, nothing less. An earl's daughter who's chosen to embrace the fringe of society while helping others navigate wading into the middle."

His fingers curled around her wrist as he leaned in until she could see specks of gold swirling in his eyes. "What if I said I don't believe you're anywhere near that simple? And that I'm intrigued beyond measure by this theory?"

Her tongue came out to moisten her lips, a nervous gesture she shouldn't have allowed as his gaze strayed to her mouth and held, cornering them both. "I would return that it's pointless. Your interest, that is."

He laughed scornfully, a self-directed reprimand. "We're attracted to who we're attracted to, Templeton. Even if it's inconvenient." Releasing her hand to fall and brush against the fine wool of his trouser leg, he said with equanimity, "Don't lash yourself over it."

Any rebuttal to Tobias's cryptic statement, should Hildy have had one crowding her mind, was lost as a tawny-headed boy entered the office at a near run. Braces dangling at his hip, untucked shirt dusting his thighs, an envelope clutched in his hand. "Mr. Toby, the rye delivery is being unloaded in the alley. You told me to let ya know. And this here letter was—" He stumbled to a halt and jerked his cap from his head. "Begging pardon, ma'am."

"Toby," she whispered with a smile.

"*Don't*," he whispered back.

Hildy took his discomfiture as an opportunity to free herself, stepping around the drafting table and into the center of the room. "Well, hello, young man."

An orange cat raced in behind the boy and, astonishingly, headed straight for the Rogue King. Where he proceeded to circle Tobias's long legs in a series of familiar number eights. The feline looked delighted and more than a little enamored.

Tobias frowned and eyed the cat, shifting his leg to disengage the beast, who continued to lovingly bump him. "He's only here to keep mice out of the grain."

The boy wrestled his braces over his shoulder. Attire corrected, he shuffled across the room and scooped the cat up and against his chest. "Nick Bottom here goes home with Mr. Toby every night. Rides along in that showy vehicle, cream still clinging to his blessed whiskers. Luckiest malt tom in Limehouse, that's fer certain. Best mouser on the block, too."

Nick Bottom. Hildy couldn't have stopped herself from glancing at Tobias if someone had paid her coal bill for the rest of the year if she hadn't. "*A Midsummer Night's Dream?*"

Tobias's jaw tensed as his cheeks lit a most marvelous shade of cherry. "Rookery boys can read, you know."

"Not many, matter of fact," the boy mumbled, his face buried in marmalade fur. As he shifted the feline, the letter he clutched in his tiny fist tumbled to the carpet. Axminster. And new, by the looks of it.

Hildy stepped in before Tobias could get there—because he rounded the desk trying to—and stooped to grab the envelope. It was the buoyant pink of a calla lily petal. She lifted the vellum to her nose and drew a surface breath.

Jasmine and passion.

Towering over her, Tobias snatched the envelope from her grasp and slipped it behind his back, out of sight. "I cut her loose as requested," he murmured for her ears only. "But I can't control the requests to continue the association."

Hildy rose from her awkward squat, smoothed her hand down her bodice, and tried to look unaffected when that nagging sting in her chest endured. "It's of no concern to me. Your fiancée is perhaps another matter."

Tobias stared, his eyes darkening to the verdant color of sunburned grass, which meant something. Although Hildy didn't know him well enough to know what.

"The rye, Mr. Toby," the boy reminded him, letting Nick Bottom slide from his arms to the floor with a dull thump.

"I'll be out in a moment, Nigel. Let the men know they can start unloading."

Nigel prepared to race from the room as fast as he'd raced in. In the doorway, he turned and dragged his grubby fist across his nose. "Lunch?"

Tobias cast a swift look at her, another piece of him being revealed like a tarnished teapot buffed to divulge the true patina beneath. "In the granary. My rucksack. Ham and cheese. And a small bag of sweets."

Nigel grinned and stretched his brace out, letting it pop back against his chest. "Thanks, Mr. Toby." Then he executed an enthusiastic bow and bounded down the hallway, his footsteps echoing off the office walls. Nick Bottom waltzed across the room, gave her an unenthusiastic sniff, jumped into the chair, and promptly fell asleep half atop her folio.

"There's also bread," Tobias added softly, but Nigel had already left the vicinity. He exhaled and gave his spectacles another shove, plainly unnerved by the spill of information. An unforeseen unveiling of the man beneath the mask.

She traced a crimson thread in the carpet with her slipper and tried to sound casual. "The boy?"

"My new valet," he murmured, depositing the perfumed letter inconspicuously on the drafting table. At her continued silence, one that expected an explanation, he lifted his hand to scrub at the back of his neck, sending that inky mass of hair sliding through his fingers. Awareness, attraction, were a pulsing rhythm through her. Less a muted heartbeat than the solid pulse of blood through her veins. She'd never experienced the like, especially with someone she hardly *knew*.

What had he called it? *Inconvenient.*

It was *bloody* inconvenient.

Tobias fiddled with the ruler on his desk, his gaze roving the ceiling, the floor. "The distillery requires labor, but many of the tasks admittedly involve modest skill. Unloading shipments, searching corn barrels for rotten kernels. Daily checks of the casks for leakage. Temperature assessments of the distillery during off-hours, which simply means someone is sleeping here all night." He pointed the ruler in the direction of the bowels of the building, where she could hear the clang and ding of the boilers she'd passed hard at work.

"We employ stills, utilizing a triple extraction method. Two hundred thousand gallons of whiskey are projected to flow through here each year when we're at full capacity." Finally, he glanced at her— just enough to read her reaction before he looked away. His expression was self-congratulatory; there was no way to deny it. It warmed her heart, the boyishness behind the blatant conceit. A sentiment she should've spurned when instead she was drawn like a butterfly to a thicket of aster.

She wriggled her folio from beneath Nick Bottom's plump feline bottom. "I have no idea what that means, and you know it. Lording your superior knowledge over me, how typically male."

"Triple distillation provides a smoother flavor versus modified double distillation, which is what's currently done in Ireland. Each drop of my whiskey is created with my grandmother's tenet in mind. The saying is slapped on every label, in fact. *Spirits for the eradication of incurable heartache.*" He winked, and the skin beneath her suddenly tight bodice glowed, moist and warm. "The Romani are big on incurable heartache, luv."

His effective dodge proved she was straying into areas where he wasn't comfortable. He'd doubtless never had anyone ask questions—only blindly follow orders. "You're quite skilled, Mr. Streeter. I'm duly impressed when I'm certain it's dangerous to admit it."

"We're not enemies, even if it feels like we are. If my self-esteem can handle the kick, you're doing me a favor, leveling what could be a rough path. I realize I was never meant for the life I'm forcing myself into. At least, I'm honest about my ambition." He shrugged and pointlessly angled the ruler neatly across his drawing. "Fermentation is basic chemistry, which I've found I have a talent for. Macauley, my partner, can sell anything to anyone, be it nun, duke, or beggar, so we make an excellent team."

"Nigel works for you, checking corn barrels and such? Part of the agreement that his lunch is to be delivered in your rucksack?"

"Don't gentlemen provide meals for their valets?"

She clicked her tongue against her teeth. *More dodging.*

He shifted, fully facing her, perching his hip against the table. "Nigel is one of about ten boys who work in the distillery. Or my warehouse. I have another seven, an older group, on the ships. They come from a workhouse a few streets over where conditions are deplorable. I almost found myself there for a short period when my mother was ill, before my navel adventure began. Now, I'm a silent patron of sorts. Nigel was working in a tarring house before he came to me, by the by. From eight in the morning until ten at night."

She shook her head in question, her grip on the folio loosening along with control of her heart as she began to recognize the full measure of Tobias Streeter's benevolence.

"Ropes are tarred so the salt water doesn't rot them. It's necessary work. As a man who owns a small fleet of ships, I can't deny this. But it isn't work for a nine-year-old boy. Nigel had scurvy when I came upon him six months ago. Terrific wounds on his hands and feet that wouldn't heal from lack of vitamins or something. Mattie's been treating him *and* going into the workhouse regularly. Which her father doesn't know about, if you please. So now, Nigel sleeps here, or *hell's teeth*"—Tobias yanked his hand through the disheveled layers of his jet-black hair—"at my townhome, if you must know. And that damned cat, too. Who may be pregnant when I named her Nick!"

Hildy brought the folio to her breast and hugged it, hiding her delight but just barely. In a roundabout, miraculous way, she was doing what she'd planned with the Duchess Society all along. Even on this most unexpected of projects. She was preparing a capable woman for marriage to a *good* man. "You're not nearly the ruffian you pretend to be. Rough edges aplenty, but what's beneath is strong. And kittens are simply the most darling thing in the world. You'll never see another mouse in this dwelling in this lifetime if Nick becomes a mother."

Tobias paused, his hand dropping to his side, surprise illuminating his eyes when she guessed people rarely surprised him. "Don't shine a hero's light on me, Templeton. One false move, and I'll snuff out the flame. I've done horrendous things to survive. Things I'll continue to do, society wife or no. When people fear you, that fear offers its own protection."

She tilted her head with a smile. "Shakespeare, cats, orphans."

He returned the smile but without humor. "Smuggling, larceny, intimidation."

Hildy found it hard to believe that the man standing before her would be married in four short weeks to a woman who hadn't the desire to shove him back against his desk and kiss the breath from him.

A woman who would *never* have that desire.

When Hildy was burning up from the inside out with it.

"How did you meet her? Lady Matilda?" she asked and gave the folio another hard squeeze. She'd never once thought to ask either of them. Ask any of her clients. When it hardly mattered now, did it?

His amusement came swiftly, as did the dent next to his mouth. "I ripped a page out of *Debrett's*, tacked it up, and threw a dart."

Her heart skittered. "Did you *really?*"

He grinned, a legitimate, one-of-a-kind presentation unlike anything he'd shown so far. She'd always admired people who could laugh at themselves, who could laugh at life. "No, luv, we met at Epsom. Her father and I have the same horse trainer. Though I can tell you, only one of us is actually paying his bills."

"Oh, of course," she whispered, her cheeks flushing.

He flicked his coat aside and braced his hand on his lean hip, staring at her as if something about the scene fascinated him. The ends of his untied cravat dangled enticingly down his chest. "I'll sign your contract." He nodded to the folio she clutched to her chest, her own brand of armor. "Get a valet and a haircut." His jaw flexed. "Go to your bloody masquerade ball."

Her shoulders slumped as a relieved breath whispered past her lips. Securing Hastings's agreement to assist his remaining four daughters through their matrimonial journeys would cover the costs for the mausoleum of a home she'd inherited without also inheriting the funds to maintain it for at least a year. Keep food on the table for her small staff, now more like family, that she'd known since she was in leading strings.

"Ah, there's the light of battle in the Mad Matchmaker's eyes. Like those races through Hyde Park, I wager. You're a gambler, luv. Enjoy a rousing fracas now and again, do you?"

She shook her head. He had it wrong. Had *her* wrong. "I'm not. I don't." She was simply desperate. And liked too much the way his accent, one tied to this neighborhood, she'd speculate, fashioned the word *luv* like it was a sweet you wanted to take and pop in your mouth.

He studied her another haunting moment until Hildy began to feel his regard like she would his touch. Then, rising from his slouch against the desk, he crossed the room and dug through a crate in the corner before coming back to her, a small vase in his hand. It had a ruffled edge like a collar gone mad and was as blue as a cornflower.

Hildy clasped the folio almost painfully against her chest, her breath leaving her.

"Take it," he directed and knocked it against her hand, his gaze clashing with hers. Twice, until she could do nothing but take the beautiful piece from him.

She tilted the vase in the candlelight, sending a sapphire shimmer over the wall. "This would be an appropriate gift for Lady Matilda, as we mentioned you need to start sending her. Presents the staff can then turn around and gossip about, validating your attachment to the *ton* and her father. Remember, the courtship rituals."

"You make it sound like a game, not love."

She swallowed, her fingers curling around the vase, an item she wanted. She couldn't lie to herself about that. Even if she *could* lie to the man standing hesitantly before her. "It's noted on the contract that I'm to help you select suitable gifts for your intended. It's not a standard part of my agreement if you're wondering, but this situation isn't standard for the Duchess Society in any way."

He knuckled his spectacles high and rocked back on his heels. "Mattie only wants medical instruments. Bottles of iodine, cotton balls, scalpels. Needles and thread." Embarrassment seemed to settle in as his gaze evaded hers. "I have an entire crate of them, the vases with a tiny imperfection in the base. They're Bristol glass, shipped direct. Anyway, I thought you might like one."

Hildy parted her lips to thank him, but the sting in her eyes kept her from speaking. She hadn't been given a gift in, well, in *forever*. Except for her friend and partner, Georgiana Munro, the Duchess of Markham, she was relatively alone in the world.

When Nigel burst into the room for a second time, chocolate smeared across his cheek, a half-eaten biscuit in his hand, Hildy pretended the magical moment with the Rogue King had never occurred.

Chapter Five

Avase.

He'd given the Mad Matchmaker a blasted *vase*.

A gift that, unknown to her but bloody well known to *him*, was strikingly similar to the one his father had given his mother years ago. Bristol blue.

Like Hildegard Templeton's eyes, if he was being romantic about it.

Possibly worse, he'd told her about Nigel. And Nick Bottom, who'd pulled the underhanded feline ploy of *I'm pregnant, therefore not a male*.

Tobias strode across the deck of his ship, *Orion's Glory*, gloomy moonlight lighting his path between a monstrous pile of rope and seven crates awaiting delivery to his warehouse the following morning. He halted at the railing, slipped a flask from his overcoat pocket, and took a therapeutic pull in hopes it would erase the astonishment on her lovely face when he gave her the vase.

So prim and yet...

A man's never given her anything, he thought dully, watching refuse float past, carried by a swift river current. Frankly, her awkwardly adorable expression had turned him to putty in seconds. She could've asked for the moon, and he'd have labored to snatch it down for her.

Frankly, it was her smile that killed him. Measured, subtle, and almost hesitant—but when it broke, it broke. Wicked and alluring, as glorious as a blazing sunset you weren't expecting that you caught sight of around a bend in the road.

He was puzzled by her. And fascinated.

She wielded her beauty less than any woman he'd ever known. Tobias didn't know how to engage in battle with people who didn't use their handiest weapons.

The longing to uncover her secrets was blinding.

"You didn't tell me about the matchmaker's dimples, mate. Prime bit of information left out of the equation, if you ask me. Gerrie said he could tuck a thimble in 'em, how deep they were. And hair the color of sunlight."

Tobias groaned and took another tug on his flask, ignoring the bait as Macauley settled in beside him at the railing, the scent of labor and Asian spice arriving with him.

"Lawks, it's freezing up here." Jamming an unlit cheroot between his teeth, he wrestled his leather gloves from his pocket and struggled to yank them on. Macauley preferred to be on a ship located in the more pleasing environs of the Caribbean. Although he'd grown up six streets west from where they now stood, he'd never been much for England's horrendous weather. Macauley struck the tinder and lit the cheroot, then expelled a stream of smoke into the hazy night. It never took long to find out what was on his mind—and Tobias was a patient negotiator. "Our man got back to me. That trifling matter you wanted him to investigate."

Tobias stiffened, his hand curling around the flask. "And?"

"Lady H's father left her in a bad way. Known for violent outbursts, a rather disagreeable sort. Gambled away the fortune before his death, the title passed to his son, who passed some years ago from typhus. Luckily or not, the brother protected her. They were close. He left the chit his terraced house off St. James's Park, one of those refined Georgians now crumbling around her, and a batch of starving domestics to support. You know the story. A distant cousin got the title and the entailed properties. Not well-liked, that bloke. A miser.

"No other siblings. Refused marriage at least twice, according to gossip. Educated alongside her brother by private tutors, so be warned.

She has a brain in that lovely head. Latin, Greek, the usual." Macauley tapped his cheroot against the railing, sending gray ash fluttering past them like snowflakes. "A tolerably attractive girl. Dazzling, Gerrie tells me. Following her all over town in a daze, he is. Though she tries to keep her attractiveness quiet when beauty shouts, now don't it, mate? A vital point you failed to impart to your trusted partner while in turn asking him to get the goods on the girl."

Intelligent. Dazzling. That about summed her up. Tobias tapped the flask against his bottom lip. "The cousin got the blunt, so she has no funds to manage the household." He silently added *desperate* to the list. Intelligent, dazzling, desperate.

"The cousin got the blunt," Macauley agreed and took another drag. "Same narrative time and again. A woman sank low by what's nestled snugly between their legs and nothing but. Being born with a rod does help in certain situations."

Tobias tucked the flask in his waistband and yanked his lapels against his neck. The evening *was* getting blustery but, by God, was the moonlight dancing across the Thames painting an enchanting picture. "But it hurts in others, my friend."

Macauley clicked his tongue against his teeth in masculine accord. "Indeed."

"So that's why she does it." For money. However, the passion on her face when she talked about her useless society was more than a need for coin.

"Only three years older than your enchanting doctor too, Street, putting Lady H maybe a year younger than *you*. If you're thinking she's on the shelf due to that bizarre idea this town has about age and matrimony, you'd be right. Smidge of irony, there, innit, that she's helping others get what she don't want?"

"No one has ever forced her, I suppose, to say yes to one of those offers."

Macauley whistled around his cheroot. "The Mad Matchmaker seem like a chit you can force to do things?"

Tobias glanced over the railing at the rubbish floating by the ship. *Good point.*

"Seems it's her decision mostly, not marrying. Although this daft club she runs propels men away like she lit a torch and shoved it up their plump arses. Prettiness can't make up for being destitute. No one wants a penniless, *clever* wife."

The wind ripped off the Thames and tossed Tobias's hair into his eyes. Hair he was getting cut tomorrow because *Lady H* demanded it. He'd already contacted an agency about a bloody valet as well. She was only a year younger than he was, younger than he'd imagined. Which made his chest constrict in a protective way that concerned him.

"Still like her, I see, from the sappy look," Macauley murmured, a shiver wracking his muscular frame beneath a coat satisfactory enough for a prince. "With Juliet sending sweet-smelling notes and whatnot, begging for you to take her back. And this doctor-fiancée. Damn, what a kettle of women you're tangling with."

Instead of lying, the truth rolled out. "I told her I was inconveniently attracted."

Macauley gave him a disgusted side-glance and flipped his cheroot over the railing and into the waves slapping the ship's bow. "You're losing all the tricks I took years showing you, Street. Your charming manner with women right down the drain and into the sewer along with this marriage business. Ruined, you are, or close to it. Blimey, but I'm disheartened."

Ruined.

Tobias thought back to the time this afternoon he'd spent with Hildegard in his cramped distillery office. They'd skipped between bickering and flirting, verbal jousting he didn't find many people capable of, the encounter leaving him slightly dazed. He wanted to dislike her, distrust her even. But he couldn't because, agree with her or not, and he mostly *didn't*, she was sincere in her objectives. She wasn't pushing the idealistic view of marriage, wasn't pushing *love*.

She was pushing freedom, decency, clarity.

Love, she'd barely mentioned.

Indeed, *he* was never going to push the topic. He'd seen what came from professing that emotion during his parent's fateful non-union. Complete and utter destruction. His mother had died penniless and, except for a son stationed four thousand miles away fighting senseless battles in India, alone. While Viscount Craven was somewhere across town right this minute, lounging with his cronies at White's, Brooks, or Boodle's. Enjoying the best brandy money could buy and the latest edition of *The Times*, ironed flat as a rose petal pressed between pages, as he liked it.

Tobias looked over to find his partner gazing at him with reluctant compassion. "Not all closed doors are locked, Mac, but mine *are*. I need this marriage to unlock them."

Macauley jacked his thumb toward the streets behind them; one cheerless dwelling stacked aside another, row upon row until there was nothing but a world of deprivation bleeding to the horizon. The scent of coal smoke and sulfur from the wharf mud wrapped about them like a cloak. "You have enough buildings you can repair right here in Limehouse. Buy the whole lot for a half crown. Or knock 'em down and create new. Your designs, your vision. You don't need this swanky project with Nash, marriage to a woman you don't love and who doesn't love you, to be who you want to be. Time to live *this* life, innit, Street? The one you've worked so hard for? Quit trying to show your father you're better. That fortune-teller crone in your tribe—"

"The Romani are not a tribe—"

"Told you that very thing. Let it go, mate. I think these toffs you're trying to pattern yourself after are more ruthless than the criminals we, as gentleman smugglers, deal with in our grimy back alleys. I'll take a knife at the throat, versus one in the side I don't see coming, any day."

Macauley was right. Tobias *was* shooting too high in a variety of ways. Being even aimlessly attracted to Hildegard Templeton was pointless because she was a mirage. Out of reach and not what you thought when you got there. If he coaxed her into bed, the act would probably be disappointing anyway, like it often was with a woman that beautiful.

Plus, she'd been surprised he read Shakespeare. Surprised he read at *all*.

A familiar sting of disapproval he couldn't entirely overlook.

Mattie knew what she was getting. A clever, uneducated, insanely wealthy, half-Romani smuggler who wished to be an architect. He wouldn't have to spend his life proving his worth to *her*. Or explaining his motives because she'd be off sewing stitches and swabbing fevered brows.

Besides, no woman could handle the darkness in his soul *and* his staggering need.

Turning, he jammed his back against the railing and gazed at a sky littered with stars, silver pinpricks embedded in an endless velvet swath unfurling over the neighborhood he loved. "Any idea what you wear to a masquerade ball?"

Macauley cursed behind the fist he wiped across his mouth. "Blast, does she have you by the short hairs."

Tobias choked on a laugh. "Mattie couldn't care less about my short hairs, Mac."

Macauley sighed and hung his head. "I meant the matchmaker, mate." He slapped his hand on the railing and reached for another cheroot. "Ask your tailor. Best in London, ain't he? Even if he does make you use the alley entrance." Tucking the smoke between his teeth, he grinned around it. "Or better yet, ask the prying chit."

"Care to accompany me? It's at a duke's or some such nonsense. Probably right down the street from my own Mayfair manse. Wouldn't that be amusing? I'll tell Lady H you're my footman. Or my valet. Do they even go to these things? Since we've had security issues of late, someone to watch my back might be a prime idea."

Macauley straightened, turning to face his partner. "Has something else happened? I increased patrols around the warehouse and at the distillery. Nigel is going home with you each night, not staying there alone anymore. And Gerrie's watching your girl."

Not my girl, he wanted to say but didn't bother. "My carriage's axle was tampered with two nights ago. The coachman noticed the wheel was unsteady when he pulled the conveyance around yesterday morning. If we'd been going at a steady clip, the blasted thing would have flipped for sure."

Macauley patted his coat pocket. "You're prepared?"

Tobias nodded. Pistol strapped to his chest, knife in his boot. And he knew, from growing up in a rookery, and later, his wretched time in India, how to use both.

Macauley pushed off the railing, his dark overcoat fluttering around his ankles and making him look like a fallen hero. "My suggestion? We discuss this masquerade business over drinks. Dice. Women. In that order."

Tobias held up a hand in warning, but his smile was daring. "A hidden nook of a public house, Mac. And I do mean a grubby hole. Nothing can end up in the newspapers. I've had enough of my life spilled in black ink." He scrubbed his hand over the back of his neck, ashamed to admit it but needing to place the truth out there so Macauley helped him stay on the straight and narrow. "The Mad Matchmaker, she's not sympathetic to scandal."

"By the short hairs," Macauley murmured and slung his arm over Tobias's shoulders as they crossed *Orion's* deck, headed for trouble.

The vase looked even better with flowers, Hildy decided and scooted it two inches to the left on her desk. Into a fat ray of morning sunlight penetrating the room from the window of what had once been her father's study. Then her brother, Edwin's. Now hers.

The windowpanes needed repair. One was cracked, and drafts continually whistled in around the casements, creating a frigid space even on a temperate summer day.

She shivered and tucked her cloak about her. This was no temperate summer day.

"I've set up an appointment with our solicitor to create a trust for Lady Nightingale and prepare the papers for her to sign *before* she signs the betrothal agreement. Baron Mercer, goodness, he's not a bad man we've concluded from our research, but he is a rather *tightfisted* one."

Hildy blinked, forgetting that Georgiana, Duchess of Markham, her closest friend and partner, occupied the room with her.

"You're daydreaming," Georgiana said from her position behind her escritoire. A castoff on loan from her husband, Dex, that she'd sent over when she and Hildy agreed to start the Duchess Society two years ago. It was a much nicer piece than Hildy's mammoth, scarred desk.

Which regrettably was like the townhouse and the cadre of servants Hildy had been saddled with.

Hers whether she wanted them or not.

Hildy traced the scalloped edge of the vase, a prickle rising in her chest as she gazed at her gift. She'd made a special trip to the market for flowers that were costly and not easy to come by in the winter. Nevertheless, she hadn't been able *not* to. "I'm merely ruminating about that awful man I sent packing this morning before I'd even managed to have a spot of tea. Baron Basildon. He arrived on my doorstep at an inappropriate hour and without a calling card. Just departed from a gaming hell from the looks and smell of him."

Georgie tilted her head in question. "Basildon? I don't believe I'm acquainted."

"Charles Trammell, England's newest baron. Saddled with the title *and* five sisters, the poor bloke. Alas, not a shilling to contribute to the Duchess Society. As much as I'd like to help those girls—"

"We're not running a charity."

"Exactly." She dusted her fingertip across a lilac petal. "Of course, my new project is on my mind as well. The Earl of Hastings's daughter and her upcoming marriage."

"To Tobias Streeter, the *entrepreneur*. Whom I'll meet at my masquerade ball if you can get him there."

Hildy brought her head up slowly, allowing any sentiment on her face to melt away before Georgie could catch sight of it. "I believe the word you're looking for is smuggler. And yes, that's the one. My job is to reform him in four short weeks, then pray a delighted earl sends the rest of his flock to us for enlightenment. My man delivering coal will thank him."

Georgie, whom the *ton* had dubbed The Ice Countess after her first marriage—though she was the least frigid person Hildy knew— knocked her quill against the inkwell in rapid succession until Hildy threw her a quelling glance.

"Out with it," Hildy demanded, folding over the corner of the foolscap sheet she'd been scribbling on to hide the sun and stars she'd drawn. She hadn't been able to get Tobias's tattoo out of her mind. Or the radiance in his sea-green eyes when he'd told her his secrets. "When you tap the inkwell, it means you're nervous. You'd make a horrific gambler, Georgie, with such blatant tells."

Georgie gestured to this morning's edition of the *Gazette* resting on the corner of the escritoire. "Have you, by chance, had an opportunity to read the gossip column yet? There was a disturbance in a public house last night. Limehouse or thereabouts."

Oh. Oh, no. Hildy shoved back her chair, flung her cloak over it, and crossed the room in three unladylike strides. Grabbing the broadsheet, she whipped to the second page, the scandal section. "How could he cause trouble in less than twenty hours? I saw him yesterday *afternoon*. We signed the contract. He jettisoned his mistress. He's cutting his hair." She let her gaze scan the lines of text as dread percolated in her belly. *Dear heaven*, she thought and let the newspaper flutter to Georgie's desk. "He and Roan Darlington, the Duke of Leighton, got into a scuffle. It says someone ended up in the Thames. Mercy, *please* let it not be a duke that got tumbled into the drink."

Georgie opened a drawer, then nudged the newspaper into it and out of sight. "His partner, Xander Macauley, landed in the river. They fished him out, Leighton and your scoundrel drunkenly laughing their heads off, their tiff apparently forgotten. Streeter and Leighton are associates in trade, you see." She dragged the quill across her lip with a chilling half-smile that doubtless scared the devil out of her husband. "I believe he may have partial ownership in one of Streeter's ships, though that could be a rumor."

"Not *my* scoundrel, not *anyone's* scoundrel," she murmured and slumped into the armchair angled before Georgie's desk. Her brother's favorite chair, as a matter of fact. This project was going to be the death of her. She hadn't been this agitated about an upcoming marriage since they'd started the Duchess Society. "How in the world do you know this?"

Georgie propped her elbows on the desk and leaned across its polished surface, eager to gossip. "Dex told me," she whispered, although they were the only people in the room. "I think my darling duke is worried I'm going mad with Anthony starting to walk *and* cutting his teeth, and he's trying to keep me entertained."

Hildy shook her head in confusion, her mind whirling. "How is Dex involved in this debacle?"

Georgie grinned and steepled her fingers, dropping her chin atop them. "The Duke of Leighton's valet is the uncle of one of our foot-men. The valet had to clean the blood off his collar and mud off his boots when he got home, and Leighton relayed the entire story. Word travels the city streets quickly, quicker than the *Gazette*. And dukes love to obtain goods on each other. Our staff knows to tell Dex imme-diately if it's tittle-tattle involving Leighton." She sighed, her lips curling into a divine glower befitting a duchess. "It's like a game. Silli-ness. Then, there they are, rolling around in the dirt."

"Then it's probable the Earl of Hastings knows."

Georgie paused, prepared to fib, then exhaled and nodded.

Yes, of course.

"That dreadful man." Hildy repressed the urge to march to Lime-house and punch Tobias Streeter in his gorgeous, hard as granite jaw. If he knew how badly she needed the Earl of Hastings's business, he might make an effort to adhere to their agreement.

Or maybe not.

"It might not be your project's fault entirely, Hildy. Roan has a temper and a rancorous reputation to match. Cares only for his antiq-uities, hence his partnership with Streeter, I'd presume. As deadly as your scoundrel in the back alley *and* the bedroom, from what I've heard. So, it isn't as if they aren't well-matched in scandalous behavior or dubious business endeavors. Perhaps Hastings will consider it as roughhousing of the masculine variety and not think thrice about it."

With a derisive grumble, Hildy dropped her head back to stare at a crack in her ceiling wide enough to shove a biscuit in. "Hastings wants Streeter to stay clean until after his first grandchild is born. Spotless business, behavior, bedroom."

"*Oh*," Georgie mused in a throaty voice. "There must be a respectable side you can present to Hastings to soften Streeter's rather treacherous standing while lessening the stink of last evening's high jinks. And when someone lands in the Thames, I do mean stink."

Hildy gave the Bristol blue vase a peek from the corner of her eye. The flutter in her chest was not merely her imagination, and the paneled walls of her father's study seemed to be closing in on her. "He employs orphans in various positions in his businesses. Even has one charming scamp, Nigel, living with him from what I could gather." She groaned and pinched the bridge of her nose, imagining the Earl of Hastings cleanly rejecting this engagement and taking his five daughters with him unless she told him things Tobias Streeter would rather she not disclose. Disclosing them to her closest friend was another matter altogether. "And then there's Nick Bottom."

Georgie's brow wrinkled. "*Taming of the Shrew?*"

"*A Midsummer Night's Dream*." At Georgie's cross look, she continued, "A cat. Pregnant. Streeter claims it's only a mouser for his distillery, but he carries her home each night. In his carriage. Along with the boy." And an empty rucksack filled with food for a child each day.

For some odd reason she didn't wish to investigate, Hildy chose to leave this endearing morsel *out* of the story.

Georgie picked up a gilt-edged envelope, tapped it once on the inkwell, then scooted it across the escritoire in Hildy's direction. "You're telling me that Tobias Streeter, fiercest negotiator on the London docks, rumored smuggler and reluctant war hero, a man feared for his dominion of a paltry, crime-ridden section of the East End, yet respected for his management of a hugely successful shipping empire, takes a pregnant cat and a foundling home each evening? To Mayfair? Just two streets over from my townhome, by the way. And he's named said feline after a diabolical Shakespearean character? Am I correct in this so far?"

"You have it," Hildy said, her gaze sneaking to that blasted vase. She didn't mention that her research, done too late in the game, after she'd already made decisions based on imprudent bias, had uncovered what appeared to be food deliveries Streeter's men made each week to various families in need. Plus, there were pleas from his solicitors for better sanitation and housing on public record.

He wasn't taking, not in total. He was also giving.

His veiled generosity changed everything.

Georgie reached for her teacup and took a reverent, ducal sip. "Are you going to tell me where you got the vase?"

Hildy circled the envelope into view. It was an invitation to the masquerade ball. Meant for delivery to a good-looking, gift-giving smuggler in a deprived district twenty minutes away. "No, Your Grace."

Georgie settled her teacup on its saucer and gave a singsong whistle under her breath. "Perhaps we should switch projects for the next week or so. I've much to do preparing for the ball and Lady Delacorte's nuptials in five days. The timing isn't ideal. And with Anthony, my darling son, deciding this week is the week to start teething, I'm struggling. Dex isn't happy about hosting a ball either. Takes away time from his study of igneous rocks or metamorphic stones or something, but I can control certain elements for the couples we're working with as hostess. Provide a protected space for them to interact." At Hildy's chiding look, she gave the cup a deliberate rotation, her gaze falling to the ledgers on her desk. "You would be doing me a favor, you see."

Hildy paused, running through the situation in her mind. It was *her* project. She'd formed a working relationship with Lady Matilda *and* the Earl of Hastings, who had the personality of a stale wafer. She'd drawn up a rather substantial list of items they needed to complete to prepare Tobias Streeter for a biddable, masked introduction to society.

Yet, she kept coming back to two words. *Inconveniently attracted.*

He to her, and she to him.

Heavens, he'd admitted it.

And she hadn't argued against his admission.

With *coward* whispering through her mind in Tobias's mocking voice, Hildy slid the invitation across the desk and officially into Georgie's domain. "He likes to meet at his warehouse or his distillery. You can't go alone. The neighborhood isn't suitable for a duchess. Have Dex accompany you. I think they'll actually like each other. For all we know, his ships have brought your husband some of his geological treasures over the years. He has reasons for marrying, solid reasons from his view, so no need to get into it. I've drafted a list to cover with him before the ball. Review of proper address, titles, and such. Suitable subjects to discuss and those to avoid. He'll be insulted but move past it. He needs to purchase gifts for his intended, and appropriate suggestions are noted. No medical supplies, please, as I've told him these are not the offerings grand love stories are built upon, and the servants will chatter more than they already are if he gives her a scalpel. He's intelligent but domineering, used to getting his way. Arrogant. Cunning."

She thought of his tender smile as he'd watched Nigel stuff a biscuit in his mouth. The bemused look on his face when he'd told her Nick Bottom was pregnant. "But he's fair, I think. Honorable when it comes down to it."

And kind, a sentiment hidden where no one could see it. Unless they looked closely.

When she finished her discourse, Hildy glanced up, realizing she'd been spinning a hammered silver ring her mother had given her on her sixteenth birthday, a piece of jewelry she never took off, round and round on her finger. Before she shelved it like she had this morning's copy of the *Gazette*, Georgie's expression was more than a little concerned.

Hildy shrugged. "It's fine, truly. We have an agreement."

"Is that all you have?" Georgie's discerning gaze shot to the vase. The duchess couldn't help it if she was dreaming up stories. People in love wanted the world to be in love, too.

To save herself, Hildy looked her dearest friend in the eye and lied. "He's a libertine smuggler set to marry in four weeks. What else could there possibly be?"

Chapter Six

Tobias wondered what he was getting himself into.

"What are you getting yourself into, mate?" Macauley muttered from lips he'd had locked to a champagne flute most of the night. At this rate of consumption, Tobias would have to pitch his partner over his shoulder and carry him home at the ball's close. "This crush is madness. My disguise itches like the devil. And for what? Your intended isn't even in attendance."

Tobias gazed about the Duke of Markham's lavish ballroom, a fair bit of his vision cut by the loo mask the Duchess of Markham had forced him to wear. He was surrounded by the aristocracy masquerading as beggars, Roman emperors, Greek goddesses, sailors, kings. The remaining were more sedately outfitted in hooded cloaks he'd been told were called dominos. Their eyes glittered with a host of disreputable sentiments behind the masks.

While he was masquerading as one of them. Looking like he belonged when he didn't. A ruse of the highest order. Surrounded by people but, as usual, alone.

The space was bathed in candlelight and the piquant scent of fresh flowers housed in vases situated around the perimeter. Many had conceivably arrived on one of his ships that week. Tables bordering the back wall were heaped with all manner of food and drink, and a crowd of revelers assembled around them. A string quartet was placed quite brilliantly beneath the double staircase, the music silenced only by the roar of conversation during a break in the song. It was a dizzying sea of sight, sound, and scent. He felt a foreigner in a foreign land for the first time, honestly, since India.

Tobias yanked at his mask's satin ribbon with a beleaguered grumble. The damned thing *did* itch. "Babies don't arrive on schedule, Mac. What's Lady Matilda to do? Tell the expectant mother she can't help deliver her child because she has to attend a frivolous ball?"

"The duchess is hovering," Macauley murmured and gestured with his flute to Georgiana Munro, who stood on the third rung of the grand staircase, giving her visibility above the crowd.

As a duchess should have in life *every single day*. Indeed, her shimmering gaze traveled his and Macauley's way more often than required.

"She's afraid we're going to start another row, even after I greeted Leighton like nothing had happened. Which is to say, a friendlier welcome than he deserves after tossing me off that bridge. Next time we gamble together, *he* enters the cut. He was cheating, slipped the queen of hearts right up his sleeve. I pointed the fact out as graciously as I could. Called him Your Grace and everything." At Tobias's laugh, Macauley cursed and drained his glass. "I smelled like sewage for a week. Four sodding baths a day! Joseph, *my* valet, had to burn my clothes."

Tobias tossed back his whiskey—not as good as his distillery's production, not even *close*—and popped the tumbler atop a tray a footman dressed as a knight sailed by holding high. What would Hildegard Templeton think, to know that her partner in crime, the duchess she'd foisted him off on like a nasty habit, seemed to like him? That he'd spent an entire evening with the Duke of Markham trading stories about India and negotiating to transport geological specimens the duke had purchased from the Dutch East Indies next month. "Joey Rum, a valet? He's a criminal, Mac. Didn't he lose two fingers in Newgate? Only reason he didn't land in the gallows is that shifty cousin of his who somehow ended up a solicitor."

"How do you know so bloody much about valets, then? Like yours didn't go to prison."

Tobias shrugged and nabbed a flute from a passing footman, his jaw clenching beneath his mask. *Yes, what did he know?*

Macauley snorted, his lips curling scornfully. "Oh, you're beat down, mate. To the bone. The Mad Matchmaker instructed you to get a valet, so you get a valet." He gestured to Tobias with his flute, spilling champagne that a corpulent man dressed as a Harlequin who passed them seconds later slipped and almost fell in. "Crack haircut, smartest clothing I've ever seen you in. Standing in the middle of a duke's ballroom looking like you fit. Don't make me discuss this ridiculous getup you made me wear. Whipped like a dog, you are. Over dimples and a set of eyes sweet enough to top a jam tartlet. And I'm whipped along with you."

He opened his mouth to tell his partner how little he cared about Hildegard Templeton, her absurd Duchess Society, and Mac's bloody itching mask when she waltzed down that glorious staircase and took the breath right out of him.

Her gown was ethereal, an ivory and silver fantasy that shimmered with each willowy step she took. A train of some wispy material dusted the steps behind her like a dewy fog she strode through, then allowed to settle back to earth. Her mask was simple, gray and nothing but, without the feathers and jewels needlessly adorning the others in the ballroom. Her hair, near the color of the honey he'd slathered on his toast at breakfast, was gathered in a refined knot at the back of her head. Only the lower half of her face was visible, but her lapis eyes caught the candlelight and held it like a ray of sunlight you wished to trap in the palm of your hand.

Halting by the Duchess of Markham, Hildy leaned in, her lips moving. Then her gaze roamed the ballroom, landing on him.

The punch of pleasure he experienced was a terrible sign.

In a distant part of his mind, he wondered if she felt it, too. With the heat they generated, how could she not?

Macauley unsuccessfully beckoned a passing footman like he was belly up to a public house bar, then stared into his empty flute as if his glower alone could summon more champagne. "Please tell me that stunning creature chatting up a duchess and now heading in our direction in that buttery confection isn't the Mad Matchmaker. Though I can see from the dazed look on your face that it damned well is. Alton had it right. A bleeding looker, she is. A gorgeous, meddling *snoop*."

"I believe there's a game calling your name in the card room, Mac. Top of the stairs, to the left. Follow the crisp smell of pound notes and the hum of drunken laughter. Try to be gentle."

"Fine by me. Don't have to ask twice, Street. Gambling is the only exciting thing in this manse aside from that raven-haired beauty dressed like a lightskirt who winked at me earlier. I nearly got a glimpse of her nipples, I did." Macauley gave his mask a rough bump that set it at a crooked angle on his face. "Be careful. This is dodgy business you're dealing in, friend. Too many women and too little sense kills a man." Advice given, he muscled through the throng on a path to swindle some helpless swell out of his inheritance.

Or the raven-haired beauty out of her skirt.

Bracing his shoulder against a marble column, his pose deceptively relaxed, Tobias surveyed the gathering, his gaze continually tracking back to Hildy as she worked her way across the crowded ballroom. And it looked like work. Her smile was tight, and he noted the chill right off. Her manner was indifferent to those who stopped her, which could have been a protective ploy. Because just as many turned their backs on her, a direct cut right in the middle of the ballroom. As an earl's daughter, she was tolerated. But her choice of profession, *hell*, to have a profession at all, had punted her like a cricket ball to the far reaches of suitability.

They didn't want her in any way that benefitted *her*.

They only wanted her for her beauty and the anemic title attached to her father, not her brains or her bravery. Her intrepid curiosity or acerbic wit.

Proving his theory, five men halted her during her journey across glossy marble, each making a valiant effort to peer down her bodice or touch her in a subtle way she couldn't readily object to. Tobias watched with a disquieting amount of ownership, his fingers curling around the flute's stem until he feared it would snap in his hand.

"Enough," he whispered when the sixth reprobate interrupted her progress, shoving off the column and searching for a place to deposit his flute. Even if that meant cramming it in the dirt of the potted fern behind him.

Hildy must have felt his gaze and the ire heating it because she glanced up, took one look at his face, and shook her head, mouthing *no fighting*.

Properly chastised and inexplicably jealous, he reclaimed his languid stance against the column when he had the overwhelming urge to march across a duke's ballroom and make a muddled situation worse. Kiss his matchmaker until this senseless attraction sputtered like a flame in a healthy gust, leaving nothing but the faint scent of smoke to show there'd even *been* a blaze.

It's what he usually did, to great effect. No one stayed in his life for long at his direction.

He'd never wanted them to.

When Hildy reached him, slightly breathless from fleeing a viscount with a disreputable enough reputation that even Tobias knew who he was, he was again struck by her splendor. Captivated by the fact that she seemed uninterested when most women considered beauty their greatest asset.

"You've been avoiding me, luv," he murmured and took a sip from his flute in a gesture he hoped showed his indifference to the attention she was receiving. Of course, the men who'd stopped her were imagining her in their beds. As Tobias did on an hourly basis. He couldn't be mad, really; it's what men *did*.

"I'm surprised. Sending the duchess to do your dirty work. And all over that trivial scuffle with Leighton. One of us tossed in the drink every so often, nothing to it. It's a friendly competition, as we're friends. Who do you think came up with the Demon Duke? I knew he'd love it, and it goes well with the Rogue King. Told one asinine baron at Epsom that it was Leighton's new nickname, and now it's official."

He grinned at the flame sparking her lovely eyes, her temper showing. He wanted her emotion to clash with his. He wanted *something* from this woman, he merely had to figure out what. "I'm surprised. I didn't think the Mad Matchmaker would run from a challenge."

Hildy gave the dance card attached to her wrist with a lavender satin ribbon a twirl and eyed him through a narrowed gaze. He bet she didn't have one name on that daft card, and she was the loveliest chit in the ballroom. "I was running from dirty work, not a challenge."

A catch of laughter spilled from his lips. She expected sparring, so he'd go another route. "Nick Bottom had kittens last week if you're wondering what I've been doing since we last met. Three. One striped like a tiger, the other two looking like paint's been splattered over them, brown, orange, white. Amazing that they arrive in such a variety of colors, none of them looking especially like their mother."

She frowned, his off-the-cuff reply sending the dimples next to her mouth digging deep. Dashed but they made him want to kiss her in front of all of bloody London.

"Do you do that on purpose, Mr. Streeter? Give an answer to a question unasked? An excellent way to divert the conversation. Part of your negotiation tactics, I'm assuming."

You bet it is, he thought but said instead, "I noticed Lindell caused you to nearly sprint across the ballroom to escape his grasp. Better you stay away as his reputation is... noteworthy. Vile enough to reach the bottom tier even." He shrugged when the thought of the man so much as *speaking* to her made him want to rip the viscount's head off. "He's known for dreadful behavior at a bawdy house near my warehouse. The kind that gets one barred entrance. And that takes a *lot* of dreadful."

Hildegard's cheeks flushed magnificently beneath the scalloped border of her mask. "Heavens. Then I'm doubly glad I said no."

Tobias paused, his flute halfway to his lips. "Said no to *what?*" The question was pleasant, but the threat in his tone wasn't.

With an impish smile, she filched his glass from him and took a sip, her lips leaving crinkled impressions on the rim from whatever silky substance was pinkening them. "He's one of the two."

Tobias's head was starting to hurt from this conversation. "Two?"

"Proposals. They're legendary, merely because I rejected them. I'd no idea that in addition to being a horrid kisser, Lindell was also a degenerate."

He reached for his flute, intent on telling her, inadvisably, that *his* kiss would knock her off her slippers when she was shoved from behind—literally knocked off her slippers and into his arms.

Tobias had been in enough barroom brawls and street fisticuffs to deduce the problem in seconds flat. Confirming his guess, the sound of breaking glass and a masculine roar that usually meant one man had transgressed on the presumed feminine property of another filled the ballroom. Holding his matchmaker against his chest—he wasn't going to spoil an unbidden chance to touch her—he glanced over her shoulder to see an irate crowd pressing in upon them.

A long enough inspection to confirm the skirmish did *not* include his partner—or the Duke of Leighton or Markham, men he might, on a good day, consider friends. Men he'd scramble in there and fight for. Luckily, this battle was between a chap dressed as a magician and the Harlequin who'd nearly busted his arse in Macauley's spilled champagne. A woman, a fairy goddess of some ridiculous nature, stood beside them, wringing her hands and appearing the guilty party.

Pressing his nose into Hildy's honeyed hair, Tobias took a cleansing breath as chaos reigned around them. Lavender and the slightest trace of soap, the fragrance sending a desirous ripple through him. He stilled, bringing the scene into his mind, never to be forgotten. They fit flawlessly while standing and would fit even *better* lying across his silk sheets, his body rising over hers. The warmth of her body seeped through layers of clothing, indeed the finest he'd ever owned. Her rapid breaths struck his neck, his jaw. Her head tucked perfectly beneath his chin, her slender body trembling.

Trembling.

Tobias released her, realizing he'd been clutching the back of her gown in his greedy fist. The mob was just behind them now, the fracas expanding to include a Renaissance knight and a Scottish lord whose kilt was swinging madly from side to side as he sought to land a punch.

Tobias looked down, prepared to find a contemptuous expression twisting her features. Instead, her cheeks were ashen, her mask askew. Her eyes filled with numb bewilderment he remembered from the battlefield. "*Gadji,*" he whispered tenderly and, acting without thought for the first time in forever, took Hildegard's arm and propelled her through the terrace doors.

Changing his destiny and perhaps hers, Tobias decided to rescue his mad matchmaker from her fright.

Chapter Seven

Hildy let the Rogue King lead her blindly through Georgie's torch-lit side garden, down a gravel footpath, and directly into the plush coziness of his carriage. Shivering because she'd left her cloak behind, she didn't think to ask where he was taking her as he placed a warmed brick beneath her feet and tucked a woolen lap blanket around her like he would have a child. After a second's pause, he reached to untie her mask, then his own, and sprawled on the velvet squab across from her. When the coach started moving, he gave them a negligent chuck out the window, the satin ribbons trailing through the air like wisps of London's fog.

Town hurled by outside the carriage as the inhabitants inside let silence command the night. His breath shallow, his teasing scent ruining any effect to ignore him, Tobias made no effort to talk. The flicker of candlelight in the arched windows of the dwellings they passed reduced in number as they entered the humbler parts of the city. Darker, grittier, louder.

She wasn't surprised when the conveyance entered the Limehouse district some fifteen minutes later.

It had been years since memories of her father's violent temper plagued her, the incident when she'd come between him and her brother the reminiscence this night. She stared at her hands, flexing her gloved fingers as if Edwin's blood was still on them. He'd had the scar on his temple and a hatred for their father until the day he died. Odd that an idiotic scuffle at a ball, a predictable occurrence, had brought the ferocious scene roaring back.

That only happened in nightmares.

Tobias didn't push for an explanation, which she wasn't sure she could give. Their relationship didn't include tales of family strife that kept her up into the wee hours of the night. He sat there calmly, the glow from the carriage lamp dancing across the hard planes of his face, emerald-green eyes roving the dilapidated dwellings they passed with a luminosity she couldn't miss.

He cherished this place. It was plain to see.

Ensnared, she gazed at his world—and tried to see it as he did. Laundry fluttering in open tenement windows, allowing frigid air inside. Seamen stumbling from public houses, pausing to gather on vacant stoops and upended carts scattered about. A chaotic mix of hackneys and drays, horses and children, shivering vendors selling sweetmeats and roasted nuts. Barking dogs, carriage wheels striking pitted paths. The aroma of rubbish and river, marsh mud and coal fires.

The area improved slightly the closer they got to his warehouse and the distillery. Fresh paint on the doors, patrols she speculated were men in his employ stationed on each corner. Less despair in the faces that met hers, fewer ruts in the road for those traveling it. A vague, very subtle sense of well-being. She was afraid to question Tobias about the transformation when her emotions were sitting so close to the surface. When she'd inexplicably shown him a secret part of herself, even if he didn't understand she had.

Only her brother and her father knew about that awful night—and they were dead.

The carriage rocked to a stop in front of the distillery. The silence was ponderous, the sound of his feathery breaths pulling her gaze from the window. His eyes glittered in the lamplight, his lips curling just enough to let her know he was amused.

Or maybe he was waiting to see what she'd do.

A gauntlet thrown, a woman challenged.

Merely another day in the life of the Rogue King.

She straightened her spine, refusing to cower. She'd been on the shelf so long that there was nothing Tobias Streeter could do to yank her off it. Even the scandal of him dragging her into his carriage and her agreeing *readily* to go. She didn't know what he had in mind, but she wasn't going to run shrieking down the street like a frightened virgin.

Even if she *was* a frightened virgin.

And an *intrigued* one.

Seconds later, his smile broke, his lips losing their battle to contain his pleasure. "The kittens, Templeton," he murmured and nodded to the three-story brick building they were parked before. "I only brought you here to see the kittens."

When the coachman lowered the creaking metal step, Hildy made a neat fold of the lap robe and placed it on the plush velvet squab, vexed because the man hijacked every agenda she set for him.

Changing *her* when she was set, by contractual agreement, on changing *him*.

Opening her mind to *his* world when she was set to open his mind to *hers*.

Tobias maneuvered smoothly past her, hopping down into the twilight lane, then turning to assist, his behavior as superb as a duke's. As charming as any man in attendance at Georgie's ball. His unique charisma wrapped the package up with a bow, fashionable clothing, hair trimmed in the latest style.

However, the *look* of him...

He appeared positively feral in the splash of moonlight, eyes glittering, skin bronzed, smile glorious. Yet, there it was, despite his forced appeal, a fact he might not even recognize. *Refinement.* The kind of elegance one was born with. Or, as was often the case, *without.*

A chameleon, able to shape himself into what was required to get his way.

The most determined man she'd ever known.

"Your turf once again," she murmured and, taking his hand, let him usher her into the distillery. Down a dimly lit hallway, past the office where they'd met the week before. Into a space warm as toast, she found, as the door closed behind them. A masculine effort at parlor design, housing a haphazard assortment of furniture. Pieces that looked along the lines of what was littered around her home, random and unimpressive, versus the king's castoffs he seemed to prefer. A sofa that had seen better days, a scuffed console table, and a carpet sun-faded to dull shades of gray. This, finally, looked like a real room.

She turned intrigued eyes to him.

He rocked back on his heels, his hand going to scrub the back of his neck. Finally, a hint of unease. *Finally*. "I sent a man ahead to light the hearth, turn up the lamps. This is where the boy, Nigel, sleeps on nights he stays. Had to furnish it for a grubby little boy. It isn't meant for visitors, but it's the coziest in the place."

Hildy laughed; she couldn't help it. "Of course, you sent a man ahead. And have a cozy nook for your misplaced orphans."

He laughed too, breaking the strain, the seductive sound taking her breath and, for a moment, sensible thought. His high cheekbones made a neat cut of his smile at the edge.

It was a grossly unjust fact, but he really *was* the most handsome man she'd ever met.

Having no idea the mad opinions running through her mind, Tobias moved into host mode. Ripping his costly kid gloves off with his teeth and tossing them on the sofa while she watched in escalating fascination. His coat was next, hitting the sofa as well before sliding to the floor. Loosening his cuffs, he rolled up his sleeves while she recorded more of him being exposed to her ravenous gaze. The word feral circled her mind again as she weakly wondered what his body would look like beneath his elegant clothing.

A question she'd never posed about a man before.

Her body quivered and tightened in response.

"What's that look?" he asked softly, his brow winging high as he lit a candelabra sitting on the hearth.

She shrugged. *Nothing*. Her stomach made an excuse and growled, loud enough for him to hear. The twist in it was lust or hunger or both; she couldn't decide which and would never tell him.

"Did you eat anything at the ball, Templeton?"

She flattened her hand atop her tummy, feeling it rumble again.

"Goodness, no. If I'd spilled one drop on a gown this color... I only have two, rather outdated at this point but serviceable, appropriate for a ball."

He paused in adjusting his cuff and held up his hand. "I'll be back. Nick Bottom and her brood are in a crate in the corner. She's rather protective, so you may want to look and not touch. Not yet."

Hildy wanted to see the kittens. She *did*. But when Tobias left the room, she rushed to pick up his tailcoat from the floor, burying her nose in the worsted wool and drawing a minute-long breath. The man smelled like he looked.

Exotic and dashing.

Delicious and *completely* unattainable.

Engaged to another woman. Not her type, and she not his. Too clever for his own good. Too attractive. She'd have to watch his every move for the rest of her life to keep someone else from stealing him. That seemed too much pressure. And a gross deficit of independence.

By the time Tobias arrived carrying a tray filled with an assortment of items as random as the furniture in the room—apples, iced buns, mismatched tumblers, and a bottle of whiskey—she was cooing to Nick Bottom and the kittens, Tobias's coat in its pile on the floor. Her expression delicately vacant, she hoped. Her gloves in a neat stack *next* to his but not touching.

With a half-turn, he nudged the console table against the sofa with his boot, deposited the tray, and dropped his long body to the floor. He poured a generous dram of whiskey into the tumblers and settled back, his gaze roving her way without comment.

She pushed to her feet, shaking out her skirt while Tobias observed with penetrating focus. "Nick Bottom is serving as chaperone. We can share the sofa. You at one end, me the other. No need to sit on the floor. As I mentioned, Mr. Streeter, I'm past the point of no return. The *ton* has given up on me and no longer cares enough to even gossip. Or not much. My phaeton races through Hyde Park, gaining scarcely a glimmer of interest. My work with the Duchess Society is talked about, certainly, but only because men hoping to marry are afraid of me. My glacial reputation is beneficial rather than being a hindrance.

And I've had no more proposals I'll firmly reject to worry over receiving."

Bending his leg, Tobias wiggled a pocketknife from his boot. "This sofa is the sort you need assistance to rise from. To say you sink into it would be stating it lightly. It provides a decent cot for a ten-year-old, but it's not for anyone who doesn't want their bum to brush the baseboards."

"Well, then," Hildy said and seated herself as elegantly as she could on the carpeted floor, resting against the bum-brushing sofa, the small table between them. An appropriate solution, she supposed, when this encounter was clearly *in*appropriate. Her train, the most pleasing feature of her gown, fluttered and settled like snow around her. Too bad it was five years out-of-date.

She nodded to the knife he held. "You thought to bring a weapon to a masquerade ball?"

His gaze journeyed over her, his expression unreadable. Instead of replying, he grabbed an apple and deftly cut it into quarters, speared a section with his knife, and held it out to her.

She took the slice and bit off a piece, chewing slowly. "What does *gadji* mean?"

He stilled, the slice he held grazing his lips and making them glisten. "A female who isn't Romani," he finally answered.

Hildy took a sip of whiskey—it was even better than she remembered, smooth and smoky and *his*—then picked at a moist corner of the bun, licking her thumb to remove a smear of icing off the tip.

Tobias paused, his gaze locking on her lips. His smile faded, and something mysterious flooded his eyes, darkening them to a deep, opaque green. "Here, I thought to have whiskey *soften* the negotiation," he said so faintly she almost didn't catch it.

"I hardly think a wee draught will render me malleable," she whispered, the liquor flowing over her tongue like a delicious flame.

He tilted his head, charming her with his delight. "In my experience, Templeton, whiskey helps *any* negotiation."

"Hildy."

His throat clicked as he swallowed. "I'm not following. Which isn't unusual."

"Call me Hildy. It's a *kinder* declaration than Templeton. Or Hildegard." She took another bite of the iced bun, realizing she'd been famished. Which she still was. Only now, the curl in her belly wasn't for food. "I've never thought of myself as Hildegard. I'm named after my father's great-aunt. She was extremely disagreeable the two times I met her. Awful, actually. A face like a dried prune and a disposition to match."

He hummed low, chewing, thoughtful. "You seem more like a Hildy." He shifted his leg, knocking her slippered foot with the toe of his boot, his smile a hundred shades of flirtatious. "Nothing like a prune-faced great-aunt smelling of camphor and mothballs."

She giggled and, embarrassed at the sound, cast her gaze to her slippers. One still touched his boot. Stubbornly, she decided she wasn't moving her foot, not an inch, no matter what good sense was telling her she *should* do. Their gazes clashed across the table, and her stomach lurched. His eyes were glowing, and she found herself holding her breath as she stared. Hardly daring to exhale, she curled her toes, trying to hide something from him that he couldn't possibly see.

Shifting his gaze, he picked up his tumbler and ran the chipped rim across his bottom lip. "Your reaction back there. The scuffle at the ball. Care to tell me what it was about?"

Leaning over the table, their heated instant gone, she took an apple slice from the plate and bit into its sweet juiciness. Wherever he'd gotten the fruit—directly off one of his ships, she'd guess—it was the freshest she'd had in months. "It doesn't matter now. Or should I say, it's in the past? What's odd to me is an incident that darkens my dreams on the occasional night should come to mind as it did. And from something as silly as a drunken brawl. There was a sound, a shout, that brought it back to me. So clearly, it was like I was standing in my father's study again, watching him and my brother fight it out."

Tobias reached to adjust spectacles that weren't there, then dropped his hand to turn his tumbler in pensive circles on the table. "It happens to many who go to war. One minute, you're standing in the middle of a market purchasing carrots when a particular smell or a loud sound, someone dropping a bottle upon the cobblestones, places you within a memory you never again want to revisit. That's worse than the nightmares if you ask me."

"India," she whispered.

He nodded and took a long pull on his whiskey. "India."

Hildy glanced at his boot, still grazing her slipper, and popped the last of the iced bun in her mouth. "Was that your partner I saw heading toward the card room this evening? A larcenous gleam in his eyes and his mask cocked at a dangerous angle."

His lips curved, that enticing hollow emerging by his mouth, enthralling her when no further engrossment was needed.

"He saved me a hundred years ago from a gang of posh youth intent on beating a scrawny half-Romani boy into the dirt. I ventured into an unforgiving neighborhood to see Spencer House, one of the first Neoclassical examples of architecture in London. A bizarre interest for a boy, I realize. Macauley thought so, too. Your brethren felt they should establish who did and did *not* belong on St. James's Place." His boot knocked her slipper again, sending a warm pulse through her. A pulse that ended dead center between her thighs. More of a thump than a tingle. "Don't look so sad, luv. The main instigator, his friend who unfortunately said his name during the incident, hasn't been a capable investor of late. I've bought everything, or close to it, that he's had to sell to survive. And he's aware who's buying."

"I'd recognize who you speak of?"

He took a vicious bite of apple. "You would."

She worked to keep sympathy from showing on her face, knowing he wouldn't appreciate it. "I have a friend like that in Georgie. And a partner. She understands my peculiar inclinations. She always has."

"Oh, Macauley's useless there. Outside of trading merchandise, he doesn't understand much beyond dice, women, and drink. To him, my ambition seems pointless and, worse, hazardous. Like the beating in St. James years ago. Far above what I should want. Or can achieve. This"—he gestured to her with his apple before taking another bite —"business with you. My willingness to alter so much as a hair on my head for it. My agreement with Mattie is puzzling to him because there's only friendship between us. When it makes perfect damned sense. *Business* sense."

"She wants freedom. And I'm happy to provide what she needs to live her life as best she can, as *honestly* as she can, while using her father's title where I need it. What do I care if my money saves another highborn family from doom? I never thought Mac a romantic until he got his dander up about me marrying a woman I don't love. When it happens every day in your world." Tobias looked to her, his eyes brilliant, blazing. "Doesn't it? While love circles constantly like London's fog in mine. Conquering nothing."

She knocked her slipper against his boot this time as his inky lashes, so long they should be outlawed, fluttered. Proving he wasn't as calm about sitting with her in a snug stockroom-cum-parlor at midnight as he made it seem he was. "You realize you're asking this question of a spinster whose profession involves making marriage more equitable for women, thereby more difficult for men? Few of the couples I engage with are in love, Mr.—"

"*Tobias*," he instructed and rose gracefully to his feet. Crossing to the hearth, he repositioned the screen and loaded more wood on the grate.

"Few of the couples I engage with are in love," Hildy murmured, pleased to say *Tobias* out loud when she'd thought of him in that way for days. The hearth fire flared, spreading golden light across the room like liquid sunshine, warmth that coaxed her into saying more than she should. "Fewer still are destined for happily ever after."

Taking the opportunity when his back was turned, she studied him when she knew she shouldn't. Recording the graceful lines of his body. Broad shoulders, trim waist. Capable hands, calloused skin she recalled from the time before when he'd touched her. His attire tasteful, his movements efficient. He knew what he wanted and went after it.

This surety burned a path through her.

He paused as if her regard stirred him, glancing over his shoulder, his tender regard inviting her to indulge. Making it feel safe to indulge.

She should have looked away, pretended, lied. Smiled stupidly. Giggled again. Climbed back in his fancy carriage and ordered his coachman to deliver her home. Promised this project to Georgie until after Tobias married instead of telling her partner this evening that she was taking it—*him*—back.

Anything to extinguish the heat snapping between them as soundly as the embers in the hearth he tended.

Curiously, Hildy didn't do any of those things. She merely stared, wondering what it would be like to kiss him. Touch him. Things she'd read about in scandalous novels and heard whispered in parlor corners. Tangled limbs and fevered skin.

Passion, need, *desire*.

Turning back, he gave the blackening wood a vicious jab and gazed into the fire. Then, with a sigh, a decision seemingly made, he hoisted himself to his feet using the iron poker as a crutch. Wordlessly, he laid the tool aside and closed the screen, ostensibly to protect the kittens.

If she'd had any doubt he would follow through, she didn't any longer. Though his face was largely hidden, she knew he smiled. Amusement or anticipation?

Crossing to her, he stood towering over her, his expression lost in shadow. His scent drifted to her, a fragrance she couldn't place. Sunlight and earth, a spicy, tangy aroma.

He sighed and dragged his fingers through his lustrous hair when *she* wanted to be the one to do that. "The way you're looking at me is almost more than I can endure and keep from kissing you. I've decided not to lie about what I'm feeling..." Rocking back on his heels, he threw his hand out in a gesture of raw powerlessness. "Because I think you feel the same."

All the reasons she shouldn't let him kiss her wafted through her mind, like a gust off his beloved Thames had set them free to drift there. She was standing at the edge of a precipice, a fantastic decision laid out before her. Further temptation because she understood it was *her* choice.

Kiss or no kiss. With a notorious, devil-may-care man who lived life to the fullest.

Tobias Streeter, the Rogue King of Limehouse Basin, was patiently waiting for her to decide. Hildy felt aroused by the control, seduced by the options.

Something fiendish flickered in his eyes. A lock of hair fell forward, brushing his cheekbone. How had she thought him austere? He seemed vulnerable and heartbreakingly young beneath armor constructed to protect him.

"A dangerous game you're playing, Hildy girl, when I rarely back down."

A long moment passed. Words crowded her throat, melted on her tongue. Thought melted into sensation along with them. She was light-headed, drunk on his nearness and the thrill of touching him.

Then he answered her plea, kicking the table aside. Pulling her to her feet, against his hard body. She caught her breath, but it only filled her with his scent. Her heart pounded, and the air lit with desire. His, hers. Eagerness and need.

She opened her mouth to say, of all things, *yes, please*, as if he'd asked permission, and he took advantage. Those rough palms cradled her jaw, bringing her lips to his.

She followed, opening hers and surrendering.

Strangely, it seemed a natural undertaking for an undertaking she'd only taken once before. A split second of awkwardness, a moment where she wondered, *Is it going to be what I'd imagined? Like the viscount's horrid attempt?*

Then, Tobias touched his tongue to hers and... *magic*.

The kiss was deliberate and unhurried, even as his chest quaked beneath the hand she'd pressed there. His tongue stroking softly, then with more insistence as he urged her to follow him down a sensual path. She slanted her head, trying to get closer. *Closer*. She may have even whispered the appeal.

He replied without words, snaking his arm around her waist and tucking her against his broad body. She tangled her hand in his hair, that jet-black, beautiful hair, shorter because she'd asked that he make it so. His scalp was warm, the silken strands thick and curling about her fingers. She tugged, bringing him to her, biting his bottom lip simply because she thought to. He released a brutal, starving groan into her mouth, his hand clenching, moving lower to cup the nape of her neck.

Their bodies melded as passion raced ahead of them, the sound of a log exploding into sparks in the hearth not registering beyond providing a clue that a world outside this kiss remained.

With fingers that trembled, he traced the silk-edged cord of her bodice. "You taste of apple and icing, luv. Bloody delicious," he murmured against her lips before sinking fearlessly back into the kiss, inviting her to a place she'd never been. A land filled with pleasure, breathtaking pleasure.

Warmth flowing through her body to settle between her thighs pleasure. Breath seizing in her lungs pleasure. Nipples hardening to tight points beneath her corset pleasure. Slippers rising two inches off the earth pleasure.

He was seducing her beyond reason.

And she was letting him.

~

For the first time, a kiss made Tobias lose control. Focus. *Purpose.* Struck him as hard as a blow to the face, so he couldn't think, only *want*. He'd never entered a passionate encounter without a goal, no matter how base.

Like one of his blueprints, a guide to follow.

This kiss had no plan, and yet it brought him to his knees.

Quite candidly, to his knees.

It was sweet and gentle, sizzling and persuasive, effortless, and the most complicated interaction he'd ever tangled himself in. Yearning at the shy touch of her tongue. Bone-deep need when she twisted her fingers in his hair. Fondness when she breathed a startled laugh—a *laugh*—into his mouth.

The kiss steadied him, guided him, brought him closer to a woman than he'd ever been while shaking him to his core.

Her tongue entwined with his until his knees went weak, and still, she demanded more. He fought the urge to rip off her clothing, crawl over her, sink inside, and never come out. Shout her name while he came, go blind with need, desire, longing. Delight her until she *begged*.

He wanted more.

More of *her*.

More of *this*.

More of *everything*.

Could give her more if she asked.

Her body was a glory, sleek curves and slender abundance, deserving of worship. If she only knew he craved the elemental things. Carnal, yet oh, so intimate. Her plump breast tucked in his hand, her peaked nipple caught between his teeth, her long legs wrapped around him as he pleasured her until they couldn't see straight.

Her juices moistening his cock before he slipped inside her.

He wanted to uncover her secrets in the hazy twilight, in a bed they creatively destroyed with their passion. If she'd let him, he would teach her to savor. And enjoy.

Ah, he didn't tell her these things. Instead, he kept his hands still when they wanted to *explore*.

But he poured his yearning for them into the kiss.

Thirsty for her, he glided his lips down the curve of her throat, stopping to suck the skin over her thudding pulse. She moaned low and responded like for like, touching him, licking, nibbling, kissing. She broke the rules he refused to, her hands roving all over him, searching for experience and answers. Not understanding this was new for him, much more than he'd given before. Explosive and unforgettable.

And real. His mind *and* body engaged.

The real Tobias Fitzhugh Streeter, a person he wasn't sure he knew well.

She didn't know she fit him as no other woman had. That it was more than physical.

This revelation, when it elbowed past his lust, chimed disaster.

Gaining possession of his wild yearning, he took her gently by the shoulders and inched her back. Before she realized what she'd done to him as his cock was hard enough to pound nails, and he didn't need her to recognize this fact. Her eyes, so goddamn blue they hurt to look at, lifted to his. Her breath skittered out across his jaw, her moist, abused lips puckering. He knew he was in trouble when she waited until her thoughts collected before she spoke.

It was the tactic of a master performed by a novice.

Cleverly, she traced the seam of his shirt from belly to neck, circling each bone button until his skin was aflame. He let her, just fucking let her have her way with him. Knowing she was tearing him down brick by brick. No reasonable argument when she could see he'd drawn back. Oh, no, not *this* woman.

This negotiation was carnal. Because at the moment, it was the only way to win. "You're going to make sure I remember this as the kiss of all kisses, aren't you?"

Smiling wickedly, her power evident in his feeble appeal, she loosened his cravat until the ends dangled down his chest, unbuttoned his collar, and leaned in to press her lips to the hollow beneath his throat. Lighting him up inside. He was hot everywhere she touched.

Her innocent caresses were turning his spontaneous seduction on its head.

"Hildy girl," he whispered in a ragged voice, his hand going to her waist, pulling her closer, not pushing her away. When he'd promised himself he wouldn't touch her below her *collarbone.* "Stop now."

Teasing him, she dragged her nose across his skin and breathed him in. "What's this you smell like? I can't place it. Fresh cut grass on a summer day. Sunlight. Earth."

He swallowed hard, his head dropping back, helplessly exposing his neck to her ravenous conquest. Her teeth nipped beneath his chin, his ear, as his vision dimmed, and his thoughts went drowsy. "Vetiver. It's a Romani soap. My grandmother's recipe."

"Why did you kiss me, Tobias?" she asked, the question tripping against his jaw. "When there can never be anything between us? It was in my mind, feverishly so, but I don't think I'd have acted on the fantasy."

He tipped her chin, drawing her eyes to his. Where she then searched his face for the truth. Her flaxen hair was like silk against his skin, a splash of sunlight miraculously entering a night-lit room. He wondered what it would look like flowing past her shoulders or laid across his silk sheets.

"Because I couldn't help myself. Because I *wanted* to. When control is never a problem. Which makes you, Hildegard Templeton, a vexing one for me." Coaxing her lips apart with his thumb, he ran his tongue over the bottom one, which he'd imagined doing since the first moment he met her. Fantasizing in his lonely bed each night.

If he was only to have this trifling bit of her, he wanted it to last another breath. Or two.

Because they could only go so far.

She sighed and wiggled against him, challenging his control. "You kiss like a gentleman when I want a kiss from a ruffian. From the Rogue King, in fact. As he's known to give them freely."

A laugh shot from his lips to dust hers. "Is that so, luv?"

Her gaze glittered sapphire in the firelight, her expression exposed. "I don't know what to do about this attraction between us. A spark I've felt since that first day in your warehouse, one I suspected you felt, too. I don't know if I like it"—she tapped her chest, drawing his gaze to her round breasts outlined beneath ivory silk and gemstones —"but I *feel* it. I don't want to run, though I may, or lie, which I'll eventually do, I'm certain.

"Tonight, however, in your balmy distillery on a narrow lane in Limehouse, with Nick Bottom purring and the fire cracking behind us, I'll admit that I've never yearned for a man the way I yearn for you. And that I'm tangled up inside. You can take this knowledge and place it alongside the memory of our kiss. Because tomorrow, we have to move past this." She skimmed her lips across his, drawing him back into her orbit. "We have to *forget*."

Tobias blinked, stunned by her honesty, her courage, her strength. Stunned by the way her words sliced his heart open and let feeling trickle out. "This is how a ruffian makes love to his woman," he whispered savagely and seized her mouth beneath his. Turning them, he guided her three paces until he had her backed against the door. Then, drawing her arms up and around his neck, he slithered his hands down her sides to cup her hips and pull her into him. Stepping between her legs with bold ownership. Letting her know what she'd done to him— hardened his body to the point of pleasure and pain.

She made a breathy, cooing sound when his rigid length made contact with her delicate folds. Even through the layers standing guard between them, he could feel her heat, and she his need. Her restless movement awakened his hunger. She was issuing a blatant invitation with each bump of her body against his, each wordless gasp against his lips, each drag of her nails across the tender skin of his neck.

If she was willing to reveal her desire, he would do the same.

He'd even promise to forget this, forget *her*, although he knew it was a lie.

This night would stay with him until he passed into the great beyond.

Their first kiss had been exploratory, a search to uncover preferences. Fast, slow, deep, cautious. What would make her moan and beg? He was a quick learner.

This kiss was born of *longing*. Moving into a turbulent sea instantly, liquefying every good intention he struggled to retain, like a lit tinder pressed to wax. Tobias arched against her, pressing Hildy into the hard wood of the door, leaving no room, not enough for a feather to pass between them. The contact was more erotic than when he'd had a naked woman atop him.

Everything that was complicated vanished until it was only *her*. The world lost and beautiful, muffled, the sound of their breathing all that drove him. Sipping her bliss, he teetered on the edge, then dove in fully because she wasn't holding back. Her hands were exploring. Kneading his hip, gliding up his chest, tangling in his hair. Then back again. And again, until he was breathless and aroused to the point of discomfort.

She was memorizing what he liked; he recognized the gambit. A harder kiss—because he preferred it. Her body engaged from chest to knee, as his was. Hips bumping, moans splitting the silence. *Aggressive*. Teeth nipping his lips, making him groan in delight. His hunger exposed. His need evident.

They were making love standing up, with clothing and no penetration, he'd tell her if he could get a word out. He kept his hands on her hips, daring himself to stop them from rising to cup her breasts. He knew his limits.

Much more of this, and any of *that*, and he'd start removing her clothing. He was only a man and, as it was, a weak one.

Or he'd be sneaky and petition her to remove *his*. After all, she'd started with the buttons of his shirt already. A fact he couldn't get out of his mind, her taking control like that.

Hildy Templeton was nothing, *nothing* like he'd expected.

She was better—and what he'd found had come close to breaking him.

His lips went to her throat, spilling muffled murmurs against her moist skin. Tremors rocked her slender frame, calling out his protective instincts. His hands tightened around her waist, his fevered mind suggesting places he could take her, make love to her. *Now.* Carriage. Townhouse. Warehouse. Chair. Bed. Floor. Desk. Standing up. Sitting. Bent over. Astride.

He'd undress her slowly, kiss each inch of skin he uncovered, his hand memorizing her curves and valleys. He'd bring her such pleasure, she would never forget him.

Never.

Lost in the haze of her, he almost didn't hear when she called him by a name—*Toby*—that halted him in his tracks. No one except Nigel had called him Toby since his mother's death. Toby was gone. Living in the past. In India or on the Romani caravans. Somewhere. But not here.

Tobias released her gradually, like grains of sand sliding through his fingers until they stood utterly separate, not so much as a loose thread touching. Hildy swayed at his sudden move, and he kept from reaching out to steady her as he sought to calm his furious breathing.

This was not lovemaking at its finest. Mac would ridicule him for ruining a golden opportunity.

But he couldn't comfort this woman *and* walk away.

Forget her, as she'd directed him to. Let her forget him.

Her eyes were dazed when they met his, blue bleeding to black. Cheeks flushed, skin moist, lips swollen. She looked like she'd been loved—and loved well.

And they hadn't even made it to the bedchamber.

"Why did you stop?" she asked, her brow pleating, those damned dimples of hers flashing. "Did I do something you didn't like?"

"End of the kiss, luv," he whispered. If he raised his voice, she'd hear the frayed edge and know he was wrecked. Know he'd liked everything *too* much. "Less to forget if we stop here. Take my word for it."

He lied through his teeth when the taste of her was haunting him. His fingertips were tingling from the feel of her silky skin beneath them. The scent of her drilled a hole in his brain. If she didn't get angry soon, indignation fueling her escape, he was going to seduce her and be done with the heroics.

To hell with their grand plans for the future.

Her courage never far away, Hildy stiffened her spine, using the door's flat as a guide. She smoothed her hand over her hair, tucking away strands that passion had led astray. It was then that Tobias noticed her ragged fingernails. So, the Mad Matchmaker was a nail-biter. An endearing, very intimate habit that made him want to toss her over his shoulder and carry her away. Carry her to the Mayfair manse he ambled the lonely halls of, precisely as Macauley had said, wondering how the hell a pitiable Romani lad had gotten there.

Feeling the intruder in his own life.

When the path he'd chosen was going to be like that, an entire *world* of lonely.

Hildy pushed off the door, shook out her ivory and silver skirt with a hand that, bless her, barely quivered. "Did you review the list of acceptable gifts I prepared for you to send to Lady Matilda? It's included in your folio of materials." Her only tell was twisting a silver ring he hadn't noticed before round and round on her middle finger. "One of my maids heard through the earl's majordomo that you sent flowers. Tulips. Rather exotic for an English winter, but that's a good start."

"Tulips are bloody hard to obtain and costly as shite, I'll have you know," he snapped, reaching to button his collar when he didn't *want* it buttoned, incensed when his idiocy was to blame. He couldn't help his frustration; she was one stubborn female. And he was *really* starting to admire her for it. "Mattie doesn't care a whit about flowers. She sent a note of thanks reminding me to locate a set of rugines, which should you like to know, are used to remove connective tissue from bone. How's *that* for adoration?"

Hildy crossed the room, picked up her gloves from where they lay in a neat pile next to his tangled ones, and tugged the soft kid over her fingers. A patent signal that the evening was over. Call the carriage, escort the lady home. He'd never had a woman react with less *fervor* after a kiss that had been hot enough to melt stone. "At least you're friends. You respect each other. There's honesty between you. That's more than most society marriages have."

He faltered, in his heart if not his intention. Her gloves were aged, faded, and frayed at the seams, calling to mind a vulnerability she would certainly never share but that he was aware of. Although he may not like it, he'd proven vulnerable to those in need. Animals, orphans, *and* women, he silently groused, throwing a disgusted look at Nick Bottom and the kittens.

He moved behind her, not close enough to touch, and snatched his coat from the floor. "I'll escort you."

She waved a hand, a rebuffing flutter. "No need. Have the man you've had following me the past few days, the young, handsome bloke, do it. I'm sure he's waiting somewhere around the entrance."

Tobias snorted, his arm jammed halfway down his sleeve. "*That* worked well."

Hildy eyed him with a ruthless smirk that made his cock twitch playfully in his trousers. "I hire men of this sort to follow and not be found all the time. I understand ways you alert someone without knowing you have. He wasn't bad, actually. I didn't realize he was on my trail until the second day. I even made a few unusual outings to keep him interested. One had him strolling along behind me, freezing his bottom off, while I looked for the perfect teapot." She gave her glove a hard yank, perturbed, *finally*, if he didn't miss his guess. "If you have this need again, let me know. An emissary, that is. I'll provide names of gentlemen who won't be spotted."

Tobias's gaze clashed with hers, his hands busy straightening his lapels when he wanted to bury them in her hair, pull the golden strands loose around her shoulders, lay her on the sofa, and crawl atop her. Even if it broke from usage and they ended up on the floor. "You are one dogged bit of baggage, Hildy Templeton."

"I'll take that as a compliment, Toby Streeter."

It was then he knew that not only had he sent a man to snoop on her and been caught red-handed, she'd also figured out the rationale behind his abrupt departure from their kiss. "So, who's showing up tomorrow to teach my lesson in gentility and suitable gift-giving? The

Ice Duchess or the Mad Matchmaker? My, the *ton* has given you and your partner impressive monikers to live up to."

"As if *you* should talk." A fierce breath slipped past her lips with the gripe. Lips pinkened from his abuse. She wiped them with her gloved hand as he stared and sent him a glare that could kill. "Send your carriage and your spy at eleven o'clock. I'll be ready."

Of *that*, he had no doubt.

Nevertheless, Tobias had decided somewhere between the smoldering kiss and the cold shoulder that he wasn't going to let this fascinating woman walk away so easily.

Chapter Eight

Hildy ripped open the velvet drape with an unladylike growl and knocked her head on the frosty windowpane. The Rogue King was late. Twenty minutes, she calculated with a scathing glance thrown to the mantel clock above the hearth. She'd bitten her nails to the quick while waiting for him to show.

And then, there were the *flowers*. Covering every surface of her father's study until it looked like a nursery. The only note included, asking which assortment was suitable to send to his intended since tulips had been frowned upon by the Duchess Society. The blasted *nerve* of the man. The heady aroma filling the room was dense enough to rest upon and was starting to give her a blinding headache on top of a sleepless night. Tossing and turning during the most erotic dream she'd ever had, which had started with her showing up in Limehouse wearing nothing but a smile.

"He's a blackguard," she said and perched on the windowsill, her gaze centered on the congested street outside. Tobias Streeter wasn't going to catch her unaware.

Not like his kiss had.

Georgie issued what Hildy suspected was a giggle behind a vibrant lavender morning glory she'd swiped from a vase, twirling it against her cheek. She'd never giggled before falling in love with a bloody *duke*. "He's flirting, Hildy. It's been so long. You've forgotten what that is. Try it. It's fun."

Hildy sneezed into an embroidered handkerchief as ideas of what she'd do to him when she saw him circled like hawks. "Flirting! Are you daft? We're trying like mad to get him *married*."

"He sent you flowers. Of every variety known to arrive at the Limehouse docks in the dead of winter."

Hildy perused the study with what she knew was a sour expression. The flowers were indeed gorgeous, damn him. "He's trying to provoke me." Because of her dig about the tulips. And her non-response to his jab about ending the kiss. He'd expected her to beg him to continue. Ladies probably begged for something every day of the week, and she would *not* be one of them. "If he's flirting, it's with the wrong woman."

The woman who'd inadvertently called him a name he didn't like being called.

Except by orphaned urchins.

The duchess trailed the morning glory across the escritoire and hummed a jaunty tune. "I saw his face when you strolled down my staircase and into the ballroom last night, Hildy. Dazed, like he'd been hit with a club."

"You *are* mad," Hildy breathed, her cheeks catching fire. *Dazed.*

"Dex likes him. And Dex doesn't like much besides rocks."

"Oh, for the love of..." Hildy hopped to her feet and circled the room. Sneezed. Grumbled. Twisted her ring on her finger, a nervous habit. One of the floral arrangements she passed contained vetiver.

That devil, she thought. When she got a whiff of its unique scent, lurid images began to tumble through her mind like a deck of cards let loose in the wind. The clumpy grass wasn't much to look at, but the aroma brought back *everything*. Tobias's lips seizing hers, his hands grasping her waist and tucking her between his long legs, and his broad, hard body pressing hers into the door. She shook her head and glanced swiftly at her partner, realizing she'd been staring into space, her lips parted in remembrance.

Yet, she'd told him to forget about it and that she would as well.

Georgie's sympathetic expression said it all. "Will you be vexed if I admit I like him? And that I think he's set to marry the wrong woman?" She brought the morning glory to her nose and gave it a thoughtful sniff. "It's a challenge the Duchess Society hasn't faced, one of us falling in love with a client, but it can unquestionably be rectified. Lady Matilda Delacour-Baynham—"

"Has *four* sisters, Georgie. Four sisters that will never work with us if I steal the bridegroom." Hildy shoved the arrangement containing the vetiver behind an incredible collection of damask roses taking up half her desk. "And I'm not in love with—"

The sound of the front door wrenching back on its hinges halted their conversation. The raised voice of Hildy's aging majordomo, Danbury, who'd been with her family for over thirty years, reverberated down the hallway. Part of her elderly staff of four, insignificant by society's standards, that she struggled to pay the salaries for.

Hildy raced out of the study before Georgie could rise from her chair behind the escritoire. The scene in the entranceway was such that Hildy paused, blinking hard to connect what she was seeing to what she was seeing.

Tobias was leaning against the wall in the vestibule, hand braced on her console table. The mail she'd stacked there to post later today lay scattered across the carpet. Danbury was arguing with the young man who'd been following her for the better part of a week, gesturing wildly and trying to shove the door closed.

"What's going on?" Hildy asked as Georgie came up behind her.

Tobias lifted his head, and her heart stuttered. His face was the color of chalk, his brow dotted with sweat, his hair a damp tangle about his head. "Close the door. Send my carriage home without me but tell my coachman to hide that fact. Get Macauley. He's got to look after Nick Bottom. And Nigel. And Mattie. Send for Mattie."

Hildy's heart sank. *Mattie.* Of course. Matilda Delacour-Baynham was his fiancée.

"It's not that, Hildy girl," he whispered weakly as she crossed to him, eating up the distance in three hasty strides. It was only when she got close that she noted the blood bubbling between the fingers he'd pressed to his shoulder, crimson drops staining her tattered Aubusson.

"She's got to remove—" He sucked in a pained breath and expelled it in a rush.

"Remove what?" Hildy helplessly reached for him.

"The bullet," he said and passed out quite beautifully at her feet.

~

Hildy threw back a shot of whiskey from the flask Xander Macauley had handed her, deciding she didn't like the sight of blood. Or observing surgery being conducted on the mahogany banqueting table that had been in her mother's family since 1750. Her stomach churned as the bullet hit the metal dish that Matilda—*Mattie* —dropped it in.

If she'd ever questioned Lady Matilda Delacour-Baynham's medical skill, she wouldn't again. After being summoned, Mattie had arrived promptly at the servant's entrance of Hildy's Georgian home and jumped into action, ordering everyone about with brisk efficiency. Hot water, towels, sheets, liquor, soap. From her medical bag, she'd retrieved rubbing alcohol, twine, gauze, and several tarnished instruments Hildy feared asking the use of. From her apothecary box, she'd dug out three glass bottles, the contents of which took immediate aromatic control of the room. Killing the scent of blood, which was welcome. Then she'd spread a clean sheet on the banqueting table, washed her hands meticulously, had Tobias moved into the room and liquored up, and surgery began.

"He'll be fine, Lady H," Tobias's partner said from his resting slump against the doorjamb of the canary yellow parlor, a space rarely in use unless she was serving tea to a new client. "Not the first bullet recovered from his body."

Hildy exhaled faintly at this news and took another slug of Streeter, Macauley & Company whiskey, then handed the flask back to its owner. Tobias was fine now, perhaps. But if wounds didn't kill a person, infection usually did. A fact she'd keep to herself because Macauley, a handsome, rugged, broad-chested brute of a man, had an anxious cast to his features that stated he and Tobias were more brothers than partners.

"He's brilliant, you know." Macauley rotated the flask in his hands, the jittery smile he threw her a glaring mix of affection and despondency. "Talked about building things since the first day I met him. Our youth was spent haring off to some section of Town that didn't want us to look at a window done in this style or a balcony created using a swank angle or something tedious like that. The shipping business is only ours because it was there for the taking. Both of us suited to managing our distinct pieces. A man with a mind like Street's can make blunt a hundred different ways, and I have my own talents. We mix well.

"The problem is, he wants a *life* rookery swells normally can't have to go with it. Because his goals blind him to the impossibility of it all, I'm there to yank him back. It's the blue blood running right now across your fancy dining table that's lighting a fire beneath his skin, hungering to get out. He can't forget it's a part of him, this world. *Your* bloody world. When I, myself, want nothing to do with it."

Uncapping the flask, he took a lengthy draught, his eyes glowing a deep burnished bronze above the silver rim. "Your deal with him has his dreams wrapped up in it. I hope you get that, *my lady*."

Hildy swallowed, wishing he'd offer her another drink. Although she was thankfully tipsy from what she'd imbibed. "Our deal has my dreams wrapped up in it too, Mr. Macauley."

"Blimey, that's a damned tangle then." Xander blew out a disgusted breath and shoved the flask in the pocket of a well-tailored frock coat. No scraps for this man. As she'd noted previously, smuggling paid well. "Cut the mister, if ya please. Just Macauley. Or Mac. The other makes me think of my dear papa, and that's something I never again want to do."

"I don't care to think of my father either," she said, the whiskey talking. Her gaze shot to Macauley, her lips opening in shock. She'd never once mentioned the Earl of Cavendish in such a way to anyone outside her family.

His amber gaze cut through her as cleanly as Mattie's scalpel was through Tobias's skin. The corners of his mouth tilted. "Interesting," he murmured with absolutely no clarification of the statement.

Hildy put her hands behind her lower back and leaned against the wall. Darkness had fallen, and her house was lit by tallow candles, oil lamps, and stray moonlight. No beeswax in this home. She was exhausted, like the few who remained to manage the crisis. "So I keep him here until..."

Macauley tipped his head, his eyes going to the ceiling. "Until he can stroll into the warehouse looking like he's just rolled out of bed with his mistress. Like he has no care in the world and the person who tried to get him missed. I know how Street thinks. Protecting the business is always top of mind. *Always*. Whoever took a potshot at him in his carriage in broad daylight, mind you, will have men posted there, the distillery, his house. The harbor, our ships in port. I have my ideas about who did this, and so will he. It's commerce, not personal. We'll tackle it as we have to." He pointed to a split in the plaster. "A crack there you'll need to address before it gets worse."

"That sounds barbaric." Although the memory of Tobias pressing her into the door with a rather boorish jostle sent heat blooming through her traitorous body. She had asked him to kiss her like a ruffian, not a gentleman. And a ruffian was what he *was*.

Macauley shrugged, indifferent, his gaze roving the walls, seeking more faults in her foundation. "Our business can be dangerous at times. The smuggling piece. Making whiskey is tame as one of Nick Bottom's kittens. About as interesting too, though Street loves it. He *likes* all the maths involved. One teaspoon wrong in the measurement, the batch is no good. I can't take the pressure."

Hildy hungered to know more about Tobias but kept herself from shooting questions at his partner when her interest might spark his. "He can stay, certainly. A guest chamber has already been prepared. Once he's moved off the dining table. No one comes and goes as we often use Georgie's home for meetings. I have minimal domestics, so his privacy is assured. However, it might be good to have discreet protection since my staff is admittedly as outdated as my clothing. Use your man, Gerrie, since he's no longer spying on me."

Macauley choked out a stunned laugh, his hand going to his hip and dusting his coat back. "You're a crack female, Lady H. We're lucky this calamity happened on Street's way here as news in Limehouse travels fast, so thank God his blood was spilled out of it. No one will guess he's here. And for some goddamned reason, I trust you. Better yet, I think *he* does."

No, they wouldn't guess. The *ton* would never connect a meddling spinster to a gorgeous viscount's by-blow who owned half of the East End.

Macauley peeled himself from the doorjamb as Mattie strode into the hallway, drying her hands briskly with a towel. She wore a butcher's apron streaked with Tobias's blood and a determined expression that gave her a ferocity no woman her age should own. She dabbed her moist brow, then her cheeks, as she halted before them.

"The shoulder is bandaged, the wound clean. I gave him laudanum, and he's out cold. It's a good time to move him. He can't stay on that table all night. Your butler is watching to make sure our patient doesn't roll off, but he looks ready to drop where he's standing, so someone may want to relieve him of duty." She flicked the towel in Hildy's direction. "I'm hoping the bedchamber you have in mind is downstairs. The less movement, the better, and he's not a small man."

No, he isn't, Hildy thought while remembering things she shouldn't. "The chamber is two doors down, rather modest but cozy. The sheets have been refreshed, the hearth fire lit. A pitcher of water was placed on the bureau. There are towels in the event the wound reopens during the night, and a comfortable chair moved to the bedside."

Mattie nodded, satisfied. "Along with the laudanum you're going to administer every four hours, you have what you need. I'll return tomorrow first thing to check the wound and change the bandage."

Hildy choked on her next breath. "The laudanum *I'm* going to give him?"

Mattie reached around to untie her apron strings, wiggling out of the stained garment. "You and Mr. Macauley. Take shifts, check for fever, keep him still if you can. Force liquids."

"But—" Hildy started the argument but couldn't finish it. The man was in her home, injured, powerless. That blasted kiss and the ferocious memory of it, visceral, like his fingers stroking her skin, was *her* problem.

Mattie sighed and rolled her eyes, finally looking like a moody young woman instead of a hardened soldier. "I can't stay. I have to be back before the servants start work at dawn. What good will this wedding be to any of us if my reputation is in tatters? And yours, Lady Hildegard, already is." This said, she marched back into the sick room, ready to direct the relocation of her patient.

Hildy fired an irate breath through her teeth. *Brat*. Gifted, sensible *brat*.

"Don't let that spoiled sprite rile you. Anyway, if she stays, the wrong chit will be there when he wakes up," Macauley whispered as he passed her on his way to move his partner.

As much as she hated to admit it, Hildy suspected he was right.

Chapter Nine

The infection took hold on the second night.

Her night because Macauley had supervised the first.

The bedchamber Hildy had selected to place Tobias in, the only one situated on the ground floor of her townhouse, was too small for a raging fever *and* a raging attraction. Even as she swabbed his moist brow and tucked the thickest counterpane she owned around his shivering body, spooned chicken broth between his chapped lips, and dosed him with laudanum, Tobias Streeter's swarthy magnificence called to her.

Mattie had cut away his bloodied shirt before removing the bullet, and they'd never replaced it. His skin glowed in stark contrast to the bleached bandage circling his shoulder and chest. Weakly, her gaze followed the line of hair trailing between his pectoral muscles. Even amid dire circumstances, his body was abject splendor. Long and lean, strapping but not too, overwhelming her meager guest bed in the best of ways. She'd seldom met a man she believed looked like *this* beneath his clothing.

Most in the *ton* were padded, either from their tailor or their cook.

Problematically, everything about him was appealing. His intelligence. His passion. His wit. His stark good looks. Coal-black hair, tousled though she'd tried to tame it with a comb, curled about his face in damp snarls. His densely stubbled jaw gave him a savage appearance that did nothing, absolutely *nothing*, to diminish his attractiveness. It only enhanced.

A tremor shook his body, and he flinched. Leaning over him, Hildy secured the coverlet, then let her hand stray to his chest, relishing the feel of his heart thumping soundly beneath her palm. He was going to survive because she'd have it no other way.

Hildegard Templeton usually got what she wanted.

Macauley's words came to her, unwelcome. *Your deal has his dreams all wrapped up in it.*

Her gaze skimmed the bedside table, where they'd placed the contents of Tobias's pockets. Money clip, knife, a pencil sketch of a building on a scrap of paper. She picked up the drawing and ran her thumb over the neat lines, imagining Tobias sitting at his drafting table or perhaps a public house, head bent diligently over his work. Vibrant green eyes lit with passion. *Passion.* She'd placed that emotion in his eyes just three nights ago. An occurrence having nothing to do with architecture.

She'd never anticipated having the Rogue King's happiness resting on her shoulders, only a sliver of his future. Complicating her involvement, he'd let her into his world, even if he wasn't completely aware of this fact. She'd witnessed intimate aspects she couldn't forget. The way he'd looked like a child with his nose pressed to the glass of a sweet shop when he talked about architecture, for one. That he took a cat and an orphan home in his carriage every night, too. Guards stationed on Limehouse corners, new paint on the doors.

Society thought differently, but Tobias was not only brilliant but *kind*. She'd seen the evidence—Nick Bottom and Nigel—he tried to sweep beneath the proverbial rug. Ruthless when the situation called for it, but fair when it did not. Decent. Industrious. Imaginative. The type of man the Duchess Society hoped to find when they conducted their investigations but rarely did. A man who wanted to succeed but believed hard work, not the destruction of the competition, should bring success. Shooting into carriages on city streets wasn't Tobias Streeter's style.

Nonetheless, there was a problem.

An enormous problem.

This mysterious, reluctant connection between them.

Which she felt—and so did he.

Splintered souls brought together by fate. Happenstance. Luck. Chance. When she'd never believed such things existed. Claptrap, rubbish, nonsense. As Georgie had said, she'd gone so long without flirting or being around couples in love that she'd forgotten what primal chemistry between two people was like. Exhaling faintly, she slumped into the unforgiving but stately chair Danbury had dragged into the room, folded her arms on her knees, and dropped her head atop them. The space reeked of laudanum and illness, but the enticing scent of vetiver clinging to Tobias's skin remained.

Haunting her with memories of a kiss she'd never forget. Of a man who was coming to mean too much to her.

She was sliding into an exhausted slumber, his light breaths lulling her, when he shifted, sending the bed ropes creaking.

"They know," he whispered, his tormented tone bringing her head up. His eyes were heavy-lidded, his gaze fever bright, irises as pale as she'd ever seen them, the color of spring grass that hadn't yet been trampled by feet or burned by sunlight.

She scooted forward in the chair, her knees bumping the mattress. "They know what?"

He blinked, his lids fluttering as he struggled to focus on her. "The troop's movement. We're trapped. Can't you hear the cannon fire?" His uninjured arm came out from beneath the counterpane, and he tossed the coverlet aside as if he meant to rise. The tattoo on his wrist was stark against his ashen skin. "Staying here is the sure way to death."

Heavens, he was out of his mind on opium and in the midst of a waking nightmare. Danbury had gone to procure another bowl of broth, so she was alone with a raving man. "Tobias, you've been injured. *Please*," she pleaded, pushing against the center of his chest to keep him in the bed. "If you rip your stitches when we're trying to fight this infection—"

"Fight?" He went to his elbow, a ragged breath slicing from his mouth. "They're set to attack on two fronts across a frontier of more than 1,500 kilometers, from Sutlej to the Koshi."

Panic lit a fire inside her chest. If he removed himself from this bed, she and Danbury might not be able to get him back in before they were able to summon Gerrie, who stood watch in the vestibule. By then, he could gravely reinjure himself.

"*Toby*," she whispered and cupped his jaw, drawing his frenzied gaze to hers. His skin burned hers where she touched him. "No more of this nonsense about a war long over, do you hear me?"

He swallowed, his throat pulling taut. "*Toby*." Closing his eyes, he fell back with a tortured sigh. "Hildy girl, what are you doing in India?"

A relieved laugh sputtered free. "I came to find you, of course."

A knowing smile curved his lips, and her heart skipped a beat. Even in this state, he could seduce. She was simply mad for him.

His lids lifted to reveal glassy, bright eyes, his pupils as round as the moon. "You like me. Even though you shouldn't. I thought you did. It's the cat." He lifted his hand and brushed his fingertip over her bottom lip. "And that kiss. God above, that *kiss*."

Her smile was unexpected and almost as drunken as his. Georgie was correct; she wasn't used to flirting. Moreover, she'd never been good at it. "I do *not* like you. In that way. You're my *client*."

His finger trailed across her cheek. "I've never seen such dimples. And to think, you brought them to a battle in the middle of the Meerut."

She took his hand and pressed it into the counterpane. Horrifying but true, the triangle between her thighs was heating up with his touch until she decided a walk around the block in the frigid London air was an excellent next step. "You can have another dose of medicine in one hour. Until then, try to sleep."

"You be my medicine, *Gadji*," he murmured, patting the space next to him.

Flustered, she rose and crossed to the bureau, dipped a length of cloth into a bowl of water, squeezed it out, and returned to the bed. As he eyed her with a drowsy expression, she placed the damp rag across his brow. "Sleep."

Again, he patted the bed. "You came all the way to India, after all. No one will think to look in my tent."

Knowing this was a hazardous plan, Hildy nonetheless perched her hip on the edge of the mattress, went to her elbow, then her shoulder until she was stretched out alongside him. There was some protection, as she was atop the counterpane while he was underneath. Too, he thought they were in India. In a tent.

He was as helpless as a pup, and she nothing but an enamored, daft bluestocking tripping along after him.

With a weary exhalation, he fit his good arm beneath her and brought her weakly against his side. His body was cooking, on fire, and she'd no idea how to help beyond curling into him and murmuring tender, meaningless words against his flushed skin. Soothed, he settled deeper into the mattress, sighed out her name, and drifted away.

One more minute, she promised herself and closed her eyes. *Let me comfort him for one more minute, then I'll give him up.*

Two seconds later, Hildy fell into an exhausted slumber snuggled next to the Rogue King.

Tobias woke with a start, a latticed band of sunlight rolling across his face.

With a muted groan, he rose to his elbow, gazing around a bedchamber he didn't for the life of him recognize. However, the room revealed much in his five-second review. Tattered velvet drapes, faded wallpaper curling at the corners, a pale spot where a painting had once hung, sold to appease creditors, he'd guess.

His shoulder screamed like the devil when he reached for the glass on the bedside table. Halting, he inhaled a painful gasp.

Ah, there she was.

Lifting the counterpane to his nose, he breathed deeply.

He might not recognize the room, but he recognized the *woman.*

The taste of Hildy Templeton, the touch of her, the scent of her lingered like smoke long after a blaze had been extinguished. Their kiss had dismantled him in a way he'd never been taken apart before.

A kiss of promise. A kiss of affection, obsession, exploration.

A kiss of the *soul*.

Interrupting his musing, a knock sounded on the bedchamber door. Still, before Tobias could say enter, Dexter Munro, the Duke of Markham, strode into the room, absurdly balancing a tea tray in his hands, looking as out of place as if he'd painted himself red and run down the street naked.

Tobias scooted up until he was resting in a crooked slant against the headboard, his wound throbbing in time to his heartbeat. "She bailed, did she?"

Dex nudged the door closed with a side kick, the tray wobbling in his hands, the teapot sliding precariously to the lip. "Like a dog with a tail between its legs. *Her* legs, in this case." He set his bounty on the bureau, poured tea with an elegant twist of his wrist, and brought the cup to the bed, sheltered like a baby bird in his fist.

"Many thanks, Your Grace," Tobias muttered and gulped down the finest tea he'd ever tasted. His voice was frayed from disuse, like shards of glass being dragged over stone. "Any food on that tray, by the way? I realize I was near death's door, but now I'm merely in a moderate level of pain and utterly famished."

Dex strolled to the bureau, buttered a piece of toast, then returned to the bedside. Sprawling in the chair Tobias's fuzzy memory placed Macauley *and* Hildy in while they'd cared for him, the duke presented the meager scrap with a stylish shrug. "All you're allowed until we wean you off the opium and your fever has returned to normal."

Snatching the toast from his hand, Tobias tore into the slightly stale offering like it was mutton. "Didn't think I'd start my day with a duke. Or a bullet wound," he said, chewing greedily. "Damned if I'm not taking two steps forward and one back. But such is life, I'm finding."

Dex buffed his nails on the leg of his woolen trousers in a show of ducal tolerance. "You counted on starting your day with the woman you're lusting over, fawning all over *you*. A woman who, regrettably, is not the chit you intend to marry. Does that sum it up efficiently enough?"

Tobias straightened his upper body, twisting his injured shoulder, pain stealing his breath. Dex continued to eye him with a parental gaze as Tobias struggled to collect his words through the agony. Hildy had a protector, and thank God for it. "Why does *everyone* seem to oppose a practice employed by society toffs every bloody day of the week? This marriage makes sound business sense for me and the lady involved. No one is being deceived regarding any aspect of the agreement. I feel like one of those colorful birds in the Caribbean, repeating the same philosophy over and over."

"Funny you mention a bird. You're in a cage, too, only it's one of your making."

Tobias swallowed the last bite of toast and washed it down with the last spot of tea. "I'm not going to try to decipher the patrician wisdom behind *that* statement. Suggestions from a peer of the realm. I'm so appreciative."

"Lucky for you, I'm not the only peer here today. I brought along Leighton. For fun. You can 'Your Grace' yourself into a stupor."

Tobias jerked his head up, vision spotting. Bracing his hand on the mattress to steady himself, he whispered, "You didn't. Not after that bastard threw Macauley in the Thames." Though it *had* been the funniest event he'd seen in years. Better than Drury Lane.

Dex fiddled with his cuffs, his delight nowhere *near* concealed. "He's still vexed about the Demon Duke thing. Sorry to say, but Leighton's lounging in the yellow parlor as we speak, chatting up that aging butler of Hildy's. Not a young staff managing this home, bless her. Which adds to the cost of direction in medical bills and pension planning. No protection either, I should add. Therefore, Leighton's kindly offered to put you up in his manse until you're ready to saunter back to Limehouse looking like nothing, certainly not a bullet through the shoulder, is slowing you down."

When Tobias started to argue, Dex held up his hand. "There's talk on the docks about someone felling the King. Your partner is calming your investors, shipping merchants, dockworkers, ladyloves. Such a fervor in the East End that I found myself unaccountably intrigued. Halted my study of this incredible black jade I acquired last month to do a little digging. Solid plan, I guess, seeing as my duchess is working closely with you. And you and I are discussing your Australian contacts supplying me with Mookaite Jasper. *If* they can get their hands on it."

"I can get my hands on *anything*," Tobias ground out between his teeth, his shoulder screaming for him to quit *moving*. The Duke of Markham investigating his businesses wouldn't be a first. Let. Him. Look.

"No idea you were so successful. Rich as Croesus, Streeter. Ducal money is a pittance in comparison. People actually like dealing with you, too, except for the bloke who shot you, of course. He's displeased about something." Dex tapped his lips in thought. "Maybe I should move from geology into smuggling since it pays so well. Although I have a solid aversion to bullets entering my flesh. I'm odd that way."

Tobias held out his teacup, glad his hand wasn't shaking too badly. Dex stared at the floral ceramic like it was a snake, then he sighed, shoved to his feet, and came back with the teapot. He intentionally poured to the rim, so there was no way Tobias could get the damned cup to his mouth without spilling.

"Tell duke number two thank you, but I'll stay here until I can walk to Limehouse," he said as tepid liquid splattered his chest and neck on the way to his lips. "For your edification, Your Grace, smuggling accounts for *two* percent of my business. And could account for nothing with one word from me tomorrow. I do it for *fun*, not profit. If I wanted to build on that piece, trust me, I bloody well could. When I started, smuggling was ninety-eight percent. I've spent years building a legitimate enterprise." He saluted the duke with his cup. "Should give lessons on how to do it to the toffs in your set who can't keep a bloody townhouse in Mayfair afloat."

"Stop it, then. Tomorrow." Thumping the teapot on the table at his side, his gaze lingered on the thick bandage swaddling Tobias's shoulder. "Legitimate businesses might be less perilous. Architecture, for one. You can trust my advice. I have no agenda. Beneath my titles and this peer of the realm foolishness, there lies nothing but a humble geologist."

"My enterprises are your concern, why?" Tobias asked, the tea reviving him in a way he'd not thought possible. Most assuredly, his head was swimming, and his vision was going gray around the cusp, but he felt like he was going to survive for the first time in days. He was deuced if he'd get angry about Hildy discussing him with the duchess, who'd then discussed him with her duke. It was the gossiping way of women.

He'd bet a shiny half crown she hadn't told anyone about the kiss.

Dex spun the teapot around by its handle, ostensibly searching for something to do with his hands. "I placed guards on your properties, the warehouse, the distillery that, I hate to admit, makes the best malt whiskey I've tasted in perhaps never. Placed them on this house, doubled the protection on my own. Lady Matilda's home. All clean but here. Someone is watching Hildy. A man's been seen lingering around the side garden, the servant's entrance. Gone in a flash, however. No idea who it might be. Not yet."

Tobias's mind cleared like someone had blown a breath of mint through it. "Move me now. Keep her guarded every damned second."

Dex smiled, his head tilting slyly. "I thought you'd see it that way."

Tobias rested the teacup on his belly. "I only agree, however, if I deal with Lady Hildegard for the rest of this project, as she calls it. Don't try sending your wife. Tell the Duchess Society's delegation this is *my* requirement. A bridegroom's predilection, as it were. If someone's going to prepare me to enter this tangle of a highborn world, it's going to be *her*."

"You know, you speak like no smuggler I've ever met. Reminds me of this professor I had at Cambridge, a foul-tempered but brilliant, quite boozy poet."

"I'm no poet."

"No, you're a smuggler-cum-architect. How does one *do* that, exactly?"

Tobias raised a brow, an intimidation tactic that didn't take much strength as he was close to crumpling into his pillows. "I don't know, how does one become a duke-cum-geologist?"

"Actually, it's geologist-cum-duke." Dex trailed his finger across a spider crack in the teapot's belly. "The wedding's still on, then?"

Tobias took a gulp of tea, close to pleading for more laudanum as the pain in his shoulder was starting to cloud his mind. Bollocks, he'd forgotten, but getting shot *hurt*. When he found out who'd done this, they were going to wish they'd killed him.

Dex snapped his fingers in front of Tobias's face. "Remember that event in three weeks where you say 'I do' and then stroll off into the sunset a wedded dupe?"

"Yes," he ground out. "I recall."

A wedding. In three weeks. He was supposed to marry Mattie in *three* weeks.

When he didn't want to marry anyone except maybe, perhaps, possibly *Hildy*.

In his mind, he hastily reviewed the plans he'd submitted to Nash's committee. They were fantastic, the best work he'd ever done if he did say so himself. But unfortunately, work he couldn't accomplish without a partnership with someone as revered as John Nash. And to be accepted to Nash's team, he needed a titled father-in-law to sway the vote, an aristocratic bride with a spotless reputation. Which, even with the unsubstantiated rumblings about her delivering babies, Mattie had.

While Hildy Templeton, with her white-hot kisses and very publicized profession, was beyond redemption. Her father's reputation was still loathsome years after his passing. The dukes who'd befriended him, Markham and Leighton, not much better. "It's on," he murmured, dread curdling in his chest.

Dex yawned into his fist and gave his shoulders a negligent roll. "Probably for the best."

Tobias's temper flared, his fingers curling around the cup with such pressure he was surprised the delicate bone china didn't crumble. "Are you implying that the lady isn't meant to be with a man like me? Rookery born, bastard bred. If you are, thank you, Your Grace, but the notion already occurred to me." He took a fast sip and choked as the tea snagged in the back of his throat. "When visions of any woman but my fiancée should be verboten. I know what you're thinking. All this is a sign that I'm attaching myself to the wrong woman."

Dex's eyes fired with their own intractable blaze. Tobias knew there was a reason he *liked* this man. The duke wasn't used to backing down either. "My advice is completely self-serving, Streeter. Did you think I'd miss the overpowering floral scent emanating from that depressing study down the hall? Flowers *you* sent. Hildy is my wife's closest friend, nay, almost a sister to Georgie. And Georgie is the most important person in *my* life aside from Anthony, my son. As the old saying goes, happy wife, happy—"

"Keep *me* happy if you want those Australian rocks," Tobias snapped, his vision dimming. His shoulder was separating from his body. "Kindly take your advice and shove it up your ducal arse."

Dex paused, then he threw back his head, and laughed. He snaked his arm around his belly and curved into his amusement. The bloody bounder.

"What a mess you're in, Streeter. Almost as grand a one as I was with Georgie. Hell's teeth, did I make a muddle of that. She loved me from the time she was a child, and I let her *marry* someone else. How's that for stupidity of the highest order? When I can't imagine her with anyone, *ever*, but me." He flicked his hand in a regal show of tolerance, waving off Tobias's rejoinder. "I have a proposal. Invite me to your distillery, show me how to make a robust batch of malt whiskey, and I'll tell you the story. We'll get so soused they'll have to wheel us home in a costermonger's cart."

Tobias slid his teacup on the table with a grimace. "Sure, sure, I'll show you. Blazes, it's basic chemistry."

Dex rocked back in the chair, the spindles creaking. His smile was cheeky, set to enthrall anyone he met when Tobias knew better. "You are, and I genuinely *never* say this, someone I want to know better."

A wave of exhaustion rolled over Tobias, pulling him under. Closing his eyes, he rested his temple against the headboard. The scent of linseed oil drifted past his nose. "Protect her, Markham. And in the morning... I'll go to Leighton's."

He felt the counterpane being lifted to his shoulders. If he'd been stronger, he would've been mortified by the fraternal consideration. Conversely, if Tobias's eyes were open, the Duke of Markham likely wouldn't have made the gesture.

The duke's footfalls sounded as he crossed the room, then the door creaked open. "You can go in," Dex whispered. "But let him sleep. Finish your iced bun, then make yourself a pallet on the floor. And no more hiding under carriage seats, young man."

Tobias cracked his eyelid to see Nigel doff his cap to the duke and stroll into the bedchamber like he owned it, his clothing a calamity and his hair worse. When Tobias had been forlornly hoping for Hildy.

He pretended to be asleep when Nigel paused by the bed, although it wasn't far from the truth. His small hand brushed Tobias's chest in a touch set to break hearts.

The boy was getting attached.

But then, so was he.

To a bedraggled orphan, a cat with an erroneous name, and a matchmaker who kissed like a courtesan.

Chapter Ten

Hildy watched Tobias cross the crowded avenue with a loose-limbed stride, nimbly dodging carts and carriages, sidestepping a well-appointed matron who gave him a lascivious side-glance. The way he tucked his arm against his ribs was the only suggestion of an injury. Dressed in stark black from head to toe, glossy Wellingtons on his feet, frock coat whipping about him with his stride, he seemed ready to do battle with the shops on Bond Street.

Or perhaps merely ready to do battle with *her*.

He stepped up to the stone pavement three stores down from where she stood shivering in the frigid morning damp, the tremors sweeping her body having little to do with the cold. Once again, his lean grace, his economical elegance, consumed her. Not a move wasted, nor a gesture overstated. She'd rarely seen the like among the posturing *beau monde*. But he was much more than those men. Tobias Streeter had a sharp mind that his attractiveness cleverly harbored.

She wanted to ignore the way her heart fluttered when he glanced up and caught her staring. Ignore the way his step faltered, slowing before he shook off the reaction and strode forward as if nothing— certainly not an *inconvenient* attraction to a bluestocking matchmaker who couldn't help him build grand buildings—was going to stand in his way.

He halted when he reached her, tipped his beaver hat with a deferent bow, his eyebrow winging high in mocking opposition. The dent beside his mouth folded in. He played the gentleman's part this day, except for the careless expression and the crooked smile. Those belonged to the smuggler. However, his skin was pallid beneath its olive tone, grooves of sleeplessness marking the area around his eyes.

Hildy knocked aside the hood of her cape to see him more clearly, but a brutal gust tearing down the street knocked it back. "It's too soon for you to be up and about," she said, stepping aside to make room for a cluster of ladies exiting the arcade. "I should have refused your invitation. Truthfully, I can pick out gifts as well as you can. I merely thought your involvement would make the giving more personal."

"Just get Mattie a new apothecary case and be done with it," Tobias countered, sending that crooked smile in the direction of one of the ladies who'd stopped on the sidewalk with the pretense of dropping her glove on the grimy stone. A widowed countess, if Hildy wasn't mistaken. All the woman wanted was a second glance at the Rogue King. "Besides, I have to make a performance of my return. We're going to parade from Piccadilly to Oxford Street because rumors of my demise are bad for business, you see. What better place than the godless Burlington Arcade to do that very thing? Soulless conversation and the frivolous expenditure of coin sounds just the ticket to prove I'm a living, breathing Londoner."

"It's only been five days since your accident, Tobias."

He took her arm and moved her through the entrance into the arcade, shielding her from a group of men who rushed past. "I'm aware, Hildy girl, of the time that's passed. The memory of a bullet lancing one's skin is hard to forget." Pausing, he glanced over his shoulder, his beautiful lips falling open in wonder. "Is that a *chaperone* accompanying you?"

Hildy jerked her arm from his grasp, shoved her hood off her head, and started down the glass-enclosed promenade. Zelda, her maid since

Hildy was in nappies, shuffled along behind them, cane in hand, a woolen cloak wrapped so severely around her reed-thin body that all that could be seen of her face was the rosy tip of her nose and a wrinkled upper lip. "Don't sound so surprised. I can obey the rules of proper etiquette when required. When I *want* to."

"*Obey*. Sure you can," he whispered with a roguish laugh and fell into mocking step beside her. She wasn't about to tell him Zelda couldn't hear a blessed thing without her ear trumpet. "Personally, I think you're scared to be alone with me."

"Is that yours?" She nodded to the hulking beast of a man who had, despite his fearsome size, sneaked up alongside them.

Tobias shrugged, then forced a pained breath through his teeth. "Death threats and torn flesh require increased security." He fluttered his fingers like he was spreading seed. "Pretend he's not there. But if he tells you to run, *obey*. Since you're so good at that."

She snorted softly beneath her breath. "Oh, yes, of course."

They passed a bootmaker and a tobacconist, feigning interest at each stop, with Hildy staying silent on the subject for as long as she could. "Are you well?" she finally asked, pausing before a haberdashery and peering in the yellow and green bay window without seeing a single item of clothing on display. Temptation swirled while walking alongside Tobias—the scent of his grandmother's soap drifting from his skin, the memory of his lips seizing hers. Forget about making actual conversation.

He inspired a knot of arousal and need unlike any she'd ever experienced.

Lying awake, staring at a crack in her ceiling *need*. Placing her hand between her thighs and finding satisfaction while picturing his body atop hers *need*. Knowing she was a dreadful person and wanting him anyway *need*.

He flattened his hand to the windowpane as if he was looking in when she could see he was holding himself up. A bead of sweat worked its way from beneath the brim of his hat to make a lazy trek down his temple. "I'm marginally well."

Her heart thumped, but she kept herself from reaching for him. "You've been seen shopping for gifts with your matchmaker. Verified as alive should the people who want you dead chance to inquire. Let your henchman summon your carriage, then make your way back to Limehouse or Leighton's—"

"Henchman. Saints love you, Hildy girl. You do make me smile. A razor-sharp wit in a stunning package is a rare thing indeed." Turning to lean his uninjured shoulder against the storefront, his gaze met hers. His eyes were as rich a green as the sour apples she bought in the market in the spring. "I have an idea. Let's go somewhere that *isn't* godless. Have tea and soulful conversation while I regain my strength. Then I will dutifully return home, to *someone's* home. A duke's or a smuggler's, I haven't yet decided."

Stunning. He found her stunning. While she found *him* stunning. A misplaced pair, they were.

Hildy rubbed at a grubby spot on the windowpane and affected a benign tone when she'd like nothing more than Tobias Streeter revealing another slice of his world. "There's a jeweler down the way who crafts lovely earbobs I thought Lady Matilda might appreciate."

"Apothecary case. Scalpels. Gauze. Iodine. In that order."

Pulling her lips between her teeth to hide her smile, she dipped her head. "Those are not romantic choices."

He reached because he seemed unable to stop himself, grazing her jaw with his knuckle. The caress bloomed, heat spreading through her body like tinder set to kindling. A blaze neither of them could contain. Even through the soft layer of his glove, she *felt* him. "It isn't a romantic story, Hildy," he whispered, leaving the rest unsaid.

But this is. Or could be.

The sentiment vibrated between them, as real a presence as Zelda or Tobias's henchman. Frantically, Hildy wondered if their chaperones noticed the attraction.

When she believed all of London should.

❦

Tobias was playing with fire. Risking his ten-years-in-the-making plan to work with John Nash. Risking this bloody marriage he didn't think he wanted anymore. An arrangement his fiancée didn't seem to want either.

Risking his heart by showing Hildy a part of him no one, aside from Macauley, had ever seen.

But he was helpless. When he'd never been helpless.

Not since his boyhood, anyway. Working in that godawful tarring house, coming home with burn-spotted hands and an empty belly, only to find a vacant cupboard, a chilled hearth, and an ailing mother waiting for him. And another letter to his father returned unopened, the unbroken wax seal a profound reminder of the futility of love.

Thinking about the past was making him antsy and in need of a cheroot. To soothe himself, he sneaked the bamboo toothpick from his waistcoat pocket and slid it silently between his lips.

As the carriage rolled to a stop before a tidy cottage on the outskirts of London, after circling Town enough times to lose anyone following them, he glanced at Hildy to gauge her reaction—because he couldn't thwart the need. It was the first structure he'd ever owned, purchased for his Aunt Esmeralda, using funds scraped together during his first year in India when all he'd known of business were tawdry dealings and inane negotiations. When his mother died, his aunt's requirements had been few. A garden. A hearth made of stone. A kitchen she didn't have to dismantle every morning when they were forced to move. She wanted permanence and, while not the Romani way, a piece of land to call her own. She'd gotten the idea from his mother. She'd stayed in their squalid flat because she believed that someday his father was going to return for her. But it had been *hers*, that flat, at least.

He was thankful Hildy's gaze was focused on the bustling lane and the admittedly charming cottage, her exquisite face tilted into the coal-thickened sunlight piercing the window. He wasn't sure what sentiments had crossed his face with the recollection. Nevertheless, her companion, the sour but vigilant Zelda, noticed his regard, her frown deepening until it nearly split her cheeks.

He wasn't fooling *her* with his aplomb.

As Tobias was a bit shaky, his injury announcing its wish for him to remain seated, he let his henchman, better known as Tommy Dogs, owner of a Limehouse boxing academy and former heavy-weight rookery champion, engage the step and assist Hildy and Zelda to the twisting footpath leading to the door. Leaning into the carriage, Tommy crooked a bushy eyebrow that had a faded scar splitting it through the middle, his scowl saying, *You brought her here?*

Tobias grunted and knocked aside Tommy's hand, his vision dimming at the fringes as he hoisted himself to his feet. As Mattie had advised during the daily changing of his bandage two hours ago, he likely should have stayed in bed.

But he'd been desperate to see his mad matchmaker.

Hildy's gaze made a deliberate review when he moved to stand beside her and the ever-observant Zelda. She wiggled the ring on her finger, hidden beneath her glove, her only show of apprehension. He admired her pluck. The pack of female wolves they'd encountered as they entered the arcade had cut Hildy as the *ton* did him every day. He'd been enraged on her behalf, although he'd hidden it well. They were jealous crones, layering their disregard as intolerance of her profession.

An occurrence made lovelier by the fact that she'd no idea how damned beautiful she was, how much *more* she was than any of her acquaintances. In looks and intelligence. In kindness and common sense.

Hildy turned as they neared the porticoed entrance of the cottage, painted vibrant crimson because his aunt liked it that way, causing him to stumble into her, reaching with his good arm to steady them both.

It was a mistake to touch her.

Heat seeped through his gloves to mark him indelibly, and his yearning roared like a hungry lion in his chest.

Her gorgeous cobalt gaze dropped to his lips, then rose, the flush lighting her cheeks making him think of crawling atop her and sliding inside. Tangling his hands in her flaxen tresses and bumping his hips against hers as he fully possessed her—and she him. Sinking as deeply as they could, physically and emotionally. His desire for her was a lurid and astonishing thing to behold when he'd been numb for ages.

"Why have you brought me here?" she whispered for him alone.

"When you're on the verge of collapse? When you're getting married in a little more than *two* weeks."

He let his arm fall to his side, his sigh barbed but his words candid. "Because I couldn't help myself, luv." Throwing his toothpick to the ground, he reached around her and knocked. Three brief raps, a code he'd created years ago so Esmeralda would resist the temptation to cock her pistol, shove it between a crack in the windowpane, shoot first, and ask questions later. He'd suffered that indignity *once* before devising another strategy.

"*Chav!*" his aunt called, using the Romani term for boy. Then swinging the door wide, her ash-gray eyes flashed at the sight of two women, obviously of quality, standing awkwardly on her front step. She eyed her nephew with a canny glance—his anemic stance against the portico column, his ashen skin—and ushered the group inside without any of the proper introductions Hildy and Zelda were accustomed to.

Her tiny home was an explosion of color and fragrance, a passage to another world. The air livelier than that found in a spice market and the furnishings more suited to the Orient than England. Vivid silks tossed haphazardly across a massive sofa that had taken three men to transport off his ship. Fluffy pillows and glass baubles, porcelain figurines and Asian vases. Petite statues of Buddhas and Greek gods.

Esmeralda had rejected a lifetime of transient living one knick-knack at a time.

It was only when Hildy turned to him with a wondrous expression on her face that he realized why he'd brought her.

Additionally, he hoped Hildy would—for reasons best not to examine too closely—get to know his beloved aunt. He wanted them *connected* in the mystical way that was life. That person you met on the street, then noticed every day after that because they were now a part of your world.

Tobias made carelessly informal introductions, then signaled to Tommy Dogs to guard the entrance, his aunt giving him a somber glance after witnessing the exchange.

"Trouble?" she asked in Romani.

He leaned to kiss her cheek, hoping he would be permitted to sit soon. That, or collapse to the costly carpet he'd had shipped from

China last year. "What trouble could there be, darling Esme?" he returned in the same language. A petite woman with ebony hair and mysterious eyes, she was beautiful enough to command an army. But she'd never married, and Tobias wondered if she was lonely or simply grateful for her freedom.

He imagined she was both.

"Sit, please," Esme directed, indicating the sofa, mindful that she didn't know how to coordinate a proper exchange, so she went with a lighthearted Romani one. If she found it odd that Tobias had brought someone to her home when he never had before, she kept it to herself.

"I have Russian tea and fresh cevapcici. Oh, and some wonderful blackberry jam from the market." She held out her hand and wiggled her fingers, indicating they should give her their coats. She wore a glittering array of rings, the stones winking in the candlelight. "Off with those layers. The hearth is blazing, the room warm as a Mediterranean summer. We'll make an afternoon of it since my darling *chav* has come to visit."

Zelda's eyes were round as saucers, and Hildy's smile curled adorably at the edges, bringing out those unique dimples. The ladies unfurled scarves, wrestled out of capes, and tugged off gloves until Esme's arms were full, the pile of clothing nearly obscuring her face. She shuffled from the room to do what with the garments, Tobias couldn't guess.

After gingerly removing his coat, one deliberate limb at a time, Tobias took two steps and collapsed in the armchair guarding the hearth.

Zelda gazed around the parlor, her mouth forming an amazed O. "Shall I help her with the tea?" she asked in the deafening voice she used when she was without her ear trumpet. Which Hildy had finally told him the woman needed after he'd yelled and not gotten a response from her at least five times. "Looks like she may need it."

Hildy sputtered a laugh—and he joined in, his heart quivering dangerously in his chest. Oh, he was *ruined*.

Zelda glanced between them, sighed out what sounded remarkably like a curse, then left the room, following in Esme's wake.

Hildy sat cautiously on the sofa, smoothed her skirt, adjusted her sleeves, her gaze circling but never landing. She seemed entranced by his aunt's home and jumpy enough to leap from her slippers. Then finally, her gaze settled. On him. "Your skin looks the color of parchment, Tobias. Especially in contrast to the mountain of color in this room. I hope to heaven you haven't popped your stitches. When you said tea and soulful conversation, I'd no idea you were taking me to the country."

"We took a circuitous route. We're only in Dartford, which officially falls in the county shire of Kent but is just outside the city. Never fear. I'll have you back to your manse and among your brethren by nightfall." He stretched his legs out, stacking one glossy boot atop the other. "And why do you care about my popped stitches, Hildy girl? What's it to you if I bleed all over my aunt's rugs? Even if I did go to great trouble to ship them here from the Dutch East Indies."

She sniffed, trailing her hand over the lip of a vase on the side table that had cost him a bloody fortune. The vase and the table. "Your sustained good health, until you repeat your vows, is part of my *job*." Fidgeting, Hildy circled her silver ring on her finger, round and round, and his smile bloomed. He loved making her nervous. Loved that she was as aware of him as he was of her. Loved that the heat between them stoked stronger than the fire at his back when they weren't even *touching*.

Imagine the heat if he touched her again.

"Quit smiling," she hissed and shot a glance toward the kitchen to see if they were being observed. "You like this. Sketching the moment like it's an angle in one of your blasted blueprints! I'm beginning to see how your mind works, and it's frightening."

"Is that right? Then you'd be the only one who's seen it, besides Mac maybe." He laughed straight away this time; there was no corralling it. "I do like this, luv, oh, I *do*. It's sparring without the agony of getting punched in the head. Your lovely mouth is stuck somewhere between a giggle and a glower. It's enchanting."

"I don't giggle."

He only hummed softly beneath his breath while she scowled.

After a lingering moment, he braced his elbow on the armrest and propped his head on his closed fist. Bloody hell if he couldn't drop to sleep right there looking at her, his dreams filled with their potent kisses. Visions of drawing her skirt to her waist and slinking his fingers through the gap in her drawers. Sinking one inside her and curling it in a beckoning motion, over and over until she cried out in ecstasy.

A trick of his that he wanted to share with her.

He wasn't only detailed with his blueprints. He'd paid attention to what women liked and bet he could make Hildegard come in less than ten minutes if he put his mind to it.

Maybe five if he worked very, very hard. Which he was prepared to do.

Her tongue came out to moisten her lips, and his cock twitched in his trousers. At least the pain was no longer going to be all about his shoulder. "What's that indolent smile of yours about?"

Lifting his head, he ran his thumb over his lips, pretending to touch hers. "Do you really want to know?" A fierce light flared in her eyes, a mix of lust and some extraordinary emotion he'd never had directed at him. "Do you, *Gadji?*"

"*Yes*," she breathed, her suggestive tone enough to have him looking to the kitchen to gauge how much time they had if he crossed to her and kissed her until she released a breathy moan into his throat. Those insatiable sounds of hers had driven him *wild*.

Placing the soles of his boots on the floor, he sat up, his gaze locking with hers. His shaft was now painfully hard, his pulse skipping in his veins. He was literally going up in smoke. "I was imagining lifting your gown to your waist, running my hands down your thighs, between your legs, my fingers finding the gap in your drawers and sliding inside. One finger, mind you, unless you asked for two. Then I'd caress you until you begged me to stop as I kissed you breathless. Until you couldn't take another moment of pleasure."

He brushed his hand across his cock, shifting it in his trousers, the way her gaze tracked his every move lighting him up inside. He wasn't willing to hide his arousal from her. He didn't want to hide anything from her. "Or maybe I'd drop to my knees before you and make you come with my mouth. There's a nub there that holds your gratification. Maybe you've even found it during your experimentation. I'd take it between my lips and suck gently. Only harder when you asked me to. I think you'd like it. And I know *I* would."

She gasped, her lips parting. Shocked, *yes*, but it wasn't revulsion seizing her features when Esme and Zelda tromped back in carrying tea trays, breaking the sensual spell holding court in the room.

Regrettably, it was *desire*.

A desire that spelled disaster for both of them.

Chapter Eleven

H ildy ate Esmeralda Gray's delectable cevapcici, which she
learned were small meat rolls seasoned with paprika and
garlic. Drank dark Russian tea laced with lemon and sugar
in a sitting room that looked to her like one in a high-class bawdy
house would. She was captivated by the entire afternoon, entertained
with stories about Tobias and his escapades growing up while watching
his cheeks pinken as he recuperated, the traditional food and drink
reviving him. He laughed easily and often with his aunt, his gaze never
straying from Hildy for long, his hat placed strategically on his lap to
hide evidence of his desire.

As he'd promised, soulful conversation and tea in the least of
godless places.

The façade he'd constructed to protect himself was being chipped
away, exposing the true man beneath. A process he allowed. That he'd
offered this revelation to her and not his intended was startling and
inexplicably wonderful.

And a nightmare because he wasn't *hers*.

Nonetheless, hungrily, Hildy seized the seconds, recording the
aroma of cardamon and citrus scenting the air; the splash of color on
the floor, the walls; the feel of raw knotted silk beneath her fingertips.

Vases and statuettes and ornamental gewgaws scattered about like pebbles on the shore. A vivid crimson door that opened to another world.

Tobias Streeter's world was unlike any she'd ever visited or imagined.

And his words...

His carnal suggestions circled her mind, closing in with sharp teeth until she tripped over her words, finally giving up and letting the others carry the conversation. Only Zelda recognized this was not the norm.

Then I'd caress you until you begged me to stop, drop to my knees before you, and make you come with my mouth.

As his carriage bumped along the gravel thoroughfare on their return to London, these erotic statements moved through her like a summer squall, sweeping away the chill until Hildy felt as exposed as Tobias had let himself be this day. Her tattered gloves offered no protection. Neither did her years-out-of-date woolen cloak or the lap blanket Tommy Dogs had handed her when she climbed inside. Her skin tingled beneath her many layers as if Tobias had trailed his fingers across her body, just as he'd suggested he'd like to. The area between her thighs lit up, a sudden melting sensation.

An area he'd let her know he wanted to explore.

With his fingers. His lips. His tongue.

"Your ring, luv. You're never without it."

Torn from her musings, Hildy glanced to the bench seat across from her, realizing she was spinning her ring beneath her glove, a senseless habit. Tobias was sprawled in the corner of the handsome carriage, his hat lying on the velvet squab beside him, no longer a necessity to have in his lap. She shifted, squeezing her thighs together and praying he didn't notice.

What could she do to make him have to use his hat as cover again?

"The ring," he whispered, his gaze dusting Zelda, who dozed beside Hildy. At some point during the visit, he'd put on his spectacles, another chink in the armor set to protect her against his charms. The scent of his soap drifting from his skin was another. "You got my stories today. Now I want one of yours. I would've asked the night I kissed you, but I was blinded by desire." He shrugged a broad shoulder, his smile rueful. "I simply forgot everything in that moment but the taste of you."

Hildy looked out the window, the glow from the carriage lamp gliding across her gloved hands, her slippered feet, his bent knees, the tip of his boot. Her heart was hammering, her skin flushed beneath her bodice. "You shared the stories you were willing to share."

He laughed, a chiding rush of air from his lips. "I shared my *life*, luv."

"With the wrong woman," she said, finally admitting what they both understood, though the utterance was so faint he might not have heard it. Looking to him, his eyes darkened until they shone the color of the emerald in her grandmother's brooch, an item she'd sold long ago but could still picture clearly.

"The ring was a present on my sixteenth birthday. I can't part with it, and it has no real value if I thought to. The other family pieces went to creditors. I'd be quite content with a modest cottage like your aunt's, but regrettably, I inherited a beast of an unentailed obligation and an aging staff. With no funds provided to support either, leaving me to conduct business. Trade is a crime in the eyes of the *ton*." Her tone roughened, ragged even to her ears. "My *matchmaking*."

Tobias exhaled and dragged his hand through his hair. He had beautiful hair. She was utterly entranced. Black as the sky unfurled above them, the glossy strands glistening blue in the lamplight.

She wondered if Mattie cared about his hair. Somehow, she doubted it.

Muscling inside his frock coat, he yanked out a flask, took a measured sip, then lowered it to tap against his thigh. "I could keep you. I have enough money for a thousand lifetimes. Enough for a thousand of *yours*."

Hildy's hands clenched in her lap. She threw a hurried look at Zelda, who was lost to slumber and couldn't hear them anyway. Although her maid was superb at reading lips.

She waited until her voice was strong enough to rise above the pulse throbbing in her ears. "*Keep* me?"

His fingers clenched around the flask, and he groaned, reaching to rub his injured shoulder. "It's done. Every damned day, Hildy. Don't act like it isn't. After that kiss where we almost burned the walls down around us, you can't be surprised I'd suggest it."

She crossed her arms, clasping them tightly to keep from reaching for him and saying, *Yes, keep me*. Make love to me. Wake with me every morning. Show me your sketches. Tell me your dreams.

Tell me everything.

She tugged her glove free so she could spin her ring without kid leather in the way. "What was the last one's name? Julia?"

He snorted and took another drink, his smile razor-sharp and slicing through her criticism. "Juliet. And she has nothing to do with what I'm proposing. I propose to share my *life* with you, without the benefit, or the burden, of marriage. But I would give you everything else."

It was Hildy's turn to issue a sarcastic snicker. "Rumor is you gave *Juliet* a diamond tiara as a parting gift. It's not a castle like the Duke of Winchester gave one of his paramours, but it's unique, I will say. Usually, men go with a necklace from Bentley & Skinner and call it a day."

"They were pearls. Still, if we're equating how much I want you in comparison to any woman I've ever known, then I'd need to give you a thousand tiaras, *Gadji*."

Hildy felt a hard pinch in her chest, and she dropped her head to her hand. "Stop, *please*."

"Mattie and I are never going to—"

"*Tobias*," she snapped, glancing at a snoring Zelda and thanking the heavens her maid was partially deaf.

With a vicious oath, he shoved his flask in his frock coat pocket and turned to stare out the window, anger radiating off him like heat from one of his malt stills. She could see circles of light reflected in his spectacle's lenses, but the glare successfully hid his eyes.

From the corner of hers, she watched him fidget. Rub his shoulder, tap his toe. Graze his finger over a streak on the glass pane. She realized the feelings claiming her were deep-seated—and genuine. You didn't choose attraction; attraction chose *you*. Besides, how could she *not* be attracted? He was so handsome sitting there, contrite, annoyed, bewildered. Fondness for him overflowed the banks of her endurance until she was carried along in a tide of affection. "The problem is, you're too used to getting your way."

"You're right, I am," he fired back without looking at her.

Hildy stretched her leg and bumped the side of his boot with her slippered foot. His gaze was molten when it met hers. "I can't, Toby. My thoughts about you are bad enough." She swallowed hard, the images roaring through her mind, causing her nipples to harden and scratch against her corset, but she pushed past the discomfort. The pleasure he'd promised he could give her. Pleasure she *wanted*.

"My fantasies. My yearnings. Our kiss shook the foundation I've always stood serenely upon. Now I understand that I stood sanctimoniously upon them. When I'd never felt actual desire for any man, I know that now." She held up her hand when he straightened from his negligent slouch, intent on persuading her, the light of battle in his eyes. She couldn't forget that Tobias Streeter had built an empire on the shoulders of his negotiating prowess.

"I can't reject every tenet of the Duchess Society for you. And I don't want to. It sounds mad, but I'm proud of myself for choosing *me*. Which is what I want my young ladies to do. It's a modern concept, a woman choosing herself, but I'm hoping to start a trend. Now, young ladies are only beneficial to society if an advantageous marriage places them there. I want to change that thinking. One union at a time."

"Your dreams are as extremist as my own." He sighed in defeat, his shoulders slumping as he fell back against the squabs. "The kiss shook my foundation too, Hildy. I've spent nights gazing at the ceiling, longing to repeat it. Imagining my hands all over you. When you believe that isn't possible, my need is earmarked for you and you alone. You don't realize..." He spread his fingers wide and gazed at his hands as if they held answers. "You don't realize how magnificent you are, how intelligent and clever and interesting. How much I want you."

Her smile was instantaneous, plumping her cheeks. His need was for her and her alone. Yet, to think bluestocking Hildegard Templeton had aroused this lean, long lion of a man to the point of rupture.

"Don't look so pleased, luv. Because I want to be furious with you. If it wasn't for those adorable dimples of yours, I'm sure I would be."

"I'd be of no assistance in gaining acceptance to the Nash project, should you think my father's title of import. My reputation is almost as dappled as yours. My family is not well-regarded. My father was unpleasant. Destitute at the end. He would have ended up in Marshalsea had he lived much longer. My brother was able to stabilize our affairs for a bit."

Tobias grimaced and rubbed his shoulder. "Maybe I don't care anymore. Maybe I never cared, and my notion of marrying is nothing but a bad dream. A nightmare, like those I have of India almost weekly."

She shook her head, her townhouse rising like an apparition in the distance, their delightful day coming to a close. "You care."

He looked away, closing himself off, miles away. If he was hers, their futures linked, their feelings for each other confirmed, she'd have made an effort to lure him from his bleak mood. Maybe with another kiss. Or more. Climb on his lap and do the things she'd heard one could do in a moving vehicle.

It would have been her commitment and her *privilege*.

As it was, Hildy nudged Zelda awake as the Georgian house she didn't want to live in anymore centered itself in the carriage window as they rolled to a stop.

Tommy Dogs was at the ready, leaping off his seat, lowering the step, and opening the door with a crude swagger before she could shake out her skirt. A footman minus the colorful livery or courteous bearing.

"Stay in the carriage, boss," he said and waved Tobias back when he started to rise. "When your doc wife-ta-be finds out you've been visiting your aunt, shopping at arcades, possibly ripping stitches and such, we're in trouble. She said one hour of activity was the limit, and we went way past." He jacked his thumb over his shoulder. "I can escort the ladies up just fine."

Hildy let Zelda step out before grasping Tommy's beefy hand and descending to the sidewalk, Tobias's gaze scorching her back. She took two steps, then turned and went back, leaning into the carriage. The wind tugged at the hood of her cloak, tossing it against her cheek. The air no longer smelled like Romani spice, and for that, she was genuinely sorry. "What did Esmeralda say to you when we left?"

"Unbelievable," Tobias murmured and let a tripping chuckle slide past his lips. Then closing his eyes, he tipped his head against the velvet squab, clearly exhausted, with no intention of answering.

But as Hildy walked away, his whisper flowed to her, riding the current of a wintry gust.

"When at last it happens, it happens."

Chapter Twelve

Two forlorn days later, Hildy glanced down the fetid alley behind Tobias's distillery, fog swirling around her feet in an atmospheric presentation snatched straight from a gothic novel. The moon was full but struggling to reveal itself through the dense, coal-smoke miasma blanketing London's sky. The air was frosty, an evening as cold as any they'd had all winter. Her breath leaked out in snowy, frothy puffs.

Still, she stood frozen in uncertainty when a warm dwelling was on the other side of the door.

"Go ahead, darling. You made it this far."

Hildy drew her cloak about her face and lifted her hand, ignoring Xander Macauley's jibe. Daughters of earls didn't arrive at distillery back entrances in the dead of night, seeking the companionship of smugglers. Unless they were mad or desperate.

She was neither.

She turned, caustic when she was the one tangled in the net. "Don't you have a key? Your business, in part, isn't it?"

Xander chuckled, the cheroot anchored between his teeth twitching, his broad body angled neglectfully against the carriage he'd brought her in. "Oh, I have a key. Could have escorted you right through the front door if I'd a mind to." He flipped the smoke to the ground and stamped it out beneath his boot. Around the corner, the sound of breaking glass and drunken shouts whistled down the narrow passage, a clear reminder that she was where she should not *be*.

Only, she'd been watering the flowers in her vase before bed, that bloody blue vase, and her mind had drifted away until she found herself fantasizing about Tobias. His wicked kisses and his scandalous remarks, the shocking things he'd said he wanted to do to her creating an explosion of yearning within her. The now-familiar burst of heat between her thighs. An itch she couldn't seem to scratch. Not quite, although she'd tried. Twice this week already. Frustrated and pacing, she'd acted without thought, changed into an ugly black crepe gown, and found herself creeping along the mews behind her townhome intent on flagging a hack when Xander Macauley intercepted her.

"If you have a key, for heaven's sake, Macauley, *use* it."

"Nah, waste of good time. *My* time. Street's going to boot you out on your lovely arse the moment he sees you. Dressed as you are in what looks like funeral garb. Then I have to return you to bloody St. James in the middle of the bloody night when I hate traveling through the posh areas of this city more than I hate being thrown in the Thames. Return you covert like too, so no one in your high-class cluster sees you and decides you have an interesting life after all. More so than *they* do, anyway. Which they'll hate you for."

"I don't need you. You can go," she growled and turned back to the door, praying Tobias's partner stayed right where he was until she got inside the brewing establishment.

"If I left you out here to fend for yourself, he'd kill me, and that's a fact."

"That's preposterous." Although it wasn't. She *knew* it wasn't. A fact that had heat swirling through her belly and doing a languid slide to pool right back between her thighs.

Who could have guessed that Hildegard Templeton would appreciate a man who showed the occasional possessive streak?

Xander scraped his bootheel across the cobblestones and cursed.

"Had to be my night that his girl decides to sneak out. Just had ta be. I knew I shoulda taken Sundays. No one pulls shifty moves on a Sunday. Why is that, do you reckon? Gerrie got the quiet night. And I'm left with the night Lady H sneaks out into the mist."

"I don't know why you're watching over me. I really don't," she said and raised her hand to knock, ignoring Macauley when he replied, "Oh yes, darling, you do." Three sharp raps on the scuffed oaken door leading into the bowels of the distillery; the same announcement Tobias had used with his Aunt Esmeralda.

She hoped he recognized the dare.

When Tobias opened the door because, of course, he was the one who opened the door, she was unprepared for the rush of emotion that swept through her and seemed to leap to him, widening his eyes, a stunning emerald glow in the hazy moonlight.

Oh, she was in trouble.

He was dressed as casually as she'd ever seen him. Untucked shirt fluttering at his hip, unbuttoned halfway down his chest. No cravat. Sleeves rolled high on his forearm. Graphite pencil tucked appealingly behind his ear. Hair disheveled as if he'd run his fingers through it moments before.

His spectacles rested on his patrician nose, the lenses catching a stray glimmer of light. Blast, but she liked his spectacles.

Expelling a harsh breath, he took his time studying her, likely noting her skirt molded to her hips from her lack of a petticoat. Her hair was down, as she'd released it from its containment before bed. She'd left her townhome in a hurry, without a bonnet or an overabundance of undergarments. A frosty draft was at this moment rushing under her skirt and up her legs.

She'd brought only her yearning and her trepidation—and a hideous mourning gown and cloak she hadn't worn since her brother's passing.

"What's with the dowdy attire?" He perched his shoulder on the doorjamb, crossed his feet at the ankle—goodness, they were *bare*—and settled in to make her suffer. To further her punishment, he took a toothpick from his trouser pocket, a habit she'd suggested wasn't one he should continue to embrace, and slipped it coolly between his lips.

She drew her cloak protectively around her, sneaking a look at Macauley, who hadn't turned away to let them speak privately but stood watching as if this exchange was the most amusing show in Town. Which it likely *was*. "Black is what one wears when one is hoping to blend into the environs. Or maybe I wear the color because it lights my wick."

Tobias's lips tilted, that alluring dent beside his mouth flickering to life. But, amused or not, he made no move to let her into the distillery.

She frowned, his evasiveness starting to chafe. Macauley's gaze burning into her back beginning to chafe. "Are you going to invite me in?"

He shook his head and mouthed the word *no*.

Going on instinct, she tucked her face into the hood of her cloak and made a faint sniffling sound. Then another, just in case he didn't hear the first one. "I only came to hear more about triple distillations," she whispered raggedly for his ears alone.

Tobias came out of his slump against the door. His feet—long, perfectly beautiful feet—flattening on the stone step as he rose to his full height beneath the makeshift portico. "Thirty minutes, then you're taking her home, Mac. Meet me back here. Not one second longer," he instructed, then took Hildy by the hand and yanked her inside the building, the malt-tinged air fondly familiar. Like that blistering heat that kept scalding her thighs.

"You can do a lot you shouldn't in thirty minutes, mate," Macauley muttered as the door shut on his statement.

Hildy released another sniffle for good measure as she stumbled along the darkened corridor, nearly running to keep up with Tobias. She planned to contain her glee for as long as she could.

"You're a lousy actress, luv," he whispered and tugged her past the manly parlor where they'd shared their first kiss. Through the open doorway, she saw Nigel stretched out on the bum-brushing sofa, immersed in the bottomless slumber only a child can attain, a drowsy kitten tucked under his arm. Tobias drew her into the office, where she'd first stumbled upon him working on his blueprints, and closed the door quietly behind them.

He locked it. As if he had a plan for those thirty minutes.

Which did nothing to quiet the awakening going on inside her.

Wordlessly, he stalked to the drafting table, rolled up his blueprints, tied them with twine, and stacked them in a shipping crate in the corner. Going to his knees, he peered under the desk and made an adjustment, lowering the flat plane several inches. Then he removed his spectacles and slid them in the pocket of the rucksack lying by his adorable bare feet.

Silence reigned, drawing out like a sigh until he blew out the taper, and moonlight was suddenly their only illumination. Then he turned to her. There was a fearsomeness about him, intent she couldn't discern. Because no one had ever looked at her that way before. "Come here, Hildy girl. We have about twenty-seven minutes."

So she did.

Nothing on earth could have kept her from Tobias Streeter at that moment. Not engagements or societal disparities or even honor—such was the wild yearning pulsing through her veins. When she reached him, he pushed her cloak off her shoulders and let it hit the floor with a thump, never once going to catch it.

"You want to know more about triple distillations, do you?" he asked and circled her waist with his broad hands. Lifted her against his chest and, turning, placed her bottom on the drafting table, her feet barely grazing the floor. Before she could take a breath, he stepped between her legs, pushed her knees wide with a hip bump on each side, knowing, she realized with a slithering shot of arousal, precisely what he was doing. His shaft was stiff, outlined in glorious relief beneath his buckskin trousers.

He wasn't hiding from her this time.

"Your shoulder—"

"Is healing, and you're light, luv. You're my medicine, remember?" His words proved he recalled some of their fevered conversation. Leaning, he snagged her gown's ragged hem and drew the stiff black crepe to her knee. A rush of chilled air hit her thighs as he worked the skirt brazenly up her legs. "I've dreamed of making love to you with your luscious body spread across this very desk, your juices staining my sketches."

Hildy hummed an inaudible bit of nonsense and braced her hands behind her, afraid she would tumble to the floor if she didn't.

When he got her skirt to her waist, he tucked the ugly fabric beneath her bottom, his breath leaking from his lips in a belabored sigh. She was left with nothing but a whisper-thin chemise sheltering little from his hungry gaze. No stockings, no drawers. In fact, she'd come directly from her bedchamber to the Rogue King, driven by a rising tide of shameless insanity. When they clashed with hers, his eyes were seething, the color of boundless oceans and fallow moors. Limitless and intoxicating.

So green she wanted to dive into them and never come out.

His hand skated from her knee to her hip as he tugged her to the edge of the desk, wadding her chemise in a wrinkled roll at her belly. Leaving her exposed for the first time in her life before anyone aside from her maid. "One can only store their need for so long before it crests its banks, overflowing despite good intention. Rational thought. Society's expectations. Morals. *Rules*." He sounded breathless, provoked but wickedly in command of the situation in a way that made her *melt*. She'd never released control to anyone, ever. "My need for you, my bloody *want*, is threatening to torch me from the inside out. Filling my waking moments with obscene fantasies, my sleeping ones with obscene dreams. And here you are, showing up on my alley stoop in the dead of night, leading me to believe you want me as much as I want you."

She grasped his arm, dragging her thumb over the tattoo on his wrist. Brought his hand to her lips and placed a sucking kiss on the moon and stars inked there. "I *do*."

He released a fierce breath through his nose and did an unexpected thing, dropping to his knees before her. When she'd been naively expecting a kiss. Then her mind flashed to the carnal words he'd spoken. *Oh*. His mouth on her...

"I'm where I said I would be at some juncture in our relationship. Between heaven and hell." The adjustment to his desk made sense when she understood it placed her hips level with his face. "Just a taste because you came to *me*, and I find I can't deny you. So you know what it's like. What *we're* like." His hot breath struck her core, although he didn't touch her. Not yet.

She groaned, powerless, a panting gasp. Her hips lifted, closer to ruin. Pleading. She should have been mortified when, instead, she felt formidable.

"Hildy girl," he whispered and traced his finger along the smooth skin of her thigh, eliciting a shiver that rocked her body.

She blinked and gazed down at him through eyes gone misty. Blood was rushing madly through her veins, a measured cadence resonating in her ear.

Touch me. Touch me. Touch me.

He kissed her thigh—*finally*—and trailed his lips to the crease between thigh and mons. His eyes were dark, hooded, the hand that gripped her hip trembling. "I'm not marrying Mattie," he murmured, then he placed his mouth on her.

His shocking statement flowed through her ears and out of her mind without penetrating. His lips, his tongue, his *teeth* assaulting her and vaporizing coherent thought. She fell back until she lay spilled like ink across his desk, her arm going over her eyes to hide the sight of him kneeling before her. Hide the expression of raw pleasure surely twisting her features.

She couldn't feel this *and* see it—and retain hold of her sanity.

Strangely, the display was foreign yet familiar. Instinctive. One she wanted *instantly*. Not a thought to push him away.

His tongue traced her folds, sucking, licking, biting gently as she writhed, hips doing an elemental dance her body knew even if her mind didn't. She was begging without words—asking for more and getting it.

Intent on making her crazy with desire, he breathed on the button of flesh she'd found during her own exploration, then his tongue followed course. She moaned, hand going to his head to direct his movement, her fingers tangling in the silky strands and tugging.

"So that's it, yes?"

"*Yes*," she breathed. "*Yes.*"

The rest of the episode was a mindless rush.

Fevered sensation, her skin flaming one moment, chilled the next, so sensitive she implored him to stop only to immediately pull him back. Imprecise fragments of the present filtered through, enough that she'd possibly remember them in the future. His stubbled jaw scraping the inside of her thigh. His arms wrapped around her, fingertips digging into her bottom as he brought her to his mouth. The edge of his drafting table cutting into her skin. Their mingled moans and panting exclamations ringing through the room. His masterful directives to spread her legs. Tell him what she liked.

Here? More? Harder? This?

The aroma of her passion tainting the air. Her ears filled with the sound of her arousal and his—and nothing more. The world outside the distillery was a misty, forgotten vapor.

He brought his hand between her legs, a tickling caress, probing gently before sliding one finger inside her. Thrusting slowly, determinedly. Like a design for a building, his plan coming together.

Licking, biting, stroking until she couldn't think, breathe.

This addition to the game was all it took to push her off the ledge and into mindless pleasure.

The cry was ripping from her throat when he brought her up and into his body, pulling her off the table, seizing her mouth and catching her shout. She melted into the kiss, tasting herself on his tongue, melted into *him*, boneless, as microscopic lightning strikes assailed her from head to toe. His lips left hers to trail her jaw, nip the tender skin beneath her ear.

"You're the most fascinating creature I've had the blind good fortune to meet," he whispered into her tousled hair before moving back to her mouth.

If their first kiss made her believe in passion, their second made her believe in love.

Unsteady as well, Tobias let Hildy slide down his hard body until her feet touched the floor, her damp, wrinkled skirt and chemise spilling free from their imprisonment to dust her ankles. Then he curved over her, holding her steady at her hip and the back of her neck as he deepened the kiss, refusing to let her go. His ambush, one she craved to her *core*, sending blood rushing through her body to pool between her thighs, weaken her knees, dry her throat.

Again, she was aroused. Again, she could have taken him. In some other way not yet known to her, taken him. The act wasn't finished with her climax. Beneath the placket of his trousers, his shaft was rock hard against her hip, his pleasure unfulfilled.

There was more to be had, more to *have*.

Her fingers twisted in his shirt, bringing him closer when he could *get* no closer. "Toby," she murmured against his lips, hoping he knew what she asked for.

Because she didn't.

She dropped her head to his chest and drew his unique scent into her being. Slid her cheek over the crisp cotton of his shirt and thought to never let go as an aroused body—*hers*—fluttered down from its flight to the moon and landed back on earth.

"What about you?" she asked, truly curious. She'd heard it whispered that leaving a man's member in such a state caused irreparable pain and possibly even *damage*.

Bracing his hand on the drafting table, Tobias pushed off and away from her, taking a stumbling step back. His chest was rising with his staggered inhalations, his cheeks flushed, his midnight hair hanging in his face, an unholy mess. He held up his arm, shook his head. *A moment.* He paced to the sideboard, poured a drink, then laughed softly and glanced over his shoulder, his molten gaze taking in her motionless stance in the middle of the room with poise she was amazed he could express. "I don't want to wash away the taste of you. Not even with the best whiskey in England."

She massaged her temple, her thoughts an absolute snarl. Her body was circling somewhere between heaven and hell, just like he'd said.

What had Tobias mumbled before he—

She gasped as his intrepid statement flooded back, along with the remembrance of his finger sliding inside her. That she would never, ever forget. "You're not marrying Mattie?"

The contrasting emotions this presented were horribly contradictory.

Joy. Angst. Joy.

"I can't very well marry her when..." He stared into his glass, hesitated, then took a drink instead of completing the thought.

Hildy bumped back against the drafting table, spinning her ring round and round on her finger. The scent of his skin was clinging to hers, drifting into her senses and tossing her emotions about. This night had turned her wishes upside down. "What about my plans for the Duchess Society?" she whispered in confusion, her gaze going to her slippers and a metal-edged ruler that had ended up on the floor. She knocked it into the corner with a kick.

If he didn't marry Mattie, it would ruin everything.

If he married Mattie, Hildy would never forgive him.

Tobias polished off his whiskey and slammed his glass to the sideboard, a sound with a decided finality to it. "Your plans? What about *my* fucking plans? Not marrying Mattie, although she doesn't *want* to marry me and I don't seem to want to marry her, will destroy everything I've set in motion with Nash. It will destroy Mattie's plan to be *free*. I have her to think about, to consider, like Nigel and Nick Bottom"—he sighed angrily, his voice frayed—"and *you*."

Hildy glanced up, recognizing two things instantly. One, she'd voiced her concern aloud. A problem best kept to herself after the intimacy they'd shared. She'd utterly ruined the post-glow, as it was called. Two, she'd somehow hurt his feelings. The Rogue King's surprisingly vulnerable feelings.

Leading her to believe that he felt more for her than he'd shared.

Just as she felt more for him than she'd shared.

Flustered and alarmed, she crossed to him, her arms held out in appeal. "I didn't mean that how it came out. Or rather, I did, but it's not all business—"

"Please, Templeton, for the love of all that's holy," he growled, "stop while you're ahead." Stalking around the room, he found his boots behind an armchair and, without locating stockings to go with them, wrestled them on, hopping gracefully from one foot to the other while her thoughts traveled down two paths. Panic and lust. He grabbed his jacket from where it lay on an overturned crate and punched his arms through the sleeves, then cursed, rubbing his injured shoulder. Without comment, he jammed his shirt in his waistband, leaving it bunched around his lean hips and belly, all told a sloppy, frighteningly erotic presentation.

She'd never imagined the act of putting on clothing could be so fascinating.

He threw her a black glance. "Stop looking at me like a roasted duck being served up for dinner. Your thirty minutes is up." Then he quit the room, expecting her to follow.

She chased him into the hallway, grabbing his arm before he made it to the alley entrance he meant to pitch her through. But he continued on, dragging her two paces until she was forced to step in front of him. "I only came because of the blasted vase! So *you*"—she stabbed a finger in the firm muscles of his chest—"started this more-than-friendship arrangement. Not me."

He shook her off, his eyes frostier than the wintry air taking hold of the night. She realized at that moment what it felt like to be on Tobias Streeter's bad side. On the *outside*. When you'd been warmed by the light of even one of his smiles, it felt dreadful.

"Oh no, luv. You came because my lips were pressed to your quim, my finger buried deep inside you. Because I know what I'm doing down there, thirty minutes is twenty longer than I *need*, truth be told." He yanked his hand through his hair, looking poleaxed. "Honestly, it isn't that. My experience or your lack. You see, we generate heat unlike any I knew existed before you stumbled into my warehouse. But don't fret. I'm happy to feign business if it keeps your bloody plans intact."

"Toby—"

He moved her gently but firmly to the side and wrenched the door open. "Don't call me that, not *ever* again," he gritted through clenched teeth and bounded down the stairs and into the alley. "It's Mr. Streeter to you."

The carriage door opened, and Macauley hopped from the conveyance, his breath icing the air around his head like wisps of smoke. "One more minute, Street, and I was coming to get—" His words slithered away as he got a close look at his partner's cross expression, then her contrite one when she lurched into the alley behind Tobias. "Hopeless, you two," he muttered. "Utterly hopeless." Turning, he lowered the step with his boot and held out his hand to assist her inside. "Best you leave, matchmaking harridan. He's not coming back from this mood anytime soon."

"Tobias," she pleaded, trying once more. But he was already halfway down the alley, improperly clothed for the cold, heading in the direction of a public house or a bawdy house. Gaming den or opium den. She really didn't know him well enough to say. Of course, with his good looks and that strikingly sullen expression, there'd be willing women at either. Which made her stomach clench until she wondered if she was going to lose her modest dinner of potatoes and boiled ham upon the grimy cobblestones. Not the first time someone had cast up their accounts behind a distillery, she'd imagine.

She stared as the fog literally enveloped him until Macauley grasped her elbow and forced her into the carriage. "He's not dressed for this weather, and he's still healing," she murmured with a sniffle that wasn't fake this time. "Although he can certainly find someone to keep him warm."

Macauley snorted and shut the carriage door, rapped on the roof to alert the coachman, and settled back when the vehicle began to move. "He's circling the block and going in the front. That scrawny waif's asleep on the sofa. Street won't leave the kid alone, not when we have competitors discharging pistols into our vehicles. And those blasted cats are climbing all over everything. We have to watch 'em every minute, or the little buggers get into something. Scratched my ankle until it bled, one of them did. That tiger-striped bastard! Everyone knows orange cats are inhospitable."

Hildy trailed her finger over a blackened hole in the plush velvet squab she imagined had been created by one of Macauley's nasty cheroots. "How do you know?"

Macauley swung one knee over the other in a languid sprawl and yawned into his fist. "You're not the first chit he's shoved out the back door, only to circle around to the front."

Hildy tipped her head so the tears would flow into her eyes and not, disastrously, down her face. An image of Tobias kneeling between her legs chose that second to appear in her mind. Along with a surge of what felt disastrously like devotion. "Of course. Certainly. Brilliant."

When she would never forget this night for as long as she *lived*.

"But it's all bollocks, a bloody disaster."

She swallowed, praying she could hold it together until they arrived at her home. "Excuse me?"

"A disaster, Lady H, because you're the first he's fallen for."

With that astounding statement released into the narrow confines of the carriage, Macauley closed his eyes and pretended to sleep, leaving Hildy with a host of unanswered questions circling her mind and her heart.

Chapter Thirteen

T obias spent the next twenty-four hours negotiating transactions that had nothing to do with architecture, shipping, or the production of exceptional malt whiskey. From one end of London to the other, dreary docks to formal parlors, he pursued his objective with as much fervor as he'd stalked the Maratha in India.

It didn't keep his mind off the debacle with Hildy, but it did give him a renewed sense of confidence in his business acumen.

The ease of his success underscored how terribly good he was at the art of the exchange as he sat across from the Earl of Hastings at White's, a club where Tobias was decidedly *not* a member, detailing why he wasn't marrying the man's eldest daughter.

And why that decision was a stroke of good fortune for the earl.

Tobias simply presented the case as he would a revised shipping route due to extreme weather or increase in pirating in the area to a business associate. Facts laid out neatly, no hint of emotion even as a pulse of emotion he didn't want to name thrummed through him. Damn Hildy and her enthusiastic kisses. The taste of her sweet skin blooming on his tongue even now. The desperate little sounds she'd uttered as she crested, her juices flowing between his lips and down his throat like the river of life. Nectar he'd gulped like wine. Tonic meant to keep a man *alive*. The first and last taste of *happiness*.

Mac was wrong. Completely wrong. Hildegard Templeton didn't have him by the short hairs; she had him by the short *heartstrings*. Which was, in itself, a much crueler situation.

Hastings coughed into his teacup, yanking Tobias from his musings, the earl's bushy salt-and-pepper eyebrows winging high. "Matilda agreed to this?"

Tobias ran his index finger around the rim of his tumbler, his gaze fixed on the fire dancing in the stone hearth across the room. When he absolutely knew the answer to a question, he often waited a beat to give his response more credibility. "She will," he finally murmured, his gaze meeting the earl's so there was no assumption he didn't mean what he'd said. "I'll stand by her as a friend every day of her life. But perhaps she should be given the chance to live the one she wants to live. Not the one she's forced to."

The earl grunted, his opinion evident in the way he indignantly tossed back his tea. "This Capper fellow is respectable?"

Tobias nodded. "The most well-regarded physician in England. Plus, he dabbles in the apothecary side, which Lady Matilda takes an interest in and would like to know more about. She'll find no better tutor."

With a low grumble, Hastings cradled the cup in his broad hands. "I'd never wished my daughter to be in need of one."

Tobias's clenched his jaw. He was willing to forgo his self-esteem in this dimly lit, dusty study in a club that wouldn't have him. A club he didn't wish to *have*. He'd take every bit of himself back once White's imposing alley door—because that's the one he'd be directed to—closed behind him.

"I wouldn't have suited as a husband for Lady Matilda. The Duchess Society did their best. I've learned much about genteel behavior, proper address, and"—he swallowed, searching for the appropriate word when there wasn't one to be found—"decorous conduct. But a man can't rise above his humble beginnings. Or not, as far as he'd hoped to."

"Too true, Streeter. As we'd known all along," Hastings said without a hint of remorse. Then he frowned and slid his teacup on the side table. "And Matilda, my darling, brilliant, complicated girl, may need you as a protector and friend more than a husband. In my experience, those relationships have a better chance of surviving. If she loved you, however, my decision would be drastically altered."

"As would mine," Tobias said with no little rigidity lacing his tone. "I care about her happiness." *And my own*, he left unsaid.

"And I care about saving my family, my estates, my legacy. Which I have bungled alone and without assistance." The earl gave the garnet signet ring on his pinkie a spin, which made Tobias crazily think of Hildy twisting her ring round and round on her finger. In a moment when he wanted to forget her, she bloomed like a rose in his mind, fragrant and unforgettable. "You know, in a town where I wouldn't take the word of most for a half crown, I'm surprised to say I believe you."

Tobias scooted forward in his chair, preparing to rise. Breaking an engagement was actually making him feel quite lightheaded. "We have a deal then."

The earl smiled without humor. "If my daughter agrees. Am I right that you'll require her consent?"

"You are."

"You're almost as defiant as she is, Streeter. You young people are botching up our ordered society."

Hell's teeth, I hope we're making an absolute hash of polite society, Tobias thought as he made his way to his carriage parked off the alley entrance, as requested.

The arrangement tied up in the prettiest packaging Tobias could wrap it in, he set out to find Lady Matilda Delacour-Baynham and explain the same to her. If she loved him, he wouldn't change course, direction, plan. He would spend his life protecting her, abiding by his pledge to be her husband. But she didn't. And she never would.

Somehow, in the past twenty-four hours, he'd been shown what love *could* be like. Not that he'd ever have it for himself. But he'd been shown what it could be.

Knowledge which changed everything.

When he arrived at Mattie's home on Manchester Square, snow drifted lazily from the sky to dust his face. Winter was well upon them.

He hopped the gated fence off Hinde Street when the rusted lock wouldn't turn and strode down the twisting gravel lane and through the unkempt side garden, striving to keep his mind on one woman while obsessing over another. With every breath, Hildy's taste and those weak sounds she'd uttered when she came moved through him like oxygen. Her lips plump from their kisses, her fingers twisting in his hair. The silky skin of her thighs whisper-soft against his cheek. Her breasts heaving, and when he'd gazed up from his crouched position while pleasuring her, her nipples pebbling tight as she stared right back at him without regret.

While he stood there in a lustful daze at the domestic's entrance, a maid with a crooked mobcap and a dismayed expression opened the door and, overlooking her censure, told him exactly where to find the eldest daughter of the residence.

"Lady Matilda's in the kitchens, sir. Stitching up chickens."

Tobias halted, pausing in removing his hat and coat as no butler stood in attendance at the servant's entrance, his body nearly numb from the cold. "Come again?"

The maid gave him a gap-toothed smile and did a dancing sidestep he couldn't begin to decipher. It might have been flirtatious, but he wasn't sure as she was old enough to be his mother. "Stitching up chickens. Says it's her most useful and called upon skill. Stitching up folks in need, that is. Not chickens." She glanced over her shoulder as if revealing a family secret, the skin around her lips crinkling like crumpled foolscap. "The doctoring business," she whispered around a cupped hand. "Odd, the gel is. You're a fearless lad to take that one on. As gutsy as they say in the gossip rags, true enough. My sister lives down Limehouse way. I've heard the stories."

Unfortunately, Lady Matilda Delacour-Baynham wasn't the woman Tobias wanted to *take on*. However, when he thought of Hildy and the astonished look in her eyes as she pulsed and tightened around his finger and his tongue, the way she'd pressed her cheek into his chest and breathed the calmest, surest breath of her life, he experienced a squeeze near his heart that presented all manner of gruesome possibilities.

The likeliest of which was that he was falling in love.

With a matchmaker who didn't believe in marriage. Or love, perhaps, as they'd never introduced the topic. A woman who, unfashionably but admirably, wanted success more than she wanted *him*.

A woman who kissed him like she wasn't planning to kiss another man as long as she lived.

As much as Hildy would loathe it, this had been apparent. At least to him it had. Likewise, he'd been complete in her arms—and bereft out of them. What he'd done, dropping to his knees and feasting on her, shocked him when he thought back on it. When they hadn't even made love yet. That was usually a move made later in the sexual negotiations, if at all. But he'd been unable to help himself—when he also wanted to make love to her more than he wanted his next *breath*. In the end, he'd chosen her pleasure over his. He'd never been more compelled to touch someone. Give. *Take*. The choice had been unavoidable.

Now, making love to Hildegard Templeton wasn't going to happen. Not after the way he'd acted. She'd be a fool to let him touch her again.

Hat and coat in hand, his heart somewhere in the vicinity of his knees, Tobias followed the scent of roasted meat and boiled cabbage and indeed found his fiancée leaning against an abraded butcher's block, a stack of poultry parts scattered before her. Mattie glanced up when he entered the deserted space with absolutely no surprise, her gaze going instantly back to the needle, thread, and thigh in her hands. She was without doubt the most composed female he'd ever had the pleasure to meet.

Her fortitude, he'd found, came in handy for stitching skin *and* removing bullets.

He knew he should start with a discussion about the weather (foul) or the latest production on Drury Lane (horrid), but the past day had beat the charm from him like a stick to a dusty rug. "I need you to jilt me, Mattie, darling, and it would be best if you did it soon."

Mattie tilted her head, catching her tongue between her teeth and executing the neatest suture any chicken had a right to receive. Task accomplished, she sat her grisly project on the butcher's block, peeled off a pair of gardening gloves he was grateful she'd thought to wear, and crossed to a washing station situated in a dimly lit corner. She soaped her hands, dipped them in a bucket of water, picked up a faded length of linen, and dried her skin, all without saying one word in response to his rather shocking pronouncement.

When she turned, her smile was playful, and he knew the jig was up.

With a sigh, he tossed his hat and coat on a stool, going on the hunt for the hidden bottle of brandy. He'd never known a kitchen to be without one and located it in the second cupboard he tried. "How did you know?" he asked and ripped out the cork with his teeth.

"That you're planning to toss me aside for Hildegard Templeton?" She laughed and snapped the damp linen in her hands with a pop. "The air sparks when you're in the same room, like lit magnesium, very bright but quickly extinguished. Also, when you were ill, you called out for her. And then there were the flowers filling her home as if you'd bought out an entire nursery. I'm happy for you if fate has brought you the person you're meant for. Sometimes, two people meet, and it's simply... serendipity. I understand as it happened to me. She's my found person, too. Although we'll be the only two who will ever know this."

Mattie held up her hand when he started to dive into the pitch he'd practiced the entire carriage ride over. "I can't go from veil to grave with you either, even if I thought I could. With *any* man. I'm sorry I suggested it when I merely thought it would benefit us both. That I had been honest about myself and my unusual life circumstances. At least we're discussing this before one of us left the other at the altar."

"I wouldn't have done that." He spit the cork to the floor. "Left you anywhere."

"You're a wonderful man, you truly are. I hope Lady Hildegard realizes her rare find."

At a loss, Tobias took a fast sip of brandy and grimaced.

Mattie laughed again, strolled to him, worked the bottle from his hand, and lifted it to her lips. Her grimace was just as marked. "Lands, that *is* horrid. The good stuff is never in the kitchen, you know."

He wiped his hand across his mouth, his throat burning from the rotgut liquor. "I have a plan. A solid one."

Mattie rested her hip against the butcher's block and lowered the bottle to her side. "I never doubted that, Tobias Streeter. Not once since I met you on a dreary day at Epsom. I'm an excellent judge of character, and you pass with flying colors. You're a good man. Stubborn but good."

He circled the room, nervous now that it was time to illustrate his plan. He wasn't going to marry Matilda Delacour-Baynham, but he was going to change her life. And his, in part. "You've heard of Thomas Capper, I assume?" He nicked aside a threadbare curtain gracing the lone window in the room and saw snow clinging to the ground, coloring the world a wondrous white. This house needed an infusion of capital and needed it soon. In a neighborhood not far away, he pondered if Hildy was watching the snowfall and thinking of him. Remembering what he'd done to her on his drafting table.

Just a start, really, to the list of things he'd like to try. His cock shifted beneath his trouser close at the thought of reviewing that list.

"Thomas Capper? Of course, I have. I've read everything he's written about surgical techniques and contagion. He trained at St. Bartholomew's as a physician *and* an apothecary. His work is remarkable."

Tobias let the curtain fall and turned to her. "It's good you approve because he's going to be your teacher."

Mattie slapped the bottle to the butcher's block, her cheeks paling. "Teacher?"

He shrugged, then winced as pain shot down his arm and radiated out his fingers. He was healing, but the injury was still tender. "Don't," he said when she started to approach in doctor mode. "I'm fine. You removed the stitches. It's not infected. The scar isn't even that ugly. For a female physician, you did a nice job. I'm going to live, thanks to you."

Mattie's lips curved, her pride evident. "You're right, you are."

"Capper and I have a business affiliation. I supply him with items he can't easily find in London. Medical equipment, herbs, spices. He's been after me to fund a clinic for going on two years. I agreed last night over drinks at a disreputable public house in Shoreditch, a nego-tiation for which I now have a throbbing headache." Tobias massaged his temple, dragging his hand over his tired eyes. "I agreed if *I* chose the location."

"Let me guess. Limehouse."

Feeling absurdly shaken by this entire morning, Tobias wiggled a toothpick from his trouser pocket and popped it between his lips. "In return, he brings you in as an assistant. An apprenticeship of sorts. Low level, don't expect grandeur. You'll be left to treat those who have no choice in the matter of the physician being a woman. Workhouses, factories, hell, maybe even Newgate. It won't be easy. It won't be without friction.

"Capper isn't sure you're truly willing to work for this. He *will* test you. But you'll be free, if you're discreet, to live the life you want to live, love the person you want to *love*. The salary will be enough for you to make your own choices. Lease a cottage outside London and live peacefully, perhaps, if your father chooses not to fund your future."

"Incredible," Mattie whispered and sank back against the block. "How did you get him to agree to this?"

Tobias removed the toothpick before it tumbled from his lips. Her naivete astounded. "Darling Mattie. Really?"

Mattie picked up the bottle and took a swig, coughing when the brandy hit her throat. "So, he sold me."

Tobias jabbed the toothpick between his lips and rocked back on his heels. "What do you care if it secures your dream and lets you be who *you* are, not who society has dictated you be? Your father has unpaid markers with every gaming hell from here to Portsmouth. He, like your future patients, doesn't have the economic wherewithal to refuse a sound proposal. You secure a scandalous but respectable position that the *ton* cannot question, such is Thomas Capper's sterling reputation. Your father retains his reputation, his home, his remaining daughters' futures. The numbers are in his favor. He only missed out on the peculiar one. The *ton* won't blame him for it. They'll lump that disfavor on *you*."

He exhaled raggedly, dejection sinking unexpectedly into his bones. "I've paid off so many people in this town, for any number of reasons, that I've long lost count. What, I ask myself, is another? Your father has promised to do better, by the way, leave the gambling behind. I'm a guardian angel all of the sudden on top of everything else."

Like a typical woman, somewhere beneath the audacity, she rattled off a list of questions. "What about your dream to work for Nash? What about the Duchess Society?"

What about Hildy, neither of them dared to ask?

Tobias's chest constricted, and he turned to gaze out the window. Snow was still falling gently, carried to earth without issue. London looked exquisite with ivory coating the everyday misery of life.

"Lady Hildegard and the Duchess of Markham will be credited with instituting the opportunity for you to work with Capper. It's a brilliant if outrageous solution which won't hurt The Duchess Society. In fact, they'll probably become advisors specializing in highborn wallflowers and cultured bluestockings. The revolutionaries in society will embrace them with what I'd expect will be anonymous funding. For scholarships and that type of thing. Your father also promises to diplomatically publicize how grateful he is because marriage to a by-blow of dubious origin wasn't what he wanted for his daughter, and everyone knew it. Hildy's society will be credited with talking you *out* of a potential disaster and finding a workable solution to your medical problem." Tobias trailed a drop of melted snow as it trickled down the windowpane. "Then he'll award the Duchess Society his four remaining daughters to shepherd along on their joyless marital journeys."

Mattie stepped behind him, her hand going to his shoulder, comfort where he had none. They were friends, he and this unusual young woman, and he didn't have many souls he counted as friends. "I find myself taken by your generosity, Tobias Streeter. The Rogue King is much kinder than he lets everyone believe. Giving up your dream to build buildings for love. For friendship. That is quite something in a world of often nothings."

Tobias issued an acerbic whistle between his teeth. "I'm giving up one rendition of my dream. *And* the girl. But I'll keep the friend." He wouldn't give up the *memory* of Hildy, however, even if she'd destroyed him with her ambition. Which he realized was hypocritically arrogant. A dogged male mindset, if there ever was one. Anyway, his plan wouldn't work if the matchmaker turned around and married the rogue. "Don't thank me yet, Mattie. Some will cut you for this and never look back, put you on a lower step, closer to where I stand. But the choice is yours, at least. The life you lead yours, not anyone else's."

She squeezed his shoulder, the aroma of medicinal herbs and raw poultry drifting from her. The least enticing scent he could imagine. "I don't understand, but I can only say thank you. From my heart, thank you."

He couldn't look his friend in the eye, not yet. So, he kept his gaze focused on a bleak London winter.

His heart, from neglect, was unaccountably exposed.

Chapter Fourteen

T hey were bound to run into each other at some point.

In a city the size of London, Hildy understood that you never encountered the people you wished to, only those you didn't.

Although, in all honesty, she'd desperately wished to see Tobias. She'd searched for him on every street corner, in every shop. Peering from her carriage window for his tall form until her eyes stung. Until desperation turned to anger with his rejection of her apologetic notes, because *yes*, she'd sent them. *Three* over the course of two months. Written on unscented vellum, unlike his mistress's. Julia or Judith, she couldn't recall. Didn't want to recall.

Perhaps that had been the problem. No dash of lavender.

Hence, a chilly April marched into a temperate May without a word from him. The Duchess Society, due to Tobias's clever dismissal of his engagement, only increased in popularity. It seemed she and Georgie gained a new client each week. Family after family arrived on their doorstep with a young lady who didn't *quite* fit society's mold of the accomplished, biddable, eager-to-marry female. They'd even been offered anonymous funding from a widowed grand dame and an aging countess who supported women's rights, such as they were.

Georgie said they should consider changing the society's name to the Bluestocking Brigade. Or the Wallflower Warriors. Hildy answered back with the Contrary Countesses, which Georgie had been before becoming a duchess.

Meanwhile, Hildy stared forlornly out of carriages and shop windows, or tossed and turned in her bed, tangling in sheets, dreams of Tobias's hands on her, his mouth doing wicked, wonderful things she never wanted him to *stop* doing. She missed his touch, his laugh, his smile.

She missed her clever friend *and* the man she'd wanted to be her lover.

She worried about what had become of his hope to work with John Nash and the sacrifices he'd made for her. For Mattie. She worried about the wound on his shoulder. Nigel. Nick Bottom and the kittens. The new batch of malt he'd been perfecting. But most of all, she worried about how she'd hurt him, how he'd sealed his heart in an instant when he thought she'd picked The Duchess Society over her feelings for him.

When she had not. Truthfully, she wanted *both*. A wish society found unacceptable.

Which made her furious, a cycle repeated daily.

Consequently, on this balmy spring morning, the first mild enough to do so, Hildy decided to race her phaeton hell for leather along King's Old Road to lift her spirits. The vehicle and gray attached to it were the only luxuries she employed outside of firewood in each hearth of her townhome and meat three times a week from the butcher. Mainly for her majordomo, Danbury, who had a weak constitution.

On this day, when her mount began to limp, she guided the phaeton off the gravel roadway in Hyde Park and alongside a footpath to investigate the problem. Dust rose to sting her nose and coat the creamy kid of her gloves. She was crouched beside the conveyance, in a somewhat compromising position, when Tobias and his lady of the week stumbled upon her during their promenade.

Oh, she'd read about his associations in the *Gazette*. Following his jilting by the capricious Lady Matilda Delacour-Baynham, the Rogue King was remarked as going through women like water. Or excellent malt whiskey, rather. His being rebuffed made him a more desirable commodity, proving the insanity of the *ton* and the unfairness of *life*.

The only gratifying element for Hildy on this fine morning in Hyde Park was Tobias's blatant shock at seeing her.

And that she was wearing a lovely new riding habit.

She'd been wrong: luxury number four.

Phaeton, firewood, mutton, riding habit.

"Lady Hildegard," he said faintly while looking down at her, that blasted dent in his cheek engaging and making her belly clench. Eyes as green as grass in Kensington Gardens glinted in the weak sunlight. With a subtle move, he detached his arm from his companion's as if Hildy had caught him doing something naughty.

Hildy pressed her hand to the moist earth, taking a shallow breath and a moment to collect herself. From her three-second review, she'd noted that Tobias looked breathtaking as usual, dressed in black like a phantom, his hair a shade longer than when she'd run her fingers through it while he brought her to the pinnacle of pleasure, crouched there between her legs. It was a passionate moment she would never in her life forget.

Wrathfully, she wondered if this week's flavor had been similarly serviced.

Picturing that for even one second was how Hildy came to find her strength hunkered there on a small spot of park terrain. No matter how handsome the display or how hot the memories, she'd be damned if she showed one *iota* of appreciation. Remembrance. Fondness. *Nothing*.

"Mr. Streeter," she returned as he'd asked her to address him during their last discussion and grasped her bay's hoof, turning it slightly to dislodge the stone from its shoe.

"Do you need assistance?"

She glanced up, her gaze, she knew, fiery enough to melt metal. Rising, she smoothed her hand down her bodice, the military trim that was all the rage bumping roughly beneath her palm. "Thank you, but no. I have it." Unable to halt the move, she slapped her riding crop against her leg. The sound was not delicate and cut through the tense air like a saber.

His smile slipped, a muscle in his jaw flexing as their gazes clashed. She watched in glee as his fingers rolled into fists at his side. Tobias was not good at hiding his temper; and Hildy was excellent at inciting it.

The woman he was with—a delicate blonde, icing-atop-a-cake type —tugged on his sleeve with a purr of impatience. "The Bread House is around here somewhere. I should like to go. Iced buns what they're known for, isn't it?"

Hildy smothered her laugh with her glove. "The *Cake* House. It's on the north side of the Serpentine. Take this footpath until you hit the lake. They make delectable cheesecakes. But I'm certain their iced buns will be wonderful, too." She caught Tobias's eye, licked her bottom lip as his pupils flared delightfully. *Oh*, she did want to make him suffer. "So delicious they melt in your mouth, I imagine," she whispered, leaning in to allow the words to drift past his ear. Then, without another word, she turned her back on him, as rudely as she'd ever treated anyone, and climbed into her phaeton.

She was gone before another ten seconds had passed, dirt and leaves flying around her and hopefully enveloping the adorable couple.

She wasn't known as the wild terror of Hyde Park for nothing.

Thankfully, the tears over her love affair that *wasn't* didn't arrive until she reached her Georgian tragedy of a townhome.

～

Hildy woke from a hollow sleep to sleet pelting her bedchamber window.

She frowned and rose to her elbow. Sleet? In May?

Kicking her counterpane from her legs, she stumbled to the window and jerked aside the curtain to find Tobias pacing back and forth across her untidy back lawn. He was bundled in a long woolen overcoat, a hat rakishly tilted on his head. It could have been any man in the darkness, in the distance, but it was him. She couldn't mistake his deliberate stride or the way he knotted his hands into fists as he did when he was vexed. Opening the casement, she leaned out, her heart doing an unqualified dance in her chest.

A mix of emotion—joy, fury, fondness—flooded her.

When he looked up, she realized he was wearing formal evening attire—top hat, tails, the entire rig—and had likely come directly from the opera or the theatre. Conceivably escorting the creampuff he'd had on his arm in Hyde Park. Exasperated, Hildy muttered a curse that was unladylike but therapeutic and reached for the casement's rusty hinge, prepared to shut Tobias Streeter from her life once and for all.

"I haven't touched a woman since I met you, *Gadji*," he yelled before she could close the window, sounding as if he'd had a drink or two before arriving on her lawn. "It's been only you since that night." He tipped his hat back on his head to better see her, his lips twisting into a scowl. "Since the first time I saw you, actually. And today, bloody hell, in that exquisite riding habit, your eyes spitting fire, I wanted to toss you over my shoulder, ride off in your sassy phaeton, and be done with missing you. When I was left to escort another someone I don't want to escort anywhere all over town looking for the perfect iced bun."

"Shh!" Her finger went to her lips as her body started an internal debate she wanted no part of. Invite him in? Shut him out? *Remember what he can do with those hands*, the devil on her shoulder intoned in a silky voice that sounded strangely like her own. "Do you want to wake the servants with this discourse?"

He laughed, his teeth a pearly flash in the milky-mooned light. "Wake? How? Aren't most of them deaf?"

Maddened, she turned on her heel, snatched her dressing gown from the lounge at the end of her bed, and shoved her arms into the sleeves. Knotting the ties over her belly, she rushed from her bedchamber, taking the servants' stairs two at a time.

"Of all the snide, arrogant—"

Tobias didn't let her get the door fully open after throwing the latch before he forced his way into the cramped vestibule and pressed her against the wall. His body was blazing and in such contrast to the cool plaster that she shivered. "I want every part of you," he whispered against her neck, his lips trailing her jaw to seize her lips. "Every bloody part. You fill my dreams, pushing aside the nightmares and making me delirious with yearning. A minute doesn't pass without the thought of you intruding. The memory of touching you, your ragged whisper ringing in my ears. Your body melting beneath mine. I'm begging you to let me in. Invite me upstairs, Hildy girl."

He caught her against him and stepped between her legs, positioning his hips so that his shaft angled against her core. Getting right to the heart of the matter with her able assistance. They moved together, groaning and writhing, their desire a dull echo racing along the deserted corridor. Defenseless, she twined her arms around his neck, tilted her head and let him in, as he'd asked her to. Her tongue brushed his bottom lip because she knew he liked it, and the kiss roared away from her, as everything with this man seemed to. His arms came around her in a desperate clench, securing the fit, exposing his need.

The sensations overwhelmed her, coming from all sides. His deliberate touch, his whispered pleas. The groans rising from deep in his throat. In response, she moaned in frustration and need, shifting to get closer, pressed between his hard body and the wall.

The more he gave, the more she wanted. Intensifying the contact until she *ached*. Her heartbeat thumped in sync in her chest and between her thighs.

She made a sound, a rough gasp that elicited his own. Elicited a shudder that shook his body. He murmured an inaudible oath against her lips, his tongue inviting hers into playful battle. His hand swept high and dove into her hair, scattering the hairpins she used to contain the thick strands at night. The other went low to her hip, where he clenched his fingers and drew her dressing gown and night rail in a frenzied fistful to her waist. A rush of air swept beneath the layers, soothing the folds that had begun to pulse and heat between her legs.

Again, that familiar sensation she was now addicted to.

He slanted his head as he plundered, his kiss *owning* her. His scent and his taste owning her. This was the Tobias Streeter she knew, a man with a plan. A man with purpose.

His plan tonight? Why, he'd come to make love to her.

The question was, would she let him?

"Mr. Streeter," she gasped and edged back, allowing a sliver of chilled air to slip between them.

His moist breath struck her cheek, the scent of mint and brandy capturing her want and turning it back on her. "Mr. Streeter. Ah, luv, is that all I'm to be allowed after I've missed you to the death of me. Don't be cross over my foolishness," he murmured and dragged her off her feet, her skirts falling to dust the floor. His hand rose to cradle her jaw, guiding her, the kiss the most persuasive he'd attempted. He was leaving nothing to chance this time.

The fit was perfect, his technique flawless. As he'd known it would be.

She was learning from a maestro. Being taken by a master.

She made no mistake; the Rogue King was negotiating a deal.

He wished to triumph. To break her. Make her grovel. "You don't know what you want," she whispered, raining kisses over his jaw. "Only that you want to win."

He stilled, looking into her eyes. His were bright, flecks of gold flaring at the edges. "I want you. *Only* you. Don't you know that by now? There's no winning without you in my life, Hildy girl. There's only *you. Us.*"

She released a hoarse cry of acceptance and longing, and he responded by swinging her into his arms and starting up the staircase, his mouth returning to cover hers before she could tell him to turn back. An imperfect attempt due to the angle. But it was glorious. Frantic. Erotic. *Real.* Tobias had left his precision at the bottom of her staircase. The muscles in his arms and shoulders shifted and flexed beneath her hands. His silky hair danced against her cheek. The scent of his grandmother's soap and the slight sting of sweat and man blended until she would have swooned had she been standing. She might never stand again, only go through life held in his strong arms.

"Second door on the left," she murmured against his neck, pressing closer, offering herself. A sliver of his skin was between her teeth before she knew what she was about. Salty and delicious. She sucked and bit gently, and he stumbled, his breath catching.

"Don't. Not yet," he groaned.

But she refused to change course. Refused to hide her need or her hunger as her world spun out of focus, her demand surpassing even his.

She wasn't sure what, but something, with her bold gesture, had changed within him.

It was as if she'd given him leave to desire her as he longed to. Freedom to be who he was.

Juggling her in his arms, he slammed her bedchamber door shut with his boot and let her slide down his body while he turned to flip the key in the lock. Tobias held her back by her shoulders, doing a leisurely study. A stray moonbeam pierced the casement, highlighting her gentle curves beneath the thin layers. She was reasonably sure he could see everything.

"You're so magnificent that I'm stunned every time I look upon you. Stunned no man has stolen you away from me. My bloody good fortune no one *sees* you. And this..." He leaned back against the door, taking her in completely, his penetrating gaze charming her body as well as his touch would. A head-to-toe languid river of an appraisal. Slithers of arousal swam through her.

Smiling wickedly, he leaned to remove one boot, then the other, tossing them aside. Who in heaven's name needed a valet when you looked like *this* while undressing? "I want nothing else between us, Hildy girl. Yes?"

She nodded. *Yes. Yes. Yes.* I consent. I agree. I applaud the decision.

"Come," he whispered and crooked his finger. A command she was powerless to ignore. Peculiar and arousing for a woman who never let anyone command her. Never let anyone take control.

When she got close, his hands went to the tie of her dressing gown. Slipping it from her shoulders, he let it dangle before giving the creamy silk a push that sent it pooling at her feet. She trembled and ducked her head, her sigh breaking the silence as she was left standing before him in a diaphanous night rail that hid little of her from view.

"Ah," he whispered as if modesty had not occurred to him. Humming softly, he tipped her chin high and placed the tenderest of kisses to her lips. Then he brought her hands to his coat lapels. "Undress me, then, at your leisure. I'm nothing if not an equal partner. A most willing participant."

She smiled, embarrassed. However, the rush of power was startling, a blistering flood of excitement sweeping her.

She might like controlling certain aspects of lovemaking. She just might.

And when the man in question wanted her as much as Tobias seemed to want her, the risk of a misstep seemed governable.

Or in lesser language, she was free to love him as *she* desired.

Fisting his lapels, she lifted the heavy wool up and over his shoulders, dropping the coat at his feet. The same process for his tailcoat. Finding joy in the endeavor, she disrobed him in a less than straightforward manner.

Unsophisticated, indeed, but in her own way.

Taking his cravat in her hands, she wound it around his forearm and yanked tight, her gaze crawling to his to record his reaction. His chest rose and fell on a belabored sigh, his hands flexing into fists. "Finish it," he whispered raggedly, the cravat fluttering to the floor. "Or I'll finish it for you."

Teasing him, taking more time than required to remove his collar and cuffs, her lips located the tattoo on his wrist, her tongue tracing the inked galaxy as he fidgeted, keeping a promise he'd evidently made to himself not to touch her until they were both unclothed. Four flicks of her fingers and his waistcoat lay in the pile of spent clothing. She kissed her way down his chest as she unfastened his shirt until he swore a rough oath and brought her to her feet. Her hands lingered at his waistband, discovering the rigid shape beneath his placket.

"I can't, Hildy. No more," he whispered and brushed her hands aside, working the bone buttons himself, stepping from his trousers and drawers in a vigorous move and kicking the garments aside.

His body—she drew a breath and expelled it on a visceral rush— dear heaven, his body was *perfection*. Olive skin, rippling muscles. A sprinkling of sable hair on his chest. The puckered pink scar on his shoulder, a wound she'd helped care for him through, binding them in the way that catastrophes in life bound people together.

Lean hips, flat stomach.

Her gaze wandered lower.

She reached to touch, and he let her. Her fingers circled his cock as his head dropped back, and a threadbare moan ripped from his throat. "You seduce me as no one ever has, luv. But what brings me to my knees is that you don't recognize your influence. Since the day you stepped into my warehouse, you've held me in your firm grasp. Like you hold me now." Placing his hand over hers, he stroked his member, showing her what he liked. Hard, fast, tight. His breath came in short pants, his hips lifting. "Of course, you'd be a champion... right out of the gate. Together, we're incomparable. Our chemistry explosive. You know how much I appreciate a sound chemical process."

As she petted him, learning his shape and his pleasure, they kissed and teased and laughed. Sighed. Moaned. With an unsteady step, he walked her back, and her bottom hit the bed. Taking her night rail in his fist, he tugged the wispy material to her thighs. "Are you sure, Hildy girl? About me? About this?"

Hildy paused, recalling the first time she'd seen him. He'd had dirt on his face and had been half-clothed, staring at her with clever eyes and a cheeky smile. She'd known immediately that he was unlike any man she'd ever met. She'd wanted him with an intuitive awareness that had raced outside the bounds of her experience. Like Georgie had once said about her husband, Dex, *I was insanely attracted even when I wished I wasn't.*

Exactly.

Then she thought of Nigel and Nick Bottom—and how gentle Tobias had been when he brought her to the pinnacle of pleasure while perched awkwardly on his drafting table, his wondrous sketches gracing the walls and stacked on the floor.

Underneath his stalwart exterior lay a kind, intelligent, considerate man.

Hildy placed her hand over his as he'd done to hers moments ago, encouraging him to lift her night rail up and off her body. With a sense of joy and inevitability, the slip of white cotton fluttered to the floor.

Even if it was only for one night, she was choosing this, choosing him.

And inexplicably, choosing *herself.*

There would be no other man for her, not in this lifetime. Although that was a secret she wouldn't share.

Tobias sucked in a breath and quickly stepped to the side to allow moonlight to wash over her. His eyes glittered with lust and something more. Something she was sure was reflected in her own gaze. "You are unparalleled," he whispered and tenderly cupped her breast, his thumb sweeping her nipple and raising the already hardened point. Leaning, his mouth took the place of his thumb, sucking the rigid nub between his teeth as her knees shook. Swirling, tormenting. A feeling unlike any she'd felt before rippled through her. Bliss communicating itself to her entire body in one heartbeat.

Beginning to melt from the inside out, she moaned low in her throat and pressed against him. His hand came to her hip to hold her steady for his assault, fingertips digging into her skin.

Contrasting sensations assaulted her, the dawning of ecstasy. The stubble on his jaw rubbing the underside of her breast. His tongue circling her areola, again and again, as waves of pleasure cascaded through her. His length a rigid presence against her thigh. She tangled her fingers in his hair and arched into his caress. "Tobias, *please.*"

"Toby," he corrected and, with a wicked laugh, gave her a push that had her spilling back on the bed. No respite, mattress dipping, he crawled over her, hooked his arm beneath her waist and tugged her with him until he lay over her, his forearms braced to shoulder his weight, his gaze possessing her. He worked his hand between their bodies, trailed his calloused fingertips along her belly and down her thighs.

Knowing where this was going, she squirmed and pelted out a sharp breath against his neck. *There*, she thought, oh, yes, *there.*

"Do you know why I like architecture, luv?" His head lowered, his mouth seizing hers in a rough kiss. He did things with his tongue that simply destroyed her as his fingers fondled her delicate folds and probed, lightly, but with resolve she felt to her toes.

"Shapes," he whispered, nuzzling her neck, biting her earlobe. Sinking his finger inside her and working it from side to side, dipping deeper, setting her on fire. Tinder to dry wood. "Lines. Curves. Spirals." His eyes had gone as dark as the sea in the pitch of the night —and he thrust into her with casual intent, watching, recording every whisper stealing from her lips. As if they were not lying naked and tucked against each other, lungs churning, bodies beginning to moisten from the heat they were generating. "Angles. Contrast. Pattern."

Hands wandering, she gripped his shoulder and his hip and rocked against him, seeking to match his rhythm. Or increase it. Gasping, she pressed her cheek to the mattress as his free hand palmed the bed, his fingers spread wide as he balanced atop her. The skin around the knuckles paling with the exertion of holding back from truly claiming her.

Curiously, it was one of the most erotic images she'd ever seen. So simple and yet so compelling. His need, his *desire* for her drawn in lines as bold as his blueprints.

"I want you ready," he said, sucking her nipple between his lips, the dual assault nearly breaking her. "Open and pulsing. Hungry. Wet. I want you to never forget this. Forget me. I want you mindless, famished."

Her hips lifted, driving his finger in as far as it could go, his palm hitting the nub of skin he'd claimed held her pleasure and sending golden sparks into her vision. "I'll beg then since you require it." Defiant words backed by action, she tunneled her arm between their bodies and closed her fingers around his rigid shaft. Stroked him as he'd shown her he liked.

"You swindler," he murmured against the side of her breast, body quivering, restraint vanishing like mist along the Thames as his hip knocked hers. "Bloody siren."

She groaned, scoring his uninjured shoulder with her teeth as she moved him clumsily into place at her throbbing core. "Help me, dammit. You know I don't know what I'm doing."

He gusted out a laugh, head dipping, silken strands dusting her collarbone. Retreating slightly, he knocked her hand away and gripped his shaft, stroking while she stared, stunned, as if she'd never seen anything as beautiful as Tobias Streeter touching himself. Fitting himself into *her*. He shifted his hips, finding the right angle immediately and edging in enough to steal both their breaths. "Look at me, *Gadji*," he whispered, his voice shattered like crystal upon stone.

Her gaze lifted, tracking a languid path up his magnificent body to find him looking gravely determined and more than a little dangerous.

His hand cradled her cheek in the lightest of caresses. Achingly gentle. A connection to something larger channeling between them.

"I'm going to record the color your eyes turn when you crest. As I promised I would someday. The expression on your face before you fall. The sounds that rip through the back of your throat when you wrap your legs around me. In the distillery, I was preoccupied. Stunned, if you must know," he said as he rocked his hips, sliding into her, parting her body with his. "This time, I want it *all*."

Closing her eyes, she let herself go, boneless, ethereal. His weight pressing her into the mattress was the only thing keeping her in this universe. His shaft was stretching her until she imagined he couldn't sink any farther. And then he did, her core pressed against his hardness.

"Stay with me," he breathed, ragged, his plea striking the four walls of her bedchamber. His hand slid to frame the nape of her neck, directing her mouth to his. His fingers dove into her hair, fingertips hot on her scalp. His strokes were lengthy, controlled, devastating. Movement hard enough to shake the bed and send the headboard creaking. She thanked the stars for a deaf maid at that moment.

He kissed her deeply, not letting her catch her breath, slow down, draw away. Where she ended, he began. Until they were one. Legs entangled, arms entwined, fingers threaded through each other's hair. Touching, licking, biting. Recording sensations and memories, although they rolled through her faster than she could chronicle them. A shower of golden sparks lit her eyelids, a pleasing tingle erupting at the base of her spine. The scent of their bodies blending, charging through her senses like a feral beast.

Her cry was guttural and without restraint.

His mouth dropped to her ear, and he whispered roughly, "Feel me, feel *us*, luv. Every inch of me hungers for you. *Only* you. Like this. Nothing between us." Linking his fingers through hers, Tobias brought her arm over her head and pressed it into the mattress as his strokes increased in speed. She clung to his neck, his shoulder, their skin slick. Instinctively, she brought her bent leg high against his hip, allowing him to drive deeper. "That's it, *Gadji*. God, how I've hungered for you."

The echo of their bodies colliding rang through the hushed chamber. She'd never imagined the primal intimacy of the act. Sweaty, savage, engrossing. Nothing could be said or written to properly illustrate the experience. One moment tender as they looked into each other's eyes, the next depraved as they whispered scandalous longings and caressed each other with wild abandon.

Hooking her leg around his, Hildy arched her back, a quiver starting in her fingertips and spiraling outward. "Stop," she murmured against his cheek, though she wanted nothing less. Fear making her ask it.

"Not on your life," he rasped and licked a sensitive spot beneath her ear, his laugh husky and sure as it fanned across her skin. Tormenting her, he slowed to a gradual slide, tip to core, letting her catch her breath. Making her dizzy. Making her crazy. Making her blind with need. A boldly steady tempo that pushed her up the bed. His hand rose to curl around her breast, his thumb circling her nipple. "Not when I have you where I've dreamed of having you. Dash it, luv, the delight of you is more than I ever imagined."

She moaned softly, passion taking hold, taking over, words lost, thought absent. "I can't."

"You *can*. You will. But you'd"—he gasped, chest hitching, pelvis bumping hers—"better *soon*, luv. I can't go much longer. It's too... you're..."

Clinching her fingers around his, she forgot herself, forgot her problems, reason slipping away in a surfeit of fevered sensuality. The antiquated bedchamber in a home she couldn't afford. The Duchess Society. The unpaid bills. A maid that needed dental work. The worry over what the hell she was going to do now that she'd fallen in love with Tobias Streeter.

Time narrowed to a pinpoint of illumination, joy, heartache, and she cried out with the force of it. Wave after wave striking her like blows, her heartbeat tripping to match his. Her fingertips digging into his hip, her hand twisting in his hair. The strands moist, his scalp hot.

His mouth trailed down her cheek. "Open your eyes, Hildy girl. Let me see."

She did—and watched her name shape his lips as she dropped into a pool of pleasure, and he followed, plunging in just behind her.

His fingers trembled where they held hers, and his guttural moan pressed into her shoulder, her neck, the crown of her head. Wave after wave of pleasure rocked her as they moved together. He shuddered, sucking in a breath as she released one. Her body gone wet and warm, she untangled the leg wrapped around his, setting them free to float on a blissful cloud. Collapsing beside her, he rolled to his back and brought her with him, tucked into his chest. Spent, dazed, sated.

Alchemy. Kismet. Destiny.

The Mad Matchmaker had been shown a glorious world she'd thought was only written about in books. Or in the stars.

Chapter Fifteen

How long did they have to wait before they could make love again?

Tobias watched Hildy peel a tangerine and pop a sliver into her mouth, then he focused his gaze on the drop of juice sticking to her bottom lip. He released a secretive exhale, his heart dropping to near the vicinity of his feet. He'd just returned from placing wood on the hearth fire to find her stretched on her belly across the bed, her legs crooked at the knee, feet popping together in some jaunty internal rhythm. From this view, he could see parts of her body that made him lightheaded with the rush of blood to his head.

She looked sated and content, lying there naked as the day she was born in a disaster of a bed. Counterpane in a twist on the floor. Pillows scattered about. Sheets untucked, wrinkled, and damp from sexual labor.

He braced his shoulder against the bedpost, his mind in turmoil. He'd never taken someone's virginity before. Never imagined wading into that treacherous pond. His expectation had been a gross display of sentiment post-orgasm, while Hildy was humming and bopping her feet about, like her change in status was a nonissue. He tugged on the tie on his drawers, the thin cotton barely concealing the modest erection he'd carried around since finishing round two. Which had started not long after round one with Hildy stating she wanted to try being *on top*—where she'd then proceeded to climb astride him and grab the headboard. Her diligent effort made him come faster than he had since his first time out with a lightskirt named Dandelion that Macauley had hired to service him. Watching Hildy's generous breasts bounce while she rode his cock had been more than he'd been able to stand and last longer than five minutes.

He was anxious to deliver a more persuasive presentation.

"Quit glowering," she said and bit into the tangerine, backhanding a bead of juice from her chin before glancing at him slyly over her shoulder. She had the *look* about her. That devious bit women took on the moment they'd had their way with you. Once they knew what you liked and had decided to use to it their advantage. "You act as if this was your first time when I know it's far from it. Miles, eons, leagues from your first. Come to think of it, I should be the touchy one."

"We did it twice if you recall," he returned, feeling foolish and petulant. And yes, *touchy*.

She chewed slowly, those damned dimples of hers absolutely glowing. Her eyes were back to their standard, astounding blue, having gone almost onyx when she threw back her head and cried out during her release. *Two* releases, thank you very much. "Are you feeling possessive, Toby?"

He brushed his toe over a mend in her carpet. Her arse looked like two perfect pale moons winking at him, vexing him further. He wasn't sure *what* he was feeling. Yearning. Arousal. Fondness. And shades of emotion never before presented in the bedchamber. *Distress*. That he'd shown her too much. Not enough. Was falling in love. Was making a hash of things. Had been too rough. Had not been rough enough.

She didn't show her hand in the bedchamber or in life, actually, which left him feeling insecure when he was not an insecure man.

She took a sucking bite, the last of the tangerine sliding between her abused lips. "Not as if I can feel possessive of you with hundreds in the background."

His cheeks burned, and he shoved off the bedpost. "It's not hundreds."

She ticked off the list on her fingers. "A viscountess. A baron's daughter, widowed, however, so free to choose. An MP's wife, although he has a mistress or three himself. You forget, I have paid bloodhounds on the street, supplying knowledge of the scoundrels in this town."

He shrugged, nearly without pain now. The agony of this conversation was on the *inside*. "I don't want to name names."

Hildy scoffed, her teeth a flash in the firelight's glow. "Too late, as the *Gazette* has done it for you."

He sighed into his fist. Wasn't he supposed to be the experienced one? The blasé member of the party? *Lud*, he'd been a fool to imagine she couldn't handle his hunger—the experience of making love without his holding back like he usually did. So why was he surprised to find Hildegard Templeton, the strongest woman he'd ever *met*, lying there in the buff, singing a chirpy tune and eating citrus as if they hadn't nearly swived each other into an early grave ten minutes prior?

She dangled her hand over the edge of the bed, pointing to her discarded clothing. "Should I put my night rail back on? I don't want to make you uncomfortable."

Fine, he thought crossly, but with a measure of enthusiasm he couldn't disregard, *let's play this game*. When he never, *ever* played games in bed.

In, out, done, thank you being the norm.

Stepping out of his drawers, he tossed them aside and climbed atop Hildy's enormous bed, grabbed an apple from the snacks she kept for "midnight emergencies," and set into it with relish. He almost laughed when her eyes dropped to his crotch.

Which made him harder, which made her look more closely... and so on.

"The woman in the park today, she's, well, there's nothing to it." He felt he should state this. Truthfully, he believed by now Hildy should've *asked*. "Opera, tea at Gunter's." He took another punishing bite, wondering where the hell his legendary prowess, noted in said scandal rags, had run off to. If the *Gazette* could only see *this* mishap of a seduction.

"Woman in the park," Hildy murmured, finally lifting her gaze from her study of his hardening cock. "I don't recall." Quite deliberately, she licked juice from the tips of her fingers, leading him to understand she did, in fact, recall. Her calm distance sent a nagging ping of anxiety through his belly when he'd never cared what a chit thought of him after sex before.

"I reacted badly," he said, coming at it from another angle. Like the plan for a building that wasn't working—try another design altogether. "To your comment about business after the drafting table incident. When I should have pulled you to the floor and quietly, so as not to wake Nigel, had my way with you until we couldn't walk the next morn. Instead, I've spent six weeks in morose contemplation of my foolishness."

She tilted her head, her bottom lip going between her teeth. "Drafting table?"

He laughed, which was also something he never did in bed, and reached for her, hauling her alongside him as he leaned against the headboard she'd nearly taken off the wall. A neat tuck her body seemed made for. She settled in happily without resistance, again leaving him feeling slightly adrift.

She traced the scar on his shoulder and another particularly gruesome one on his elbow. He could feel her interest like he could her warm breath dancing across his chest.

"A wound from a piece of glass being used as a weapon. I was fifteen. Macauley got the worst of that battle. He came close to dying in a pool of blood on the docks."

She found the mottled one on his hip, her eyes lifting to his in question. It was a sliver of a pale thing now, though infection had nearly ended his life. "India. The last time I fought and killed for something I don't believe in."

"My father was abusive, which may not come as a surprise as he was known for having a disagreeable temperament." She snuggled against him, closing her eyes to the memory or the telling. Tobias wasn't sure which. "To my brother most of all. There was a night, a violent argument. The blood. I can still see Edwin's blood on my hands. The jagged scar on his cheek, the sadness in his eyes. Our family ceased to exist, in a way, after that day. We moved like ghosts around each other."

She pressed a tender kiss to his chest, likely not realizing she did so. "Then three years later, I was alone, living with real ghosts. Life took them all and gave me... this life instead."

He dipped his nose into the reckless abandon of her hair, the scent of lemon and lavender drilling through his skin like a needle. "Was that the memory, the night of the masquerade ball?"

She nodded, then surprised him by murmuring, "Love is a trap. Like beauty. Neither last."

He paused before speaking, resisting his inclination to throw out a teasing statement. To deflect the conversation back to shallower waters. Because there was a kernel of substance, of truth, buried in her eight words. "So, you'd rather *not* be staggeringly attractive?"

"What happens when one loses that attractiveness? That's what I ponder."

Ah. "I think love builds the bridge linking desirability with the rest. The more important aspects. But I'm certainly not speaking from experience."

She sighed, not the answer she was looking for. Not a solution he was ready to give.

She walked her fingers across his chest and circled his nipple twice, setting his body aflame. "You helped me when you didn't have to."

She fidgeted, throwing her leg over his waist, and he caught the groan in his throat lest she see how susceptible he was to her. His blood was racing through his veins with the urgent need to take her again.

"Our business has only improved with Mattie's supposed jilting, her scandalous but secretly admired new situation thought to be, perhaps, best for all. We've gained support. Support not communicated widely, mind you, from several grand dames. Patrons, who could've imagined? Enough that I was able to establish a scholarship for a young lady who doesn't have means but has everything else.

"It's been rather stunning in the best of ways. A coup for the Duchess Society, an ingenious solution *you* came up with and generously attributed to us. You gave up working with John Nash and dashed your plans to bits, and I'm still not sure why. I hope *this* was worth it. I can never repay you—and this isn't how I want you to think I tried."

Worth it? Bloody hell. Tobias dragged the sheet to his waist, although there was no way to hide what this brazen chit was doing to him. "I gave up my plan to marry. To join the *ton* in whatever patchwork way I could, a ridiculous venture from the start. That's it. I'm still going to design buildings. I'm merely going to do it in another way. Maybe a better way, all told. Mac and I have already purchased a row of warehouses on Narrow Street and are working on a proposal to submit to the district administration. Teardown or refurbish. It's unclear at the moment. Maybe both. Unlike anyone else who would have purchased the crumbling wrecks, I'm looking into what's best for the community, best for Limehouse."

Tunneling his arm beneath her, he brushed a kiss across her cheek, lingering to snare a taste of the silken skin at the corner of her mouth. "Let's settle this matter, then never speak of it again. Being with you, hearing you sigh as you tighten around me, feeling your body shiver from my touch, ah, luv, it's worth a ship's bounty. And I've transported many near-priceless ones. I know the value of *life*."

He could also admit that he'd never felt like this. Never cared for a woman in this way. So overpoweringly similar to the sensation that swept him when he completed a new building design. He'd never lain awake *after* the act, staring at the ceiling and wondering why his heart was aching when his body was sated.

Puzzling, terrifying, magical.

Meeting Hildegard Templeton had been a bit like stumbling upon the answer to a question he hadn't known he'd asked.

Hildy zigzagged her finger down his body to the ruffled edge of the sheet, which had tented auspiciously with her teasing touch. "So, we're going to continue this association?"

"Tonight?" he asked, a hopeful ring to his voice. Would a third go be too much to ask?

She giggled naughtily and burrowed against him, her knee hitting his cock and sending a jolt through his belly. The woman had no *clue* how she affected him. "I meant tomorrow. Next week even, though I realize that's a long affiliation for you."

Oh. Not another go then. But he brightened; she wanted to continue. "Hildy girl, not to put too fine a point on it, but you said you'd never be—"

"Your mistress." Her voice held a brutal edge, an edge no man on earth wanted to go against. "I won't have it. I won't *do* it."

But you won't be my wife either.

Besides, he was afraid to ask. Afraid of the answer.

What the hell did she want anyway? He really wasn't sure.

Not a Romani by-blow educated on the sea and the streets, that's what. He couldn't forget that Hildy had been shocked he read Shakespeare. Shocked he read *at all*. Looked at him like he was a ditch digger that day in his warehouse. An earl's daughter, even a disgraced earl, was shooting too high. Centuries of history wrapped up in a bloody name. He was amazed Hildy hadn't demanded he present a calling card before he seduced her right out of her night rail.

Hadn't he learned his lesson with Mattie? He and the *ton* weren't meant to intermingle. Even if they all inhabited a few square blocks in Mayfair, looking like one lovely little community, they lived on opposite sides of the world. He'd merely continue to reside amongst them, tipping his hat on the street while acquiring everything they peddled to protect their archaic titles and pretending their cuts did not make him bleed.

His jaw tensed, resentment bubbling, the familiar sting of disapproval that he couldn't seem to shake wrapping around him like London's vaporous fog. Who cared, anyway? He didn't want a wife any more than Hildy wanted a husband.

At least, he didn't think he did.

She rolled half atop him, pressing her smile to his frown. "Your lips could crack ice, Streeter."

He laughed somewhat halfheartedly and streaked his hand down her glorious body. What was he doing getting incensed? This was every man's *dream*. A naked chit who didn't want to marry him cheerfully occupying his bed.

Or truthfully, he was cautiously occupying *hers*.

"What are you offering?" he asked, using his negotiation tone, not his seductive one.

Though the tactics were similar.

She stacked her chin on his chest, her fingers doing wonderful things as she contemplated the question. Idle touches. Tickling, stroking, caressing. He would allow this for five minutes, then he was flipping her to her back and starting round three.

He was so aroused, his shaft *hurt*.

At long last, she tilted her head, solving the puzzle in her mind. "Friends. Like before. But with gains. Advantages."

"Friends with advantages," he whispered, astonished by the idea. Of course, everyone knew you couldn't be friends with women you were intimate with.

Only women you *never* wanted to be intimate with.

However, they'd been friends, he and Hildy, bustling along nicely until she'd wounded his pride during the drafting table skirmish. A *friend* he'd wanted to tup desperately from the moment he set eyes on her. Which complicated any effort from a man's perspective—and possibly placed them beyond friendship.

His feelings for Hildy were complicated. When he thought of her, one word rang through his mind. *Mine.* Embarrassing for a broad-minded man to admit such domineering propensities.

While he continued to ruminate, she huffed an exasperated breath and lifted the sheet to look at things below. "Are you honestly thinking of saying no? With *that* saying yes?"

He blinked, staring at a crack in her ceiling that she'd no funds to repair. He wasn't, was he? Honestly thinking of saying no? His hand curled around her hip and brought her close, his body deciding for him.

Humming a tune that meant she believed she'd won the battle, Hildy skimmed her lips along the nape of his neck, bit his earlobe—a particularly vulnerable spot—while her hand crept down his chest, ribs, waist. "There are more things you can show me, aren't there?" she asked, wrapping her fingers around him and stroking just like he'd showed her.

With a sense of urgency he shouldn't feel on round number *three*, Tobias rolled her over and settled between her thighs. She was moist where he pressed against her sex, her heat and the scent of their earlier sessions sending a pulse of excitement through him. He'd never in his life wanted a woman the way he wanted Hildy. "At least twenty. Thirty, maybe."

She linked her arms around his neck, drawing his lips to hers, cutting off any supplementary statement he should've liked to make.

God, could the woman *kiss*. A natural, as only some things could be taught. Hot enough to melt his drawers off if they weren't already gone.

"Not here after tonight," she whispered against his cheek, her voice laden with more than desire. "The memories are dismal, much like the house, but I'm indebted to the staff, so I remain. They've been here, the ones left, all their lives. All of mine. I can't abandon them. *Or* afford them. It's a quandary."

He braced his forearm on the bed, gazing down at her. "I have a modest flat attached to the warehouse. Private, quiet. No servants. That daft valet you forced me to hire won't step foot inside it. Won't step foot outside Mayfair, if you must know. Limehouse is crime-ridden and too malodorous a locale, according to him. We'll spirit you in, none the wiser."

He scratched his chin with his shoulder, the healthy one, an aroused flush heating his cheeks as he imagined what he could do to her in his warehouse. Lots of nooks and crannies perfect for tupping. He'd start by taking her on the roof, her clutching the brick wall while he stood behind her, overlooking all of London as they found their pleasure. "Nigel goes to bed at nine sharp. Then the rest of the night is ours."

Her smile was beatific, those blinding dimples coming to life and turning him to putty. "Nine. Got it."

This could work. What they had in the bedchamber had so far been *incredible*. And she'd proposed a straightforward proposal, a tad duplicitous but uncomplicated. Friendship with *advantages*. Not even the pretense of keeping her as his mistress, which was more of a committed grind than it appeared on the surface.

However, as the world disintegrated to nothing but a matchmaker and a rogue king making love in a lonely Georgian bedchamber, Tobias's last thought was that they were kidding themselves.

Because Hildy's heartbeat was already in steady and everlasting rhythm with his.

Chapter Sixteen

Hildy adored the look of chagrin that crossed Tobias's face so often of late when he happened to catch her staring. A habit she was unable to break when she was around him. Tobias Streeter, rookery tough, fierce negotiator, and renowned importer of exotic merchandise was a tender man beneath the armor.

When she'd arrived at his secreted warehouse flat that evening, five weeks into their advantageous friendship, she learned that Tobias had just put Nigel to bed, fed Nick Bottom and the remaining kitten—the tiger-striped one since the other two had been adopted out to good homes—and settled behind his drafting table, not *the* drafting table but another equally sturdy version they'd found out, a glass of Streeter, Macauley & Company whiskey in his hand.

He glanced up when she peeked around the door of a rambling abode falling somewhere between cottage and flat, his expression disconcerted before he erased it. The sconce above his head sent a cascade of light across his spectacle lenses that hid his expression in part from her. He was clothed in a linen shirt, open at the neck. Buckskin breeches clung to his long legs. His cravat lay in a wad on the table. His gaze dropped to the valise in her hand with an affectionate smirk. It contained the change of clothing and incidentals she brought each evening she spent with him. Which was eight evenings straight. In fact, they'd only skipped three in five weeks when Tobias had to do hourly supervisions of a fresh malt brew, and he slept at the distillery. Nights she'd nearly offered to share the brew watch, so they didn't have to be apart.

Although she'd been given time enough to uncover the key to the mystery of the man.

He'd had relations, more than she wanted to envision, but never a *relationship*.

When he looked at her in that retiring way, confounded and amused, as if he wasn't sure how he'd gotten to this spot, she imagined she *might* marry him if he asked.

But the Rogue King wasn't going to ask.

After all, they'd made it to twenty-one on his list of forbidden acts, and he didn't even have to give her a pearl tiara when they parted.

"Are you going to linger in the doorway like a waif or come inside, luv? Nigel's dreaming of sweets and iced buns. The feline beasts are snuggled beside him."

She shook herself from her daze and stepped into the flat, snicking the door closed behind her. "Gerrie said to tell you that he'll guard the entrance until six, then, um... I can't remember his name, but another ruffian is arriving to take over." Crossing the room, she placed her valise by the wardrobe. She'd just slipped her arm from the sleeve of her coat before Tobias came up behind her, assisting with the other. Then he tossed the garment aside and took her into his arms.

"You can keep a set of clothes here, Hildy girl," he whispered into her hair, his breath hot on her scalp. "The feminine essentials. Instead of dragging that beaten satchel around London like a vagrant."

Hildy melted into his embrace and inhaled the familiar scent of him into her soul. Her body recognized him as it recognized no other. But she didn't reply to his comment. It was a frequent topic of discussion, a near argument once or twice, keeping personal items at the other's residence.

She and Tobias had gotten so twisted around an agreement made in the heat of the moment—never broker settlements while naked was her new decree—that she didn't know what she wanted. What *he* wanted. Where they were going with this tempestuous love affair. Was it love? She couldn't stand to be parted from him for even one night. When she didn't know, except for it being *his* home they met in, if he'd be there in the morning.

A predicament she'd created. Lock, stock, and smoking barrel.

She stepped back, out of his arms, unable to give either of them what they needed. Fear was a strong motivator.

He sighed resignedly and turned, willing to waive the argument. Then nudged his spectacles high on the bridge of his nose, a gesture that meant he was perturbed. With Macauley or the shipping corporation or the distillery. Nigel. Nick Bottom and the kitten, whom they'd curiously named Buster. The Duke of Markham or Leighton, his bosom pals of late but still men who could one minute be laughing like loons and the next throwing punches.

Or her. Maybe he was perturbed with *her*.

Over questions they seemed incapable of answering. Decisions they were incapable of making.

Their future. Their lack of a future. Marriage. Passion. *Love.*

When she wished to strip off her dusty clothing after a frustrating day spent arguing with a baron who wanted to keep his mistress *and* his wife, crawl into Tobias's imposing bed in the corner of the room, and let him demonstrate number twenty-two on his list of perversions. Then eat cheese and drink wine on sheets they'd destroyed, whisper secrets and dreams in the darkness as had become their habit.

Instead of whisking her away to a realm of seduction and pleasure, he rubbed his eyes with his thumb and index finger and gave her a sullen side-glance. "I realize a quarrel isn't going to land you warm and willing in my bed." He moved to the stately oak bureau that served as a mock drink station, poured a glass of whiskey, and threw it back. "But that isn't all I want from you, no matter what you may think."

She frowned and began to spin her ring around on her finger. Either that or start biting her nails. His tone was frayed, the slashes beneath his eyes shadowed. Something had happened today. His cross mood, she suspected, was due to his trying to figure out if he could talk to her about it. "Toby, what's wrong?"

He exhaled, a mocking half-laugh. After pouring another drink, he turned to her, perching his hip on the bureau. Raising the glass to his lips, he sighed, then dropped it to rest on his thigh. "Viscount Craven has requested my attendance. I'm to come around at nine tomorrow with one of those calling cards you had me order, when I thought to marry Mattie, jammed in my pocket. Islington, of all places. I did some digging as I thought he was in Town. Digging being a drink at White's with a marquess who'd like me to invest in his railway. He told me everything he knew."

Tobias took a sip, a long one, and glanced into his glass, searching. "A misfortune with Craven's finances has forced him to live among the working class, though in a splendid terrace on the trendiest square one can find in Islington. Still, he must associate with clerks and tradesmen when he walks the streets. God help them if they get close enough to touch him. The man does not like to mix with the lesser class."

Hildy shifted to fully face him, but as she would with a wild animal, she kept her distance. His eyes held a strange glow she'd never seen in them before. So tormented that she was tempted to enfold him in her arms, comfort he'd reject with that stern look on his face. Tobias accepted sympathy about as well as she did. "Craven?"

"My father, *Gadji*," he whispered and saluted her with his glass.

She paused, stunned. His *father*.

He chuckled, the sound bubbling up from deep in his chest. It wasn't pretty. Except for the handsome dent beside his mouth that she loved, and the spectacles she sometimes had him leave on while they made love, none of this was pretty. Absent fathers and neglected little boys made for the saddest of stories.

"Did you think the by-blow rumor was false? A scant amount of blue blood indeed dripped on your heirloom Aubusson the night I was shot. The Craven piece is where I got my love of Shakespeare and—"

"Stop it." She crossed to him and ripped the glass from his hand, wondering how much he'd already had. Slamming it to the bureau, she grabbed his wrist to keep him close when his instinct was to flee. Fly right out of there and into a depraved night. Her instinct would have been much the same if she'd been in his situation. "You don't have to go to him. You owe him *nothing*. Less than nothing. Forget he exists."

His jaw tensed, a muscle beneath his bewhiskered skin flexing. His intoxicating scent dashed over her, muddling her thoughts. The remembered whisper of his touch, who they were when they were *together*, forged a precarious path of yearning and anguish.

"Oh, I'm going, Templeton. I wouldn't miss this show for five hundred pounds. Not when I can buy and sell him now, our roles reversed." He worked to free himself from her grasp, but she held tight. "Wouldn't you advise me to? See him, that is? If I were still set on marrying Mattie? A horror of a viscount claiming to be Papa is better than an aging valet to prove my worth in this city of vultures."

She dropped his arm and stumbled back. "I've never doubted your worth. On the contrary, I think you're remarkable."

"Of course, you doubt it. As I do and have my entire life."

Glass breaking and an inebriated shout coming from the blighted alley running behind the warehouse had them turning. Then, after a hushed silence when unspoken regret had circled the room, they turned back, drained of fury, now purely weary and disheartened. Tobias's eyes were overflowing with despair, in the far reaches where he allowed no one to enter.

"You don't need it, need *him*. Let it go, Toby."

Tobias's teeth bared in a snarl, and he gripped her shoulders, giving her a gentle shake that nonetheless rocked her to her bones. "This is *my* world, Hildy. You don't belong here any more than I belong in yours. It's best we figure that out now. Before we get in any deeper. Especially if fragments of my life that were long dead are coming back to haunt me."

She released her hold on him, in more ways than one, her arm dropping to her side in defeat. "So, this is how you plan to push me away. It's missing the delicacy of a pearl tiara, I must say."

However, she was *not* going to show her devastation. Not here. Not with his eyes as hard as moss-covered stone. His body close physically but his soul stranded on the other side of England. His feelings of inadequacy were unfounded and absurd, but *he* was the only person who could talk himself out of them. "Fine," she murmured, misery sweeping her. "I give up."

His lips compressed until a white ring formed around his mouth. Then he exhaled deeply, swallowing hard. "It wasn't going to last. These kinds of friendships, with advantages and such, never do."

Her breath caught as her heart squeezed, pain radiating through her. "You're right, they don't," she snapped and wrenched back, snatching her coat from where he'd tossed it over the wardrobe's open door. She whipped out her hand when he made an effort to assist her. "Don't *even*. I have it."

He blocked the doorway. Yanked his hand through his hair, looking genuinely bewildered. The whites of his eyes behind his spectacle lenses were bloodshot, his expression broken. "I'm making a muddle of this, as usual. If you could just... give me a moment. Although I'm right, what I'm saying is true, and you know it. I stare at the ceiling night after night, alternating between the urge to wake you to make love again or to, *bloody hell*, I don't know, tear the room apart in my angst." His shoulders collapsed on a ragged sigh. "The worst part is when I wake wanting to tell you my secrets."

She shoved her arms in her coat sleeves and drew the collar tight, hiding part of her face. Heaven only knew what her expression showed when her mind was spinning wildly, her heartbeat racing. "You've *made* a muddle of it. Since the beginning, it's been inconvenient. Your exact words. Well, now it can be *deceased*. Put out of its misery, no more. Move out of my way, Streeter, or so help me, I'll shout the roof down. That could be messy. You have the boy and the cats to think of." Without another word, she brushed past him and into the hallway.

"Take Gerrie with you, dammit, Hildy," he called. Protective to the end, the cad.

Yet, he didn't try to stop her. Made no move to keep her from leaving him.

Hence, she stepped into a mist-shrouded alley, her mind full of fury and despair, not up to processing the inconsistencies.

She should have wondered why the carriage was waiting, the step down, the door open when no one had given the signal that it should be. Should have noticed Gerrie wasn't sitting atop the coachman's seat, as he sometimes drove for Tobias. Should have noticed there was no guard in sight. Instead, she climbed inside the conveyance and collapsed to the velvet squabs, the tears beginning to leak down her face as her heart was breaking.

When the arm snaked around her neck, pressing an acrid-scented cloth to her mouth, heartache vanished, as did consciousness.

Chapter Seventeen

T obias stood beneath the portico of his father's residence, his hand poised to knock on the four-paneled Georgian. It was one of his favorites as designs went. He felt numb, the color of the door matching his mood—*black*. This would be his first encounter with Laurence Balfour, Viscount Craven, since 1802. A ten-minute review in his mother's threadbare parlor over tea and biscuits. His father had brought a toy of some sort and a book of rhymes. There'd been another meeting before that, but he'd been too young to recall. His mother had often told him about it, her words glowing, as if Tobias should have been pleased by his connection to a titled gentleman, a man that cared naught for him.

As it was, two meetings in twenty-eight years sounded about right to Tobias.

Nevertheless, it would be his first as the Rogue King. More formidable than a mere viscount, much more. His father was simply another impoverished aristocrat who'd neglected his duties, lost his fortune, and was aging out of his archaic line. A situation so commonplace it was laughable.

Frankly, the situation bored Tobias. And he loathed boredom. An emotion he layered over the flush of indignation heating his skin, like a garment protecting him from foul weather. Evidence of *feeling* he hoped to hide from the old man. The day had started poorly, his carriage for some odd reason missing, and it had gone downhill from there.

Hildy, a vacant presence in his life, being the worst of it.

An aging majordomo answered the door, jowls hanging nearly to his collarbone, canary-yellow teeth gleaming in the glow of the oil lamp he clutched in his fist. He studied Tobias with watery amber eyes, his derision predictable. Though Tobias was clothed in attire costing more than it would to lease this house for a year. He corrected himself. In Islington? Hell, he could've leased the entire block for what he'd paid for his *waistcoat*.

"I'm expected," he murmured and strolled in without formal invitation. He flipped his calling card to the empty console table and recorded its fluttering descent to the faded Axminster.

"I know who you are. Why you're here. You're the one born on the base side of the blanket, who took his mother's name, instead of the name he'd no right to, but a name what might have done some good," he stated, rolling out Tobias's history with clipped ineptitude, his voice husky from eons of cheroot smoke and unworthy counsel.

Tobias realized this wasn't a typical aristocratic butler, but a below-stairs domestic moved into the position due to the distressing state of the viscount's finances. The day was promising to improve.

"Streeter, innit? King of something or the other. I remember your mother, lovely chit. I was working in the stables then, head groom. Gads, you're going to send Craven into a tizzy. You look jus' like her."

"Where is he?" Tobias ground out between clenched teeth, ready for this review, this *charade*, to be over.

His life didn't involve the viscount or any of his lackeys, it never had, and Tobias wasn't moving forward another hour with the thought that it would. As it was, he'd *royally* bungled his relationship with Hildy over his insufficiencies at being set aside by his father as a boy, when it was time he *got over it*. Time to live this life, as Mac had advised time and again. As Hildy had advised as well, though he wished not to think on that just yet. Replaying the way he'd treated her last night was eating a hole in his belly.

But there was always the opportunity to make it right.

Tobias had stopped for flowers on Columbia Road on the way over. They had the widest variety, some arriving directly off his ships. And Johnny Plint had found a rare edition of *A Midsummer Night's Dream* two weeks ago that Tobias had been waiting to give her that he thought she might like. Or appreciate the irony of, in any case.

It wasn't a fucking pearl tiara—and it wasn't goodbye.

He'd beg his way back into Hildy's good graces somehow. He wasn't known as the canniest negotiator in England for nothing.

After all, she was *his*.

The majordomo who was really a groom squatted, joints popping, gesturing toward the stairs with Tobias's calling card. "Up there, first floor, second door on the left."

Tobias smirked, thrilled to see his father's household was being run with all the charm of a high-class bordello.

The runner gracing the staircase was aged but elegant, the wallpaper faded but quality. The banister scuffed from years of use but sturdy. Certainly, the residence was a step down from Mayfair, but not as far a step as some in the *ton* had been forced to take. Islington wasn't Limehouse. Or Bethnal Green. Or Shoreditch.

The bedchamber door he'd been directed to was open. The voice flowing out was commanding. And anemic. The smell: medicinal and dull. "Come in, boy. I know you're there. I heard you and Quince discussing me inappropriately in the foyer."

Boy. Tobias hadn't been a boy in years—had left the position sooner than most due to having to bring funds into a perishing household at nine years of age. The beginning of his career had been tarring rope for ships he'd one day own. A wretched existence. His father hadn't given so much as a farthing to ensure he'd be safe. Or happy. Or healthy. This, he would never forget.

Angry all over again, twenty years suppressed, he stalked into the ornately appointed room. *Overly* appointed. Massive mahogany pieces suited to a bigger space were now relegated to a smaller one. He bowed, the merest shift that could be considered deferential. "Sir."

A grimace twisted the viscount's visage. "My lord."

Tobias counted to ten until his ire settled and his voice would arrive cool as a spring breeze. "Craven."

Viscount Craven coughed into an initialed handkerchief he drew to his lips. It was spotted with blood, a large stain almost obscuring the letter C. "You're an audacious lad, no one can deny. Ruling your filthy part of the world like a monarch from what the gossipmongers say. Grand plans you have, more than any Romani bastard should hope for. More than one should dream."

Tobias removed his beaver hat and dropped into the armchair drawn alongside the bed. He wasn't removing his overcoat, a signal that the conversation would be brief. He had better things to do, starting with winning back his girl. "Monarchs have limited time for such nonsense, so make it quick, old man." He nodded to the crumpled handkerchief clutched in Craven's fist and popped his hat against his knee. "It doesn't look like you have much. Time, that is."

Craven peered at him and blinked slowly, his countenance a bit like an owl's Tobias had seen on the caravan years ago. Sunken cheeks, eyes bulging, so round as to take up half his face. But the eyes were a vivid, startling green. His mother's had been blue.

A biological truth that made Tobias crush his hat in his hand and send a silent prayer to keep his temper in check.

"Spitting image," the viscount whispered and collapsed into his featherdown pillows, his gaze roaming the room as if he searched for something. Or *someone*. "She was unparalleled. But ambiguous bloodlines also made her untouchable. You think I was a beast? My father rivaled the worst the world has seen. Surely you see the justification for my actions, Fitzhugh. My choices were limited in every way that mattered."

Tobias's heart hiccupped in his chest. He focused on the soothing tick of the mantel clock to steady its feral hammering. The faint scent of lavender beneath the aroma of sickness in the room. Hatred was potent and bitter and could not be allowed to control him in the way he'd allowed it to. He had a life to live, didn't he? This farewell was purely a step in the process of forgiving and *forgetting*. "I go by Tobias. I've never used that name. Or the other."

"*Streeter*," Craven sneered, his breath arriving in a fragile pant. He waved his hand feebly, and when it fell to the counterpane, Tobias was fascinated with the map of pulsing blue veins protruding from his father's skin. "She had a cousin with that puerile name. *Tobias*. Sounds like a name for a cobbler. Or a clerk. Part of the reason I never acknowledged you, our argument over what to call you. She said I had no right to decide. As if my issue wasn't *the* determining factor. So, I left her to her own obstinate devices. For which I'm sorry because you've turned out to be a man among men. A leader, a warrior. More capable than any the *ton* has legitimately produced."

Tobias dropped his hat to the floor and stretched his legs out in a discourteous sprawl. "The woman I'm in love with calls me Toby." Why this nightmare of a human being was the first he admitted this to, he reasoned, must be the beginning of madness.

The viscount's rheumy gaze shot to his, his cheeks paling until they were the color of ash inhabiting a hearth long cold. "Is she highborn? Have you managed such a feat? If she is, let her call you anything she pleases, no matter how common."

Tobias's patience leaked away at the thought that, *Yes, she is highborn,* when he bloody well wished she wasn't. "What do you *want*, Craven?" Yanking his pocket watch from his trouser fob, he checked the time. "I'll give you five minutes, then I'm climbing into the hack resting at the curb outside and heading to my Mayfair manse." He glanced around before returning his gaze to the pitiful soul huddled in an oversized bed with no one but a groom-turned-butler caring if he lived or died. "When you've had to flee that locale due to graceless management of your affairs." He looked to the window, tilted his head in thought. "Although Islington does have its charms."

Craven chuckled when he should have bellowed, pride in his offspring evident. Recognition that made Tobias want to put his fist through the wall.

"You talk the part." The viscount flicked his bony fingers up and down, assessing. "*Look* the part. If only, oh, damned bloodlines and worthlessness! You could have helped me rule my world as well as you rule yours."

"This interview is complete," Tobias growled and rose to his feet. "I hope your passing is peaceful, *my lord*."

"I can help you secure Nash," Craven wheezed, his voice discharging like a pistol. "The architectural committee. And I know who put a bullet through you. A viscount has those he can call on for favors, still, my boy. You couldn't possibly understand the power of a name and a name alone."

Tobias halted in place. *Fuck*. There were truly no secrets in London.

"I know all about your scheme, young man. And your injury." He exhaled, the handkerchief fluttering in his hand. "With regard to Nash, a friend, a baron of some note, has a nephew on the committee. Mentioned you'd been considered. *Strongly* considered, shockingly. Until the Hastings chit left you high and dry to be a nurse or some such twaddle. A scandal, clearly, but less of one than marrying you, I gather. That daft Princess Society involved in the entire predicament, when women making decisions of any kind spells disaster. Absolutely horrifying, the entire episode. And then you tossed a duke in the Thames." He tapped his temple, three soft thumps. "*That* didn't strengthen your appeal."

Tobias reached to grab his hat from a carpet that had once cost a fortune and was now so faded as to be unremarkable. He refused to retake his seat, but as an adept entrepreneur, he was willing to listen. His investigator had been unable to locate who'd put a bullet through his shoulder, so having a title *could* at times assist when approaching delicate issues. He hated the validity of the theory but could nonetheless submit it as evidence. "Three minutes, Craven."

And the Duke of Leighton had done the damned river tossing, he'd like to tell this aged fool.

The viscount stacked an arm beneath his head as if he'd won a battle, his relieved exhalation bouncing off the bedchamber walls. "Archibald Thornton. You've heard of him, yes?"

Tobias laughed softly beneath his breath. "That bastard, is it? He owns a garment factory in Shoreditch. We had a disagreement over a shipment of silk last year. I refused to provide materials after seeing how he runs his business. Children, dangerous equipment, pregnant women not being given breaks or water. Not a dispute one would kill over, however. Or perhaps that's just me."

"You're making powerful enemies, boy."

"By making inquiries into the conditions at his facility and alerting certain interested parties? It would seem so." Tobias cracked his knuckles and rocked back on his heels. He needed a new fight if things he desired with all his heart were going to continue disappearing from his life. "This is interesting news, indeed. I'll handle it from here, my lord."

"See that you do. Because I have no heir, as you likely know. Upon my death, the entailed properties go to Baron Pauling, a distant cousin on my father's side. A blundering gamester who'll lose his entire inheritance within a year. Horses are his preferred way to squander coin, though he's similarly ill-fated with cards. Just wait"—he coughed, a prolonged series that shook the bed—"and if you care to, you can buy the lot from him in, oh, eighteen months or so."

"I don't care to," Tobias whispered. *I don't care what you did to me. It's what you did to her.* His mother had never gotten over this malevolent blighter.

Never. Excusing the times he'd searched the squalid lane they lived on for his father's grand carriage, the birthdays and Christmastides that had passed without acknowledgment, what this man had done to his mother, Tobias couldn't pardon. Couldn't forget, couldn't forgive.

The viscount pointed at Tobias, his thin lips lifting in what he probably thought was a smile. "I want you to take over management of the lone unentailed estate I managed to keep in the family. Hampton Hall in Derbyshire. Land gifted to my mother's family by Queen Anne for victorious service in the Spanish Succession. Two thousand acres of farms and gardens. Tenants. Natural resources. Timber. It's profitable or could be for the right executor. That idiot Pauling wants to redesign the house in what he calls the Jacobean style."

Tobias winced. *Jacobean.*

Craven snickered, then coughed, sending more crimson spots across his handkerchief. "Whether we welcome the actuality or not, we're linked, sharing blood and the emerald eyes of the Balfour men. Sharing a gifted intellect, which I never expected from you, I must say. Therefore, on my deathbed, I'm going to publicly recognize our association, saddle you with an estate that is amazing to behold, a delightful place to raise a family, should that highborn chit you've got your eye on care to leave London and its coal-ridden charms during the off-season. A place for you to putter and rebuild to your heart's content. Gardens there are a tad shabby last I saw them but designed by Capability Brown himself."

Tobias smothered a curse and twisted his hat brim into submission. *Capability Brown.* It would have to be the most famous landscape artist in the *history* of landscape artists who designed the gardens his father was dangling before his nose like a carrot.

Craven waved his handkerchief like a flag. "Don't try to hide your interest, boy. I can see it from here. When you first take the winding gravel drive leading to the estate, your heart will drop to your feet and stay there. An obsession with a woman changes a man's objectives. Trust me on this. So, use what you have or what you don't have *yet*. It may take me a little time still to pass on. Could be months even."

Obsession wasn't the correct term for what Tobias felt for Hildy. Vicious longing, like the wound on his shoulder that had throbbed for weeks. A yearning lodged in the pit of his belly, one he feared was never to leave him. His mother had never gotten over her heartache. Maybe he'd never get over *his*.

"Why would you offer this?" Tobias slipped a toothpick from his pocket and jammed it between his teeth, almost laughing at the appalled look on Craven's face. "And why the hell would I say yes?"

"I offer because, although I know you'll find it hard to believe, I loved my mother. Much as your loathing for me shows you loved yours. I won't allow her favorite place in all of England to be mishandled by an inane fop who merely happens to be family." He folded his hands atop the creamy sheet, the bones in his wrists jutting against paper-thin skin. "Why would you say yes? My acknowledgment might be enough to secure the Nash post, that's why. Help him create another Regent's Park somewhere we don't need it or a block of those godawful terraces he's so fond of. This could change your life without you having to marry a chit who loves stitching skin more than she loves you. Plus, it removes the necessity to smuggle. Kills two birds and that sort of thing."

"I enjoy smuggling," Tobias muttered around his toothpick.

"Bloody *enjoy* it. Frankly, it's a minuscule part of my business at this juncture. More of a hobby."

Craven's lids drifted shut, and Tobias sent up a silent prayer that the man wouldn't die on his fifteen-minute watch. "Then accept my offer to prove to yourself that your business acumen is sounder than your animosity." A laugh gurgled from his throat, his fingers clenching around the coverlet. "Indeed, who in their right mind would give up a castle when they can *afford* the castle? Take this woman you *love*"—he sarcastically muttered the word, and Tobias felt a pang deep in his chest for his mother and the boy who'd combed a gritty street looking for an absent father—"there and propose, you fool."

Hildy.

She hated the home she'd been forced to assume management of, as it was littered with ghosts and dreadful memories. Tobias himself felt no attraction to any part of the city aside from the filthy ones. Not like he could ask an earl's daughter to live in his rathole attached to a warehouse. Although he recalled with an arousing pulse that communicated itself to his cock, the flat had been the scene of the most impassioned sexual adventures of his life. Before he'd bungled the situation, he and Hildy had been preparing to give number twenty-two on his list a try.

A list he'd had to be *very* creative to come up with.

Tobias fit his hat to his head and cocked it at a smuggler's slant, discomfited to find his father was an excellent judge of character—even if he had little himself. He could wriggle his way inside a man's head and his desires with astonishing exactness.

His mother had held no chance against Laurence Balfour.

"Decided yet?" Craven whispered, on the edge of sleep or death.

Yes, he'd decided.

Tobias was going to accept the castle. And marry the girl.

Chapter Eighteen

Tobias knew something was dreadfully wrong the moment his rented hack pulled into the alley behind the distillery. There were two carriages parked at crooked angles, like toothpicks that had been hastily thrown upon the floor. Ducal insignias some decorous bloke had dreamed up centuries ago adorned both.

Why would Leighton *and* Markham be here?

And where the hell was *his* carriage?

He was out of breath by the time he made it to his office, the roses he'd purchased on Columbia Road and planned to deliver this evening clutched in his fist. He avoided looking at the drafting table because Hildy was stretched across it when he did, her legs spread, her moans dancing along his skin. If he tried, he could taste her on his tongue. The scent of lavender and lemon lingered as well, only in his memories, of course. When he'd never before connected a scent to a person.

Her ghost graced every space they'd shared.

Mind, body, soul.

Macauley met him at the door, glass in hand, lines of strain around the mouth he lifted it to. Tobias peered into the room, feeling like a visitor in his own space.

There were indeed two dukes and one duchess in attendance.

They talked at once, a cacophony of voices.

Georgie: "She's gone."

Macauley: "We found Gerrie in the alley with a knot the size of an orange on his head."

Markham: "I have men out combing the city."

Leighton: "This is what comes from dealing with riffraff. I smuggle too but *well*."

Tobias held up the roses to halt the flow of words, a thorn the vendor hadn't scraped off jabbing him in the thumb through the wax paper. But he'd heard enough to get the gist. The only sentence that mattered. *She's gone.* For the first time in his recollection, above being shot at in his carriage and during military campaigns, he felt faint.

"Where?" he asked rather stupidly as if the panic on four faces didn't state, *We don't know where.*

Macauley sent a severe look toward the dukes and duchess, then stepped close and took the flowers from his hand, placing them on Hildy's drafting table with reverence. Reverence reserved for someone aged or dead.

Tobias's rage, his *fear*, was acute. "What the bloody hell happened?"

They explained in a mix of scattered comments and animated gestures.

Hildy had missed an appointment this morning with a baron she was heroically trying to persuade to give up his mistress—a comment that caused Macauley to glance sharply at him and the back of Tobias's neck to burn. Worried, Georgie had checked Hildy's home before, without explanation about *why* exactly she'd do this as her second step, the duchess moved the search to Tobias's distillery. Then his warehouse, where they found Gerrie lying on the cobblestones in the alley and Hildy's glove two paces away from him in a twist, wheel marks soiling the leather.

The quest had come full circle, landing them back in Mayfair, a plea to Markham for assistance in finding Georgie's partner. It spoke to Macauley's fondness for Hildy that he'd stooped to asking a duke for a favor. Macauley loathed the aristocracy.

Tobias wasn't sure how they'd ended up with the second duke— Leighton—and he didn't think to ask. Because as he'd learned earlier today with his dear papa, two titles must be better than one when solving a dire problem.

Ripping off his coat, he tossed it over the table and that damned knot of roses. Although a floral stench continued to fill the room like a bellow. "I'll kill whoever's done this," he snarled and went to the console table, yanked out the bottom drawer, and flipped it upside down. The notch at the back unlocked a secret compartment and the loaded pistol he kept there.

Hidden from curious boys and inquisitive women. Both of which he had in his life.

Both of which he was *keeping*.

"Whoa, hold up there," Macauley advised while the Duke of Leighton whispered, "*Exactly*."

It was Markham who had the steady head, holding out his hand for the firearm. "We're not rushing in, Streeter. You have no idea who *did* this. Unless you only have one enemy to consider. And considering the shooting incident, you may have more than one. If that's not the case, tell us his name, and we'll go round and knock on his door. Get Lady Hildegard back for you straightaway."

Back for you. Tobias threw a swift glance at Georgie, finding her eyes full of sympathy.

The truth hit him. Getting her back would be for him more than anyone in this room, wouldn't it?

While lying to themselves and each other, he and Hildy had torn apart every wall and stepped profoundly into each other's lives. His skin prickled when she walked into a room, a frisson of awareness he'd never experienced with another soul. His heart skipped when she laughed; his blood quickened when she touched him. Even the lightest, most virtuous contact set off a fierce rebellion in his body.

He suspected she felt the same.

Three days ago, after they made love with her pressed against the wall, legs wrapped around his waist, he'd stumbled to the bed, slipped into a sated sleep, and woken hours later to find Hildy, cheek propped on her hand, gazing at him. He'd never had someone look at him like that. Intimate and affectionate. His response cascaded through him until he couldn't think of another thing to do except roll her over and kiss her into acquiescence. Rather than say the three simple words that had been trying to force themselves from his lips for weeks.

He wasn't going to let her leave his life, if she chose to once he found her, without hearing those words. Then it would be *her* decision what to do with her life, as she'd always pledged to herself.

Tobias handed his pistol to a duke and moved to the sideboard, a magnificent satinwood piece he'd purchased from the second son of a marquess who'd been forced to sell his family treasures. He thought it was about time he quit buying up pieces of other bloke's existences and stick to living his own.

He stood there staring at the bottle, but he didn't pour the drink he wanted so badly. A clear mind was what Hildy needed.

A clear *heart*.

Somehow, he'd find the courage to give her both.

Hildy woke from a drugged sleep, her mouth tasting of dirty wool, a rancorous scent clinging to her hair and clothing. Beneath it, clinging to the counterpane she'd been placed upon, drifted the smell of linseed oil and dust. If she'd expected to rouse from this adventure in a rookery dwelling or a dilapidated warehouse of one of Tobias's competitors, perhaps being held by the person who'd released his firearm into a carriage, the surprise was hers.

The sounds drifting in the cracked casement were affluent ones. Lilting conversation and laughter. Wheels striking roadways in much better condition than those in the slums, where the deep pits often broke an axle mid-transit, the echoes like bones breaking.

She rose to a shaky sit and looked inanely to the bedside table and the bell sitting there. Then, giggling with what must be lunacy, she picked it up and gave it a shake that sent a jingling chime through the air.

The door opened immediately, a maid poking her head through the crack, her mobcap bouncing merrily. She looked all of fifteen, her curly hair the flaming color of a carrot, freckles scattered like pebbles across her nose and cheeks. She grinned, her teeth as crooked as a picket fence blown to bits by a storm.

"I'll bring tea right away, ma'am, never you fear. My lady, I mean! He's a nutter, he is," she whispered and glanced over her shoulder and back, "but please, for all that's merciful, be kind. He does it for the girls." Then she snapped the door shut, threw a bolt that was located on the *outside*, and stomped away, presumably to bring the tea she'd promised.

Hildy did what she did best and took a moment to analyze the situation. Acting on impulse was not her strong suit. Practicality *was*. Even in the midst of crisis, she kept a level head. Although she was conceivably as nutty as her captor, something about this situation didn't speak of danger. Though she *had* been incapacitated with a chemical, which was discourteous on every level.

Rising to her feet, a tad wobbly at first, she circled the room. Nudging aside the long-ago-faded gray velvet drape, she glanced out the window. Second floor, no way to get to the ground without risking grave injury. The street was respectable, lined with rows of residences and London planetrees forming shadowed canopies over the street. The King's Arms, a charming public house, sat across the way. Georgian, every dwelling on the street, she believed. Drawing a breath, she let it go with a sigh. Tobias could tell her down to the year they were constructed, but right now, finding a way out of this mess was up to *her*.

But her mind, although she pushed thoughts of him aside, never strayed far from him. Tobias Streeter was wrapped up in every beat of her heart, whether she wished him to hold that power over her or not. Pulses of anger were threading through her still, the arrogant beast, but soon, she suspected, her feelings would turn to heartache.

Further investigation—a wardrobe housing gowns and slippers from another era and a threadbare chaise that squeaked when Hildy sat on it—disclosed a home she'd guess was in a similar state to her own. The furnishings had, at one time, been the height of elegance and now were simply sad remembrances of a grander time.

A household struggling to survive.

When the bolt slid free and the door opened, the next surprise was that she recognized her abductor.

"Lord Basildon!" She came off the chaise in a flurry of condemnation. "You must be dotty to consider a reprehensible thing such as this!"

Charles Trammell, the newly minted Baron Basildon, stumbled into the bedchamber, a tea tray perched awkwardly in his arms, partially supported by his protruding belly. Behind his back, the ginger-haired maid wagged her fingers—hello or goodbye?—and slammed the door behind him, locking them in again.

Basildon bowed as best he could, his wrinkled cravat hitting his cheek. "Lady Hildegard, I apologize most humbly for my desperate measure," he said and slid the tray on the first available vacant spot. An escritoire, when he should have continued to the end table sitting by the chaise. "I didn't know the effects of the chemical lasted hours. My cousin, Samuel, is a dentist, a rather good one when most prefer to yank every tooth in your head right off, and he advised me how to properly use it. I only wanted to further discuss my situation, and I've been trying for a week to get my chance." He bumped his hand down his lime-green waistcoat with a hard swallow. "But you're always with the Ice Countess or the Rogue King, and to admit the truth of it, both of them terrify me."

If *this* man had been able to track her for even three minutes, Hildy had lost her touch and her mind. Being blind in love made a woman easy to hoodwink. Agreements made in the buff and ridiculous barons chasing you through the night. It was preposterous.

She huffed an aggrieved breath and crossed the room, grabbed the tray, and placed it on the more appropriate surface. Collapsing on the chaise, she poured herself a cup of tea, drank it down, and did the same with another while the baron fretfully eyed her. "She's a duchess, not a countess," she said when the taste of tea had replaced the taste of the toxic substance Lord Basildon had used on her, the *fool*. "Bloody ridiculous when there's nothing icy about The Duchess of Markham."

"Agree the nicknames are daft. The duchess, however, *is* frosty. But they do tend to stick, don't they? Nicknames and such. The *ton* are a clever bunch, though not very pleasant." He wagged his eyebrows, and she knew he was thinking of her own moniker, one that had indeed stuck. The baron's search for the Mad Matchmaker was why he'd come to her in the first place, a little over a month ago. She'd told him then that she could not help him.

Hildy deposited the teacup on the table and glanced to the window, noting the sky beginning to darken with a setting sun. The horizon was shot through with a bruised cerulean close to the color of the vase Tobias had given her. Her most cherished present of any she'd been given.

Almost a day had passed since the baron had abducted her. Georgie would be frantic as Hildy had missed a meeting with another dunderheaded baron who wished to keep his mistress *and* his wife.

She was getting quite sick of men and their fragile individualities.

As for Tobias...

He'd cut her loose without the benefit of his standard expression of regret, the infamous tiara. Which she might've liked to *have* if she couldn't have *him*. He probably didn't even know she was missing. Although she had been stepping into his carriage when the kidnapping occurred. The thought of Tobias worrying about her made her feel a tad bit better. "Where's the carriage you spirited me off in?"

Basildon jacked his thumb over his shoulder. "Neat mews tucked away behind this manse. Placid as a wallflower's kiss back there. No one will say a peep about a carriage being parked that shouldn't be. Now that I'm in the upper reaches, folks don't ask. And if they did, I'd turn my nose up and walk past them."

"What did you do with Mr. Streeter's coachman?"

Basildon dragged the chair sitting before the escritoire across the room, scraping the floor along the way. With a groan, he fell into it, dropping his head to his hands and squeezing his temples. "I panicked. Coshed him with my cane. The Rogue King is going to kill me."

"Yes, he might." She hoped Gerrie's skull was as thick as it looked.

"You'll stop him, though, won't you?" His frantic gaze met hers. His cheeks had gone crimson, the bold color of a glass of claret. "After we marry? You can't let him kill your husband, after all."

"Lord Basildon, you're trying my patience. We are *not* marrying."

He drew his finger in a tight loop through the air. "You and the duchess. Frosty."

She slammed her hand to the table, gratified when Basildon reared back in his chair. "You poisoned me—"

"It's not poison! It's medicinal. Blimey, don't tell Streeter it was poison."

Hildy was close to finding the baron's cane and coshing him harder than he had Gerrie. "I'm not planning to tell him anything."

Basildon tilted his head, perplexed. Or sorrowful. That she couldn't admit that the first thing she'd do after leaving this house was find the Rogue King and tell him *everything*.

Hildy rubbed her brow. A headache was starting to rattle her brain. "Maybe you'd better start at the beginning, Lord Basildon."

He clicked his tongue against his teeth, gripped the spindles, and rocked the chair back on two legs. He had passable teeth, granted, but she still wasn't marrying him. "The beginning being when I asked you to help me with my sisters."

She gazed at him through her fingers. "I told you no because you couldn't pay even a shilling, and I'm almost as destitute as you. The Duchess Society is not a charity. Start the tale after that, if you please."

Basildon popped the chair back to four legs, wiggled a cheroot from his waistcoat pocket, and held it aloft. "Do you mind, my lady?"

Hildy sighed. After the man had poisoned her, he thought to ask if she was offended by his smoking? "Not at all."

Rising, he lifted the globe on the oil sconce, lit the cheroot, sucked on the end, then returned to the chair, which creaked ominously with his weight being placed so swiftly upon it. "This title rubbish is nonsense. My father was only awarded his in 1817. Meritorious service in the House of Commons the reasoning behind it. Named after our family home in Basildon, county of Essex. I was unlucky enough to be burdened with the thing myself a mere two years later. Sadly, my father's heart was a fragile vessel. Do you know what it's like to assume the least established entitlement in society? Literally, the freshest barony on the block? Good for bread but not society. I'm one step above a vicar."

"Baron is one of the oldest titles in the peerage," Hildy argued, though even *she* doubted her justification. A baron, and a shiny penny new one at that, wouldn't be treated much better than a tradesman by the established order. They wanted centuries of blood payment for their respect.

"Tell yourself that if it feels more democratic," he muttered and blew a curling gray wisp toward the ceiling.

"Why this charade, may I ask? This *crime*, if I state the case correctly."

He shook his head and sucked hard on the cheroot. "Not a charade, my lady. But it *is* a crime, I suppose. The plot goes like one of those novels you hide beneath your pillow. Maybe I even got the idea for this from one. Someone catches us together, and you have to marry me. Because I'll do the proper thing straight off. Your supreme good looks, thank the gods, are an unplanned advantage. Most unruly women are not, well, pretty. Ugly as apple cores, truth be told. Only glitch is your keeping company with Streeter, who could kill me with a twitch of his pinkie. But I can easily ignore your relationship if you ignore mine, as I have a darling side project I'd like to keep in rotation."

When he could see she wasn't admitting his plan was brilliant, he bristled. "You've got a successful society to run. Can't let the untamed passion you feel for me muck that up." He flapped his hand like a magician—*presto*—ashes fluttering to the carpet. "So, marriage it is. Secure this blasted title with the birth of my progeny. The biggest boon is help with my five sisters, *five*, as my parents were extremely prolific. Too much so to my mind. Now I know why they spent so much time in their bedchamber. I'm only trying to deliver a clever sister-in-law who cares greatly about their dismal futures."

"Five," Hildy murmured, spinning her ring around on her finger. Heaven knows where her gloves had gotten to, her best pair. When the baron had begged her to help him, oh, four weeks ago it was now, she hadn't realized he was responsible for shepherding *five* young ladies through society. If he'd mentioned that point, she'd conveniently forgotten it.

"They're lovely girls. You'll see when you meet them. As accomplished as I can make them, being new to this title business and without proper funds. The eldest, Ophelia, plays the pianoforte like a dream. The youngest, Mary, is quite a looker if I'm allowed to say so. Like you. Her twin, not so much, which is peculiar, isn't it? My quandary is, and I ask with true sincerity, what man is saddled with *five* chits to manage through the Marriage Mart? A mart I didn't have to attend before my father's decoration!"

Heavens, he was cracked. Although his responsibilities *were* immense. "Who's to find us, Lord Basildon? I believe you're missing that plot point in your lurid novel."

"No, I ain't." He grunted, blowing out a milky stream of smoke. "Oscar, third son of a marquess, so he has loads of time on his hands, is set to stop by after he wakes. Played hazard all night. Could be another hour. Maybe two. We'll make it look romantic if you don't mind."

Hildy poured another cup of tea and began to think her way through the situation as she sipped. The sneaky carrottop maid made a nice pot. "You didn't tell this Oscar fellow my name, did you?"

Basildon's lips parted in shock. "I would *never*. He's no idea he's going to force your hand. He's just coming around for a chuckle. The Mad Matchmaker, why, you're famous in some circles. Feared in others. Much like your friend, the Rogue King. We shall be the scandal, ah, I reckon not of the *year*, but of the week, surely. A baron's lifelong imprisonment is worth a spot of ink spilled in the gossip rags, innit?"

Hildy tapped her fingernail against the ivy spiral on the teacup's rim. Probably one of the last remaining items of value that Basildon owned, his mother's china. No one knew better than Hildy how to make money from the desperate sale of valuable household items. "I'll do it."

He grinned and slapped his knee. "You'll marry me, then? Superb!"

"Heavens, no." Hildy sat the teacup down with a snap. "I would never marry a man who'd poison me."

"It weren't poison."

"However horrendous your judgment, and honestly *because* of it, the Duchess Society will take on your sisters." Hildy could not imagine Ophelia of the harmonious pianoforte playing or lovely Mary being afforded a secure future by *this* man. Leaving the Trammell brood to their senseless sibling was more than her conscience could take. She would find a way to finance this mission somehow. Georgie would offer to fund the project, of course, as she'd done in the past, but that was not appropriate.

Basildon's mouth opened and closed like a brim's. She could see he was trying to pick apart the insult to his character in her statement, separate it from her agreement. "You said you couldn't afford to take on freebies. And I can't pay. How will this work without wedlock?"

"Oh, you're going to pay." Hildy smiled, her throat raw from whatever chemical mixture this horse's arse had used on her. "Just not with blunt. Save that for the gowns your sisters are going to require. And they *will* require proper attire. Lessons in comportment. Contract review. Dance. Titles. English history. Appropriate topics of conversation. As will you since you'll be escorting them through society."

"*Blimey.*" Basildon sank low in the chair, the cheroot's tip glowing amber against his knuckles. "I'm scared to ask what I'll be doing as payment."

"I need a man who can follow others without being seen and report back to me. No interaction is required. You seem to have that skill." Among other things she and Georgie could have him do. There were odd jobs at her home, loose latches and rattling doorknobs that he could repair as well. If she thought hard on it, the list would be endless.

"Surveillance work." His mood lifted with his posture. "Like a spy. I'd be quite a bang-up confidence man, I would."

Hildy held back her snort of laughter, amazed by the fragility of the male species. "Of a sort. You'll work for the Duchess Society until each sister is settled and not a moment sooner."

"That could take *years*," he lamented and went back into his slump. "My plan seems better. Thought you'd like having five sisters."

"Don't fret. The Duchess Society won't disappoint. Your current problem?" She took a leisurely sip of tea, ready for a bath, food, sleep, in that order. She would survive being given the boot, Tobias scurrying off like the frightened rat he was to surround himself with creampuffs and lightskirts. Opera singers and actresses, widows and dowager countesses. Nothing lasted forever, as he'd declared. Not even extraordinary love affairs. "If you don't return me home none the wiser, our futures could change in a second. I'm ruined, *you're* ruined, now that your sisters need an unblemished association and are connected to me. Because I *won't* marry you, even if we both go up in flames."

"You're a remorseless woman, Lady Hildegard. We might not have suited, after all. I'm coming to believe you're a brazen bluestocking, just like they say."

Brazen bluestocking. That was simply wonderful.

Hildy met his gaze, putting the fear of God into hers. A smile threatened, but she tamped it down. This was the only fun she'd had this entire awful day. "Indeed. And you'd best not forget it."

Chapter Nineteen

T he collection of voices swept over Hildy the second she
stepped inside her darkened foyer. A mélange uncommon in
her home, where guests were infrequent.

One voice stuck out above all others. Deep and rich, a baritone
should Tobias have been a vocalist instead of a smuggler trying
valiantly to become an architect.

Dash it all, she thought. *It appeared her disappearance* had *been noticed.*

Thankful her aging butler routinely sought his bed before nightfall,
Hildy gathered her composure and her expression as she stood alone in
the doorway. She obviously looked a fright, but she would control what
she could. She drew a breath scented with the sting of linseed from a
recent cleaning, air that felt chilled grazing the hands she'd twisted
into fists at her side.

Idly, as she traveled in the direction of the commotion when she
should've had other concerns top of mind, she wondered if Tobias had
stopped at his jeweler on the way over to purchase a pearl tiara.

A small group of people who'd come into her life in unexpected
ways stood before the immense mahogany desk in her father's study, a
map of London spread across its scarred surface. Hildy decided at that
moment to rid herself of the piece the first chance she got.

Purging this place of ghosts might help her more easily inhabit it.

She padded behind the assembly, less an effort to startle anyone than simple and utter exhaustion. Dukes Leighton and Markham, Georgie, Macauley. And Tobias. Sleeves rolled hastily to his elbow, shirt open at the neck, buckskin breeches clinging to his long legs. Wrinkled collar and cuffs, no cravat, no waistcoat. His usual rig.

Of course, formal attire wasn't required when searching for missing bluestockings. *Brazen* ones, most especially.

She glanced over after hearing a muffled snore. Nigel was fast asleep on the brocade sofa, Tobias's woolen coat thrown over his wiry body. He and the boy had made themselves at home in this lonely dwelling. The rightness of that seized her breath at the back of her throat and trapped it there.

The assemblage talked over each other, pointing out spots on the map and ruminating about the best places to explore, when Tobias brought up a rather salient point.

"If we find the conveyance, we find Hildy." He dragged his hand through that gorgeous silken hair of his, and even in her fatigued state, her heart kicked in her chest. "Harder to hide a mere slip of a woman than a town coach with a shoddily painted-over crest once belonging to an earl."

She leaned in, noting that they were focusing on the wrong area entirely. Basildon's terrace was located in Kew Gardens. "The carriage is fairly noticeable and parked around back," she murmured, knowing no way to politely tell them she'd returned, and they could cease their fretting.

Georgie broke rank first, gasping, her hand covering her mouth. Conversation halted, a charged silence gripping the room as all eyes turned to her.

Tobias made it to her first, pulling her into his arms, his words lost in the lips he pressed to her tangled hair. She melted into his embrace —vexed with him or not, she was exhausted, *and* she loved him—his heart hammering beneath her ear, the rags of his breath dancing across her brow. He held her to his chest for a long second before releasing her to a stunned audience, who were likely realizing how close she and

Tobias had become. She didn't have the energy to battle the assumption.

"Where have you *been?*" Georgie asked, her embrace the next Hildy accepted as Tobias stepped aside, looking poleaxed, his cheeks ashen. "We've been combing the totality of London looking for you!"

The Duke of Markham took over, as dukes were known to do. "Since that decrepit majordomo had to be put to bed at sunset, let's go with whiskey as there isn't tea. You look ready to wilt, Lady Hildegard."

The Duke of Leighton sprinted into action, always ready for a lively ducal competition, crossing to the sideboard and pouring an exceptionally generous dram that, should she drink it, would require someone to carry her to her bedchamber. Tobias, if she was able to choose the person for the job.

Still angry with him, true, but he was the only man for *that* task. Ever.

She readily accepted Georgie's guiding support and Leighton's whiskey, settling into the armchair that had been her brother's favorite. In fact, it was the one he'd been sitting in during the start of the scuffle years ago with her father, an incident that routinely gave her nightmares.

Tobias came to his knee before her, his touch light as if she'd vaporize upon contact. Cast in a muted mix of candle and moonlight, his eyes glittered as he stared intently at her. So green she felt cast into the sea of them. "Hildy girl, what *happened?*"

She told the story in between draining the tumbler of Streeter, Macauley & Company whiskey—somehow a bottle of his brew had made its way to her sideboard. She was woozy and deliciously drowsy, and the plot indeed read like a garish novel. But wasn't life sometimes truer than fiction? The heroine abducted by a malcontent baron of dubious intelligence but returned unharmed to face her reluctant but virile lover.

She was laughing by the end of the tale, dabbing at the tears in her eyes, causing the group to cast worried glances at each other that she noted but didn't comment upon. Macauley even pushed a plate of biscuits before her at one point, which she thankfully consumed like a starving child, not even bothering to brush away the crumbs coating her lips.

Tobias tunneled his hand in his trouser pocket and came out with a handkerchief, extending it to her. Of the finest quality linen with his initials stitched elegantly in the corner. *TFS*. She took it without lifting it to her nose to draw in his scent, her lips silently forming the letter F. After all they'd shared, she didn't know his middle name.

"Fitzhugh," he murmured for her and her alone. That he'd known what she asked without her asking spoke volumes.

Time dissolved until it was only the two of them tangled in the force of their attraction. All she loved and hated about him was placed there for her review. The dark lashes framing his glorious eyes. The beguiling dent in his cheek. His granite jaw that did, unfortunately, match his stubborn nature. The tattoo she longed to brush her lips across every time it peeked from his sleeve. His air of assuredness, as if he knew her better than she knew herself. That trace of arrogance, a masculine swagger that never failed to set her off.

His impossible kindness. His hideous inflexibility.

They were, she suspected, still at an impasse. Tobias's expression spoke of relief and held the hint of amusement it often did when he looked at her, but wariness was lingering there in the downcast tilt of his lips. And anger, which she suspected Basildon owned. Possibly, even with the chaos of the last day, he hadn't changed his mind about them ceasing to be advantageous friends. If he expected her to forget the way he'd tossed her out on her bum because of "situations like these never lasting" or "pasts coming back to haunt" when hers had *always* haunted, he was mistaken.

With a grunt that meant he wasn't ready to talk, he braced his hands on his knees and rose to tower over her. The he started rolling down his sleeves, his expression positively frightening. "Gentlemen, who's with me? I don't need help, but I might need witnesses."

The cutthroat of the bunch, Leighton hummed in approval and marched into the hallway, presumably to locate his coat. Or a pistol. Or knife. He was known for possessing an uncertain temperament. Markham, the cheery duke, kissed Georgie on the brow and whispered something that made her cheeks glow. Macauley simply growled and began to crack his knuckles, the sharp pops echoing throughout the room.

"Oh, no! *No*," Hildy cried and scrambled to her feet. "He's our client. And an *idiot*. You can't kill him. He has five sisters!"

Tobias halted and dashed the ball of his hand against his ear. "Come again? I swear, I heard you say *client*."

"Stars in heaven," Georgie exclaimed and dropped to the sofa, almost atop Nigel's legs. "Hildy, tell me you didn't."

Hildy felt her decision made perfect sense, but she was, she realized after peering into her empty glass, what her mother would have called a trifle *blotto*. "Those girls are destined to horrid futures without us. I can't live with myself and let that happen. Basildon isn't a bad sort, really, merely a thoughtless, short-sighted—"

"*Enough*." Tobias yanked on his coat one irate sleeve at a time, still planning to pummel the Duchess Society's newest employee. *Oh*, they weren't going to love that bit of information either. That she'd, in essence, hired her kidnapper. "Hildy, this dullard *poisoned* you. A chemical stink still clings to your clothing, should you think it's gone. I'm afraid to have Mac light his cheroot for fear you'll combust. And you're thinking of helping him? This weak-willed, spineless fop of a man who abducted you from *my* carriage, from *my* bloody district." He slipped his knife from his boot and jammed it inside his waistband for easier access. "For that, I'm going to take him apart piece by blasted piece."

"This isn't a good business model, darling," Georgie whispered, "assisting criminals. Even if five marriageable young ladies are on the chopping block."

"Agreed," Tobias snapped and stalked into the hallway, Markham and Macauley on his heels. "Who cares if another bloody person ever gets bloody married ever bloody again."

Crimson crisped the edge of Hildy's vision. Though she believed her protectors were the handsomest bunch in London by far. Simply dreamy. "This isn't about *you*, Tobias Streeter. It's about *me*. That's what's vexing you," she shouted, hoping her words traveled down the hallway because she meant them. Slightly slurred, but she *meant* them. Funny, her kidnapping wasn't even about him, the arrogant bounder. When he imagined it was. "Someone thought to cross the blasted line in blasted Limehouse with the blasted King. Stole his carriage, but that was only a coincidence. Could have grabbed me from Mayfair as easily as the rookery, too."

Georgie choked on what was either a laugh or a cough and dropped her gaze to her slippers. Markham, who hadn't made it out of the room yet, groaned and rested his head in his hands. Next, Leighton's curse floated back. Then Mac's strangled gurgle of laughter and whispered taunt of "the blasted king." All were only making the situation worse.

When Tobias returned to the study because she'd left him little choice in the matter, impugning whatever manly fragment she'd impugned, everyone vacated with hushed apologies, downcast glances, muted farewells. The Duke of Markham carried a sleeping Nigel past them to presumably tuck him into one of the vacant bedchambers upstairs.

"I'm still going to exterminate that blighting baron, only now I'll have to do it alone," Tobias said and ripped his gloves off with his teeth while she stared in foxed fascination. He was unjustly attractive, she decided with a sluggish smile. She hoped he'd someday rip off her chemise with those teeth. Tear a hole in her drawers and dive inside. Her body warmed at the prospect. "Because you want to singlehandedly save every female in England from a faulty union. When faulty is the standard outcome, Hildegard."

Hildegard. My, he *was* angry. She yawned into her fist, leaning her temple against the curved lip of the chair, knowing sleep wasn't far away. Or a raging headache when she woke. "You're not going to exterminate Basildon. I won't allow it. He's going to work off this mishap he's found himself in. The Duchess Society can use an underhanded baron with scarcely any moral fiber. Better that than see him dead and those girls left with no one. From personal experience, any brother is better than *no* brother when men rule this world. This isn't the rookery, where you slash first, think later. He's a *baron*, Toby. You can't just go out and murder a member of the peerage, even if he is the least respected baron in England."

Tobias swore and flung his gloves to the table. Fished his knife from his waistband and turned it over in his hands, the metal glinting in the candlelight. "I don't fit in here. I'll always, what did you call it, slash first, think later."

She blinked, her lids as heavy as if they'd been weighted down with half crowns. The fringe around her vision was going fuzzy, too. "Is this your way of telling me, once again, why you're not good for me?"

He glanced back at her, noted the state she was in, and his mouth pulled into a frown. Then shrugging from his coat, he moved to her, dropped to his haunches before her, and covered her tenderly with the garment. She turned her head, pressing her cheek into the smooth wool.

Dear heaven, it smelled wonderful. Exotic spice and that tantalizing soap he used mixed with a tinge of coal smoke from the city he loved. The fragrance undeniably his. Her eyes drifted closed on a sigh of pure pleasure.

His calloused knuckle grazed her jaw, his lips following in delicate caresses. Her sweet, sweet man. "Couldn't let me save you, could you, Hildy girl? Just this once."

"I didn't need saving," she murmured on the edge of sleep.

His sigh rang through the room, the gust of air delightful and minty across her cheek. "You don't need me."

I do, she wanted to argue, but whiskey and an unexpected abduction had stolen her strength. "You have to accept me for who I am, Toby."

He rose, his leather boots cracking. "You too, luv."

As she'd surmised, they were at an impasse.

She fell into a deep slumber wrapped in his coat, without taking the risk of telling him she loved him.

But he'd never told her.

So, they were even.

Chapter Twenty

Hildy woke in a remarkably uncomfortable position in her brother's armchair the following day. The previous night sifted through her mind like sunlight through a cracked windowpane, and a fierce headache gave the last moments the hazy quality of a faded painting.

But she recalled enough to have her banging her sore head on the chair and inhaling a sharp breath.

The breath brought the aroma of food to her senses. Blessed, wonderful *food*.

A pot of tea and a plate—kippers, toast, sausage, and jam—sat on her father's desk. The tantalizing aromas were sending her stomach gurgling. Pushing to her feet, she stretched, Tobias's coat held close. She couldn't let it go.

Even if she'd let *him* go.

Slipping her arms through the sleeves, she climbed up beside the tray, the way she'd sat on the desk as a child, munching and sipping her way through the next fifteen minutes. She strengthened with every bite, except for the ache in her chest, which no food would lessen.

This love business was excruciating. Like a dreadful case of diphtheria.

The folded slip tucked under a book finally caught her eye, the initials scrawled on the vellum in a bold script she recognized.

H.G.

Hildy girl.

Unsteady, she placed the teacup on the saucer and extended a trembling hand, scooted the book aside, and brought the sheet close to her nose. It smelled of ink and parchment, nothing special, but she imagined the scent of man clung to the page as well.

She would one day tell her grandchildren that their grandfather courted her very romantically, using the written word as a vehicle to communicate his love.

When it started a tad differently than that.

H.G.

I didn't dare wake you from such a restorative slumber. I stayed as long as I could. I'm headed to Derbyshire to secure a castle. There are guards stationed outside your townhome. Henchman, as I'm known to employ. Not one step without them, luv. Macauley, Leighton, and Markham are all on point to check in on you. If you're resigned to working with—and here the ink had dribbled where Tobias pressed the tip of the quill too hard into the vellum —*Lord Basildon's sisters, you're not to spend one* (he underlined this word twice) *moment alone with him.*

I've left you with three things. A Midsummer Night's Dream, an orphaned boy. And my heart. Now it's up to you to figure out what to do with them.

Toby

Hildy reached for the book, her eyes stinging until she was forced to blink frantically to clear them. Derbyshire. Castle. What in heaven's name? The situation was classic Tobias Streeter. Charming and tender yet with a cunning bent, no way to contact him should she wish to beg him to return to her. The ball in her court, so-called, when it was really in *his*.

He'd left her Nigel and a tome she could see upon first glance was a treasure. Leather-bound with that indescribably musty, aged tang drifting from it. Gilt-edged spine and cover. She was no appraiser of books, but this was a rare edition.

He'd spent a pretty penny. Maybe more so than he had on the tiara.

Hildy smiled and pulled the volume close, covering her pounding heart. Tobias's coat wrapped around her like a hug.

I love him, she determined, the sentiment ringing through her mind clear as a church's bell. A possessive and exacting statement. A final decision regarding a topic she wasn't going to be swayed from. *Ever*.

Now, she only had to figure out how to *find* the man in question so she could tell him.

~

A week later, his next missive arrived postmarked *Hampton Hall, Hampton Village, Ashbourne, Derbyshire*.

So that's where he'd snuck off to.

The letter opened simply.

H.G. I hope this correspondence finds you well. And safe.

Then he tripped into a lovely description of the market town of Ashbourne and the southern Peak District, an area he'd never visited. He was staying at a local estate, which he oh-so-casually mentioned he was set to inherit from Viscount Craven, with no details about how this occurrence had occurred. Built in 1609 to replace a moated fortification, replete with added wings and enhancements, not all sound and so on, Georgian and Jacobean and others, he seemed enthralled with the bequest, even coming from a man he didn't *like*. With a soft smile, she mused that he'd be embarrassed to know his enthusiasm showed.

He also mentioned, subtly, that he'd located who'd taken a shot at him in his carriage and dealt with the matter. But that she needed to continue to have protection.

Then he concluded the message as simply as he'd started it—*Yours, Toby*—and went off on his merry way to manage a property she hadn't known existed until this moment.

When was he returning?

Was he returning?

Did he still love her?

Was the *you-have-my-heart-and-a-priceless-book* vow written in the heat of the moment?

He'd included enough information for her to reply, yet extended no invitation to do so. Or visit. Perhaps a trifling offer to wreck one of Hampton Hall's beds with their frenzied passion wouldn't have been too much to ask. A summons she'd have accepted in the time it took her to pack a valise, gather a nine-year-old orphan, and sprint to the Peak District via the fastest mode of transit available. With or without a tone-deaf maid in attendance.

At this point, she didn't care what the *ton* thought of her. Tobias Fitzhugh Streeter was a wonderful man, a brilliant architect, a generous, loving, slightly reluctant suitor—and she was *keeping* him. The Rogue King of Limehouse was *hers*.

Nonetheless, there were uncertainties remaining. She decided to reply to his letter without thinking too hard about them. Could not stop herself from responding.

But she wasn't going to make it easy on him.

Toby. I'm imagining number twenty-two on your list.

Yours, H.G.

His response arrived as quickly as a messenger could get a communication from Derbyshire to London.

H.G. Number twenty-two involves a desk.

Yours, Toby

The messages were merely penned flirtations from then on.

Written in code so, if intercepted, no one would recognize the confidences being revealed. Confidences between two people who'd shared once-in-a-lifetime intimacies and seen each other as no one else had.

For example, Tobias's nonchalant comments about Hampton Hall's hearth being constructed with Derbyshire stone mentioned to remind her of making love before the hearth in the distillery just before dawn. Number sixteen on the list, if she wasn't mistaken.

She'd never forget Tobias slinking his arm about her waist and pulling her against him as he entered her from behind as they lay on the rug, his body curling around hers. Turning her head and seizing her lips in an angled kiss that was grander for its imperfection. The following morning, she'd found a scrape on her hip from repeated abrasion against his faded Savonnerie. A wound that sent a streak of heat through her every time she looked at it. For five days until it healed, a source of delight.

Now a faint red mark was all that remained.

That and her wicked memories.

Her next note contained an offhand comment about a chair in his office and seeing a similar one in a shop on Bond Street. Of course, she wanted him to lie in bed, remembering item number twelve on the list. Her sitting astride him, legs hanging neatly over the chair's arms, hands gripping his shoulders as he worked her up and down his shaft.

His response was immediate, or as immediate as it could be from the southern Peak District. Where they'd continued this teasing, tortuous production of courting for twenty-three days.

H.G. Come. NOW.

Yours, Toby

Hildy read the note, slipped it between the pages of *A Midsummer Night's Dream*, packed a valise, dropped Nigel at Markham House for a short visit, then headed to Derbyshire to get her man.

Chapter Twenty-One

Bloody hell if he didn't miss his girl.

Tobias descended the ladder propped against the stable's ancient stone wall and drew his forearm across his sweaty brow. A fetid gust off the moors washed mercifully over him. It was decided with the absence of a letter in today's post, delivery he eagerly waited for, like he would the arrival of a newborn. He was going to London to retrieve Hildy. *Tomorrow*. Or maybe this evening. He had to come back immediately—but he was coming back with *her*.

And Nigel. And those damned cats.

He'd requested a special license from his solicitor last week. It was done.

His heart tripping in his chest, he took a breath and gazed across an endless vista of craggy hills and verdant valleys, the loveliest place he'd seen in his life. And he'd seen many places. In less than twenty-four hours, if plans went according to schedule, which for him they usually did, he would pose a question that would change his life and Hildy's.

His skin heated at the thought of her, his chest constricting. He was nervous, without reason, because it was a question they already knew the answer to.

Grunting, he tossed the ladder over his shoulder and carried it into the empty stable, tucking it away in a murky, spider-laden corner. He'd let his steward, Riley, go for the evening. Rolling his shoulders, Tobias sighed, satisfied with the day's work. He loved toiling with his hands, testing his body, stepping away from the cerebral effort that lay on his drafting table. Stepping away from the mountain of shipping accounts in need of attendance.

He'd been thinking about letting Macauley run that side of the business, asking the Duke of Leighton to step in as a partner instead of just a client. The man was born to smuggle. Because life changed, didn't it? The gift of this estate was a prime example. A gift the petty side of him wanted to toss back in his father's face. However, as soon as he'd toured the place, Tobias had fallen in love with the towering arches and worn stone staircases. Bedchambers adorned in layers of dust gone thick as snow. Vacant parlors and sitting rooms and even a library with a fearsome collection of books but no readers. Acres of verdant land as far as his gaze could take him. This rambling property needed a man who knew his way around a blueprint. And a hammer.

It needed a *family*, he realized with a smile.

Then there were the tenants' decaying homes to repair, pitted roads in the village, a church with a thatched roof that had not seen new reeds since the late 18th century. However, Tobias hadn't left his business acumen behind entirely. With the advent of railways into the area, as was being proposed for the 1830s, Derbyshire would open up to development. And he would be ready with capital.

The sun was dipping low in a bruised sky, a vibrant, warm wash across him. His damned horror of a father had been right. Hampton Hall would make a lovely place to raise a family. *His* family.

Hildy, he determined as he gazed around the modest courtyard, would love this place. It was charming but a bit rough around the edges. Like he was, he supposed. The perfect country home for a brood who lived on the fringes as they did. Mayfair could be the place they lived to work. Here, they would work to *live*.

He wasn't foolish; he knew he needed to make a grand show of his proposal. Hildy had been a part of so many, her *own* needed to be breathtaking. Rose petals scattered across the floor. A musician playing the violin from a secreted nook. An astounding gift. Unforgettable. Maybe that bracelet he'd seen at his jeweler's during his last tiara run, a gorgeous diamond and sapphire creation that he'd remembered thinking, *I would have to love someone to give them that.*

And he did, so he would.

Soon. He was lonesome and exceedingly tired of writing about lovemaking instead of *doing* it. Midnight fantasies in his mahogany beast of a bed, Hildy's latest letter clutched in one hand, his cock in the other.

There was only so much a man could amuse himself.

Though he'd enjoyed their banter. Enjoyed courting her in writing when what rolled from his lips wasn't always what he wanted to actually say. Gazing into her bright blue eyes often twisted his words into meaningless babble. Penning those messages to her had a certain starry-eyed flair that he was embarrassed to admit he liked. A story he could tell his children, how he'd been a romantic fool over their mama. A true Renaissance man.

The sound of a carriage rolling down the winding gravel drive had him glancing over his shoulder, lifting his hand, and squinting into the glow of a setting sun. He frowned, flipping through the mental list of who could possibly be arriving, as no one aside from Macauley and Hildy knew where he *was*.

It hit him suddenly. That tingling jolt of awareness that lit the air when Hildy was near.

He was running before he realized it, long legs eating up the distance, his cap flying from his head to strike the ground. Before the carriage had slowed enough for it to be safe to exit, the door flew open, and she was *there*. In his arms, gasping, murmuring ferocious endearments against his neck. He brought her close, pressing his nose into the wild tangles of her hair and taking the first full breath he had in ages. She smelled like Hildy, lemon and lavender, the subtle fluency settling his pounding heart.

Lud, he'd missed her.

The kiss was unavoidable, untamed, and precisely what he'd needed since he left her sleeping in an armchair in her father's gloomy study. Her body melted into his until he was relatively sure he was holding her up. A memory of pushing her against the wall in the distillery, her legs wrapping around his waist as he found his way to her, roared through his mind.

How soon, he thought, *can I have her again?* Exhaling roughly, he stumbled back a step and gazed into her face. Her eyes were the color of the sky today. He'd now think of them as Derbyshire blue. "What are you doing here, luv? I was on my way to London this evening, morning at the latest. I couldn't take another of those lusty letters of yours. I've missed you horribly."

Her tears were immediate—and shocking—her face crumbling.

He'd never known Hildegard Templeton to cry. Look like she was about to? *Yes.* Actually do it? *No.* Helplessly, he folded her into his chest, glancing over her head at Gerrie, who vaulted from the carriage seat with a nod to the postillions as they began to settle the mounts. "I don't know why she's weepy. We made rotting good time. Sixteen miles an hour until we hit muddy roads in Enderly. Then it was a slog. Bouncy as all hell, but I've had worse. But I ain't no lady with delicate sensibilities."

"No," Tobias agreed, "you're not. There's an archaic stable round the house, west corner, uninhabited but with plenty of space for the horses. There's a lad about, Peter, a groom of sorts, who can help you rub them down. And a cook, Mrs. Bellamy, who'll make sure you have food and know which bedchambers are habitable, as not all are. Unless you enjoy sleeping with spiders."

Gerrie shuddered and slapped his crop against his leg. "Heck no, I hate spiders. What about the sour-faced maid?" He indicated the interior of the carriage, arms crossing over his chest. "Asleep half the trip, too deaf to converse the other. Had to shout at her every time we stopped to change the horses. Add to that remarks from Miss High and Mighty, the one tangled up in your arms, about my language and my need for a haircut. Who she thinks I should marry, how many children I want to have, although I reckon it's her *job* to chatter about things like that. I want a raise if I'm going to be dealing with fussy women all the time. And from the sappy look on your face, boss, I'm going to be seeing more of this chit."

Tobias's stomach dropped. *Zelda.* "You brought that old crone," he whispered stonily into Hildy's hair, dreams of spreading his beloved like butter across his bed and having his way with her wilting with the rest of him.

Hildy sniffed without comment and burrowed deeper into his chest.

He turned in the direction of the house, pulling Hildy before him. "I repeat my advice, lad. Kitchen. Mrs. Bellamy. Appropriate bedchambers. Zelda's as far from mine as you can get."

"Aye aye, captain." Gerrie grinned and, with a terse salute, went to disengage the horses.

He and Hildy didn't speak on the way to his bedchamber. She scrubbed a knuckle beneath each eye and avoided catching his gaze. Yanking a handkerchief from his pocket, he thrust it at her, wanting to tell her she didn't have to be embarrassed about crying when he felt like crying himself.

Bloody hell. She'd mucked up his plans to deliver an unforgettable proposal. The proposal to *end* proposals. Now, the request would be slapdash at best, jumbled at worst. There wasn't one rose petal to be found on this disaster of an estate unless it was growing wild and full of thorns, and he clawed himself to pieces getting it. Too, he'd never make it the night without asking her to marry him, particularly if they found themselves twisted up in his moth-eaten sheets.

When Hildy touched him, or God forbid, put her mouth on him, which she'd gotten very, very good at, he lost what little was left of his mind.

He frowned. His proposal was going to be a disaster.

She didn't say a word as he led her down the gallery hall, the walls lined with conventional paintings of dour ancestors, a relatively unattractive bunch he hoped were not on his father's side. Consequently, not on *his*. The bedchamber he'd been occupying was sparse but clean and contained a mock parlor to the side, a shabby brocade sofa and scuffed leather armchair shoved before the hearth, a knitted rug of indeterminate origin tucked beneath.

After taking Hildy's coat—dusty—and her gloves—stained—and her bonnet—crumpled; he settled her into the chair, poured her a glass of shite brandy as that's all he had, gave it to her, then went to one knee to tend the fire Mrs. Bellamy had kept going with the smallest staff in Derbyshire at her disposal. His hands were shaking. His legs were wobbly. Because of the image that had fluttered like leaves through his mind. He'd had the notion that, after they married, he wanted Hildy to visit every shop on Bond Street and purchase new coats and gloves and bonnets, so many that she never wanted to shop again. So many that she was forced to throw out her outdated pieces. Every last one of them.

It was a heartwarming thought that punched him in the chest. He could picture it, hence the wobbly knees.

His *wife* purchasing attire and saying, *Place this on Tobias Streeter's account.* My *husband's* account. And unlike many blokes in the *ton*, he paid his bills. The shopkeepers would listen. Hildy would be treated as she'd never been treated before. Better than any duchess because blunt talked louder than *Debrett's*.

He might just be able to make her happy. Babies. Cats. Bonnets. Books.

He jabbed the poker in the fire, then glanced back at her, the woman he loved with all his heart. The woman he wanted to be his wife. This was his *choice*. Not misery over being pressed into a corner he didn't want to inhabit, like most marriages. A situation brought about by convenience or business objectives, as he'd considered with Mattie. Or scandal, as that horse's arse Basildon had thought to make use of.

He truly wanted this. He'd found the person he *wanted* to grow old with.

Wanted her, and the boy, and the cats. Architecture and whiskey-making. The rough streets of Limehouse and the meandering paths of Derbyshire. Though he might leave shipping to men with more enthusiasm for the enterprise.

When he arrived back in the moment, it was to find Hildy watching him with those vivid indigo eyes, a watery, dreamy color now from her tears. Her gaze tracked to his hand, where his fingers were gripping the tool with more force than necessary. Her smile against the rim of the glass, because it *was* a smile, lifted the edge of her lips and brought her dimples roaring to life. His favorite feature.

Fine, he thought and stabbed at the blaze until it crackled and spat embers back at him. *We're both nervous. And I'm mucking this up.*

"So," she murmured with a leisurely drink, "Capability Brown designed the gardens."

He rocked back on his heels, crouched by the hearth, wanting to touch her yet not quite ready. "Craven's going to acknowledge me, the rancorous bastard. Twenty years too late, I might add. When I preferred being connected to him in a vaporous way, like London's abominable fog." He gave the burning wood another vicious stab. "Dangled this bit"—he gestured to the bedchamber, the estate—"before my face like I was the lead horse on his team and would race for an apple."

Hildy's shoulders lifted and fell on a sigh. Tobias loved that she was judicious when she knew he was troubled. Didn't let spill the first thing that came to her mind. He'd never had anyone care enough to do that before. "But you want it."

He did. "Maybe."

"What about London?"

"What about it?" he asked, dropping the fire tool into its holder.

Her eyes flashed over the rim of her glass. "What about *me*, Tobias? What about *us*?"

He exhaled and rose to his feet. After grabbing a lit taper from the mantel, he held out his hand. The time had come to step into his future and pull Hildy along with him. "Come."

She did without question, her willingness releasing the pressure in his chest.

That picture of her buying bonnets and saying his name tunneled through him again. She wanted this, he believed, wanted *him*.

Linking his fingers through hers, he guided her out of the bedchamber and down the hallway where oil sconces threw muted shadows at their feet. He halted before a door at the end and was suddenly, unaccountably, bashful. Wouldn't London society be amazed to know that the Mad Matchmaker had the Rogue King on the run?

Terrified about the answer to a simple question.

She nudged him in the side with her elbow and laughed softly. "What's this?"

He reached around her and opened the door, trying to avoid touching her or he would lose focus. He was horribly weak where Hildegard Templeton was concerned. The doorknob had been replaced because the previous one stuck, leaving you either locked *inside* the room or out of it. Actually, the chamber had been his pet project, aside from review of rotting casements, outbuildings, village cottages, and roads, for the past month.

She brushed past him, not waiting for an invitation. Such was his girl. He shouldn't have been surprised she'd showed up in Derbyshire, pushing when he needed a push. Stopping to capture the moment, he drew her in, mind and body. The scent of her skin, the sound of her breath, a yearning he could scarcely contain filling him.

Her breath shot out in a gasp as she turned in a gradual circle in the middle of the room.

It *was* lovely. Set off perfectly with dying sunlight floating through the high windows, lighting the dust motes until they looked like shimmers of snow. A wall of windows. The best vista in the place. In all of Derbyshire, he'd wager.

"It's a study. Or an office if you prefer. *Yours*. Since the one in your home in Town isn't really. Yours, I mean. I know the memories there aren't the best, luv." He rocked from side to side, shoved his hand in his trouser pocket. "This desk is rumored to be one of Prinny's castoffs if you care about such things. Rosewood. The sofa and chair are Egyptian. The rug Savonnerie. Aubusson and Axminster are passe according to Thomas Hope."

Her hand went to her mouth, a giggle escaping, though she tried to contain it. "You engaged Thomas Hope for assistance with the design of my *study*?"

He blinked and released a sigh that threatened to extinguish his candle. Should he have *not*? "I've shipped multiple pieces from Asia for his company, so I didn't think twice about asking for his advice."

"Of course, you didn't," she returned, her amusement evident.

Stepping into the room, he set the taper on a high, round table of some sort that Hope had claimed was one of a kind while Hildy began to do that delightful trick of hers, spinning her hammered silver ring round and round on her finger. "Since I can't purchase your trousseau, or at least I don't think I can, this is my... engagement gift. To you." Strolling to the window, he knuckled aside the velvet drape to reveal a pleasing view. The best in the house. "You can see Crowden Head just there"—he pointed and felt her come up behind him, her body warming his soul instantly—"and Kinder Scout if you look hard to the left. I never..." He coughed and dipped his head. "I never expected to like Derbyshire so much. But damned if it isn't the most beautiful place I've seen in my twenty-eight years."

"Toby," she whispered, her voice breaking. Her cheek came to rest on his back, and her arms snaked around his waist. "I love it. I love *you*. You are, most unexpectedly, the kindest man I've ever known."

He turned in the circle of her arms, searching her gaze for the answer to a question he'd yet to ask. "You disrupted my plan. I'd thought to scatter rose petals. Have a musician playing from a hidden alcove. Champagne. Jewelry and candlelight. Not the rather fragile sunlight and horrid brandy afforded us here. Mac set aside boxes of tapers, beeswax not tallow, and a case of bubbly from a recent shipment for the occasion. I'd thought bellringers the next morn on the street might be a nice touch. I know you've witnessed better proposals, more formal or proper, but none are more heartfelt—"

Hildy bounced on her toes, pressing her lips to his. Hungrily, he opened his mouth and took, hands sweeping south to grip her hips and bring her against his raging arousal. Then spinning them, he pressed her into the wall and kissed her until they were panting. Until his thoughts were muddied at the edges. Until he wondered how life without her even *mattered*.

"You love placing me against walls, Streeter."

He kissed her neck, her cheek, her temple. "I do, Templeton. I really, *really* do."

"We're going to live here?"

"I'll make a place, any place for you in my life. Derbyshire or my bloody palace in Mayfair. Both, neither. I love you, Hildegard Templeton, only you. Forever, only you. My stars, my certainty, my *future*. A thousand lifetimes, and it would only be you." Then he slanted his head, seized her mouth, and took her back into the magic.

"Yes," she whispered raggedly against his fevered skin when they broke apart. "Although, I don't think you asked."

He tipped his forehead to hers, and her breath was a silken caress across his cheek. They were one at that moment. Before the children, the responsibilities, the felines, for one sweet second it was just the two them. "Will you marry me, Hildy girl? Knowing everything you do about me?"

She smiled, so goddamn beautiful and wise he imagined he must be dreaming. "It's *because* of what I know about you that I say yes. Yes, Tobias Fitzhugh Streeter, I would like to become Rogue Queen of Limehouse Basin."

He frowned, lifting his head enough for a shaft of dying sunlight to intrude. "They wouldn't dare, would they? Call you that? I hate those bloody nicknames."

She burrowed into his chest, merriment shaking her shoulders. "Darling, we're going to be the talk of Town for months. I wager I'll have a fresh moniker bestowed on me before we repeat our vows. Let the *ton* spin mad webs from their desolate drawing rooms if that's all they have to do. In the announcement, we shall not mention my father's title, only *my* name, which isn't common. In fact, I may add this to the contract for future clients. *Her* name must be listed. I'll dare the groom to argue."

"You're frightening, luv."

She sighed, thinking of poor Basildon, who was diligently trying to work off his debt of five sisters. "I've heard that before."

"Are you only saying yes because he's acknowledging me?"

"Who?" she murmured into his fine linen shirt.

He dusted a kiss across her brow. "Quite."

"Toby, about number twenty-two on your list..."

Brilliant question, he deemed, and almost sent a cheer to the heavens. His lonely bed down the way was going to be used. In a matter of minutes, if he had anything to say about it. And his body was starting to have much to say. "Twenty-two," he echoed, trying to sound relaxed when his mind was churning out *extremely* carnal images like one of his stills churned out whiskey.

"You mentioned a desk in your letter." She trailed a questing finger down his shirt, circling each bone button as his skin lit. "This one of Prinny's you've given me, it's quite large. When I adore large *things*." She unbuttoned the top two, parted the linen, and pressed her lips to a vulnerable spot just beneath his collarbone. His knees shook when her teeth took a neat, startling nibble. "Sturdy. Thomas Hope wouldn't direct you to a piece that couldn't withstand *abuse*. He has his sterling reputation to think of."

Tobias growled and slung his arm about her waist, lifting her off her feet. He made it to the large, *sturdy* desk in two strides and plopped her bottom on top. Stepping between her spread legs, he caught her lips in a kiss he hoped would halt her teasing stream of words.

"*Oh*," she sighed with an amused wiggle that knocked her pelvis against his. "A leather top. This is going to work exceptionally well. Traction."

"Stop, luv," he whispered, laughing along with her. Rampant desire was draining his ability to effectively debate. "You're making me crazy. You know I can't negotiate worth a tinker's damn when you do that thing with your hips."

Hildy reached to cup his jaw, turning his gaze to hers should he miss her next statement. Then, taking his hand, she pressed his palm over her beating heart. "It's yours. From the first moment, yours. My stars, my certainty, my *future*. A thousand lifetimes, and it would only be you."

"Mine," Tobias vowed, only the start of the vows he would make. "Forever mine."

Epilogue

Happiness in marriage is entirely a matter of chance.
    -Jane Austen

Hampton Hall, Derbyshire, 1823

"This desk is delightful. Best purchase of your *life*, Streeter," Hildy murmured in a voice that, even to her, arrived sounding like a purr. She danced her fingers down his chest and over his ribs, the sapphire ring her husband had given her on their first anniversary sparkling in the sunlight, piercing the not-quite-sealed curtains. "Prinny would surely approve."

Tobias rolled to his side, brushing a strand of hair, damp and tangled from their amorous adventure, from her brow. He could point out that they lay *beside* the desk, not *on* it, she supposed. Where he'd moved them when he'd said his knees were threatening to buckle. But what man wished to argue over semantics when he'd just, and she was quoting, "Died and gone to heaven"? Her husband was a shrewder spouse than that. "Nick Bottom watched us the entire time. And Buster swiped my ankle at a critical moment. We've got to keep the felines out when you summon me into your private domain to *talk*, luv.

227

I engaged the lock so Nigel wouldn't burst in, but we left the cats on the wrong side of the door."

Hildy swiveled to face him, propping her chin on her fist. She was still amazed that this affectionate, gorgeous, intelligent man was *hers*. "Why do you say *talk* as if I invite you in for other things? Like I'm a spider setting a web for you."

"You do realize we're naked?" He stroked his fingertip down her side and over her hip, his gaze smoldering. "In your study. In broad daylight. When I was merely expecting to review last month's expenses for the Duchess Society with you."

Once a smuggler, always a smuggler, she thought. Playing fast and loose with the truth. "Don't play coy. You gave me the *look*, Toby."

He raised an eyebrow, all innocence. Then stretched like one of the cats he wished to boot from her study. Her breath caught in her throat; his body was a *glory*. "I have no idea what you're referring to," he said, knowing exactly what she was referring to.

She was weak, absolutely *weak* with desire for him. A happy, mad fool in love.

Nevertheless, this game, for once, was *hers*. She held the winning chip. Feeling victorious and wicked, she pressed her lips together to hide her smile. "There *is* a tiny wee thing I wanted to discuss. Nothing urgent." She walked her fingers from his belly to his hip, his muscles tensing and rippling beneath her fingertips. "If you can tear yourself away from renovations for the new warehouse. Designing terraced houses in Islington. Plans for a second distillery. Am I forgetting anything?"

His lids fluttered as she continued to tickle and tease, shading eyes that had darkened during their lovemaking to the color of jade. Dark green meant delightful things in her household. Delightful things in her *bed*.

"I was actually writing a letter to Mattie. The workhouse conditions are deplorable and getting worse by the day. She gives me better updates than the inspectors. Markham is going to propose a bill in the House of Lords for stricter review when he, Georgie, and the children return from their estate in Ireland. Leighton got into a row with a marquess at the last session over an opera singer, and Markham feels it's better to exclude him as he's temperamental at the moment. Though two dukes fighting the same fight would be a marvel." Tobias reached to adjust spectacles that were sitting on her desk, not the bridge of his nose. "Leighton is a beast of a shipping partner, but he's the worst diplomat I've ever seen. When I imagined *we* cared little what the *ton* thought."

Hildy drew a figure eight on his thigh, idly wondering how much time they had left. Nigel was out riding with their groom, Peter, but he'd be banging on the door soon, wanting lunch. A growing boy, his appetite was remarkable. "It wasn't an opera singer Leighton was brawling over. It was Helena Astley. The marquess said something impertinent, and the duke knocked him on his bottom. Basildon gave me the entire overview as he was there. I believe the duke is infatuated."

"Your amiable spy. A bloke I tolerate only because I love you to pieces. And it's arse, luv. Men knock each other on their arses." Tobias frowned. "Astley? Ah, yes, Astley Shipping. Lady Hell. Thank you, but no. Termagant doesn't begin to describe the woman. Tried to negotiate shipping routes with her once. Never again."

Hildy tilted her head, considering. "Georgie and I could—"

"Don't *even*. The Duchess Society couldn't make a success of that rowdy chit if you and Georgie spent a year on the project. Wears breeches in her warehouse, which *is* slightly intriguing. And horrendous. Worse than any wild phaeton race through Hyde Park, this one."

"Leighton's intrigued. I saw the way he stared at her at Epsom. The air around them crackled like that charge before a thunderstorm. You know, the kind that raises the hair on the back of your neck? But she detests him—and her antipathy seems about more than business. You can see where this is going. I couldn't write a better romantic novel if I tried. Smitten duke, apathetic hellion. It could be true love."

Tobias snorted softly. "No, luv, he isn't intrigued. Or in love. He's vexed. And it's not. Going anywhere, that is. The girl sold an antiquity he had his eye on to Viscount Davies-Finch, an Indonesian statuette or something equally tedious. Or one of those fossils he's so fond of. Stole it right from underneath his patrician nose." He trapped her hand against his thigh to still the movement. "Hildy girl, if you keep this up, we're never leaving this room."

She exhaled gently. It was time to tell him. "You know I've been sleeping more. And having minor digestive complaints."

His gaze shot to hers, his cheeks paling. "Are you ill? Is that why Mattie stayed an extra day last week? I thought it was because her lady friend, Miss Powell, wanted to further explore the moors."

She lifted his hand from where it rested on her hip and laid it on her belly, in the general area of where their baby was growing right this very minute. "Not ill, Toby. But I fear I'm adding to your responsibilities. Two cats, *two* children. In about seven months."

His features slackened, his lips parting. "A baby," he whispered reverently, his fingers trembling against her skin. "Our baby." His breath left him in a rush. "Oh, shite, I feel faint."

Her heartbeat stuttered, her chest constricting. For one second, she'd seen fear sweep his face. Although, she was also nervous. Elated. Worried. Overjoyed. "Say something, Toby. Are you happy?"

His gaze lifted from where it had dropped, his eyes moist when they met hers. "Hildy girl..." He swallowed hard and wrapped her in his arms, murmuring against her temple, "I'm delighted. I *adore* you. I want the blasted cats *and* the children. I'd like to fill Derbyshire with our brood. Seven sounds about right."

She relaxed into his embrace, her own sigh rushing forth. A family. They were building a family. Not seven, she'd tell him later, but maybe three. Three children sounded perfect.

Pulling her to a sit, Tobias stood and found his trousers in a wrinkled pile behind the desk and shoved his legs into them. Wrestling with the buttons on the close, he strode to the sofa and came back with a beautiful shawl knit by a local craftswoman—a gift from Nigel for her birthday—and tucked it around her. Then he was off, searching her desk for a quill and foolscap. Finding what he needed, he gave her a swift kiss and resumed his seat next to her. Knees bent, he scribbled away and mumbled vaguely, his bottom lip caught between his teeth.

She stared with her heart near to bursting. *This* was Tobias Streeter, the man she loved.

"Esmeralda." He said this out of the blue as if he'd shared the rest of the thoughts circling his mind at high speed. "She'll need to be here. We have the vacant dower house. She's skilled with birthing. And Mattie." He scrawled another note. "Definitely Mattie. We can't leave anything to that deaf maid of yours. I'll also need to rearrange some business dealings to be free for at least the last month of your... whatever it's called. Containment?" He drew a line underneath a word, then circled it for more emphasis. "When are you due again?"

"Confinement." Hildy laughed and reached for his hand, halting his furious writing. "Are you going to be like this the entire time?"

He glanced anxiously at her stomach and nodded. "I expect I am."

She tipped his chin until his magnificent eyes caught hers. "I'll be fine. I feel wonderful. Joyous. I can't wait to tell everyone. Georgie will be thrilled! If we have twins, we'll have caught them in one try!"

Tobias tapped the quill on his sheet, leaving a blotch of ink above the word *nursery*. "You flash those dimples and think they'll win your case. I know your merciless tactics, Mrs. Streeter."

"Is it working?"

He tossed his list aside and pulled her onto his lap. "It's working. My brazen bluestocking."

She kissed his neck and whispered into his ear, "I've heard they make the best wives. And rogue kings, the best husbands."

THE END

Thank you for reading *The Brazen Bluestocking*!

Are you excited about *The Duchess Society's* next project? In book 2, *The Scandalous Vixen*, a duke stumbles upon the duchess of his dreams. If only he could make her say yes...

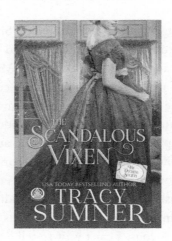

Acknowledgments

Orange cats are a delight! Macauley was wrong, as men often are. (I
know from experience!) Adopt don't shop, reader friends. Support your
local animal shelter.
And thank you, ALWAYS.

Also by Tracy Sumner

The Duchess Society Series

The Ice Duchess *(Prequel)*

The Brazen Bluestocking

The Scandalous Vixen

The Wicked Wallflower *(coming April 2022)*

League of Lords Series

The Lady is Trouble

The Rake is Taken

The Duke is Wicked

The Hellion is Tamed

Garrett Brothers Series

Tides of Love

Tides of Passion

Tides of Desire: A Christmas Romance

Southern Heat Series

To Seduce a Rogue

To Desire a Scoundrel: A Christmas Seduction

Standalone Regency romances

Tempting the Scoundrel

Chasing the Duke

About Tracy Sumner

USA TODAY bestselling and award-winning author Tracy Sumner's storytelling career began when she picked up a historical romance on a college beach trip, and she fondly blames LaVyrle Spencer for her obsession with the genre. She's a recipient of the National Reader's Choice, and her novels have been translated into Dutch, German, Portuguese and Spanish. She lived in New York, Paris and Taipei before finding her way back to the Lowcountry of South Carolina.

When not writing sizzling love stories about feisty heroines and their temperamental-but-entirely-lovable heroes, Tracy enjoys reading, snowboarding, college football (Go Tigers!), yoga, and travel. She loves to hear from romance readers!

Connect with Tracy: www.tracy-sumner.com

Made in the USA
Monee, IL
13 December 2022

21595081R00146